S

The Salvation of Tempestria

Shifting Stars
Gathering Storm
Shadows Fall

Shadows Fall

The Salvation of Tempestria
Book 3

Gary Stringer

First paperback edition December 2021

Cover Design by BespokeBookCovers.com

ISBN 978-1-8382777-4-1 (Paperback)
ISBN 978-1-8382777-5-8 (eBook)

Published by Gary Stringer

Chapter 1

Sara and Jessica were on full alert. There was an intruder in the portal room, and they had tripped a silent alarm.

The black-robed figure of Dreya the Dark stepped out into the long corridor, unconcerned, unhurried. She sensed them before she saw them, hiding at the far end. She had taken no more than two steps when two purple catlike alien girls stepped out from where they thought they were concealed, each pointing a weapon at the woman in black, who continued to walk slowly forwards, regardless.

"Sorry, love," Jessica spoke up, "but I don't think you're meant to be here."

Still, the intruder's steady pace continued.

"In the interests of fair play," Sara advised her, "in case you're unfamiliar with guns, these things can kill from a distance."

"In the interests of fair play," Dreya countered, still not stopping, "in case you're unfamiliar with wizards, so can I."

"Oh well," Jessica accepted with a shrug, "can't say we didn't warn you, dear."

With a shared glance, they both fired at once. To their astonishment, however, the beams seemed to hit some kind of invisible shield surrounding the intruder, which filtered the energy, allowing some to penetrate, while keeping the rest out.

"Thanks for the energy top-up," called out the sorceress, who finally did stop walking. "Just what I needed after a long journey. Now, I believe it must be my turn."

Bolts of electricity shot out of both hands, striking the two defenders, but they were equally unharmed.

"Magically resistant body armour," Sara explained, "which means you can't do anything to us."

The two Chetsuans drew swords and rushed down the corridor, but with a flick of her shoulder-length hair, Dreya caused the weapons to fly from their grasp. Undaunted, they switched to the knives they had strapped to their wrists and closed the gap, but all they struck was a shadow.

They scarcely had time to recover from that shock, before a large linen cupboard flew across the corridor to slam Jessica

1

painfully against the wall. Sara cried out her sister's name, but her breath was knocked from her lungs as the grandfather clock flew out, catching her full in the face and pinning her against the wall on the opposite side. Struggle though they might, they could not break free. The swords they had dropped floated in the air, threatening their owners.

"Lesson learned, I trust?" Dreya remarked, materialising before their eyes. "Magic resistance only stops direct magic. I still have a thousand ways to kill you with indirect magic."

The Chetsuans weren't ready to concede defeat yet, however. They didn't get much chance to use their telepathy. Earth humans couldn't do it, and they knew each other so well, they really didn't need special powers to know what their sister was thinking. But the mental abilities of two Chetsuans together, especially twins who were naturally in harmony with each other, were considerable.

Staring intently at Dreya, from where they were pinned, their eyes glowed with amber light, as they chanted, "You don't want to harm us…You don't want to harm us…You don't want to harm us…"

Dreya felt the assault on her mind and raised her eyebrows, intrigued. She hadn't experienced such a ferocious mental attack in a long time.

"You two are powerful," she acknowledged, "and I don't often say that. If any other wizard from my world came through that portal, they would find you a serious threat, but your telepathy won't work on me for two reasons.

"First, in addition to my own mental discipline, I am protected by a sympathic link."

Upon hearing that word, the girls stopped chanting.

"Wait, sympathic link?" Sara wondered, a puzzled look on her face. "I've only ever heard that once before."

"From a certain half-Faery druidess called Catriona Redfletching, no doubt."

"You know Cat?" Jessica asked.

"Better than most, or so I like to flatter myself. Which brings me to the second reason your mental attack was always going to fail: I really *don't* want to harm you."

"You don't?" Sara checked, tentatively.

Dreya shook her head as the swords clattered to the floor. "I never had any such intention. I'm not a tyrant, despite what some on my world might think. I didn't come here to kill you. If I had, we wouldn't be having this conversation. As I said, I have a thousand ways to kill you, yet I haven't used any of them. You attacked me, and I don't generally react well to that, but you were defending your home, and I respect that, so I'm willing to give you both a pass this once." She raised a warning finger. "But only this once, is that clear?"

They both nodded.

"Excellent. Now, I'm going to release you both. When I do, I suggest we put this misunderstanding behind us and start again. Agreed?"

"Agreed," they chorused.

True to her word, Dreya cancelled her magic and allowed both Chetsuans to free themselves. They immediately sheathed their weapons.

Stepping forward in a non-threatening way, Dreya offered her hand and introduced herself.

"So, are you, like, Cat's friend or something?" Sara asked.

"A friend, yes," Dreya confirmed, "and more besides."

"More besides?" Sara wondered.

"Of course!" Jessica cried. "Don't you see, Sara? That's why she wouldn't get into a relationship with Daelen – she was already in a relationship with Dreya, here."

"Jess!" her sister hissed in warning, worried that Dreya might not take kindly to the news that her girlfriend had feelings for someone else and she might take it out on them.

Guessing her fears, Dreya smiled, reassuringly. "Don't worry, I know all about that. It's not a problem."

"Then why wouldn't she just tell him she was with you?" Sara wondered.

"An unintended side-effect," the Faery woman explained, regretfully. "Keeping me a secret via a magically backed promise was a strategy. It was never supposed to cause her emotional distress. Believe me, I would never do that, and I would have met up with her to remove the block any time she asked. She chose to keep it because she still believed the strategy was sound. And just to be clear," she added, "the magic never stopped her from doing whatever she wanted. It didn't force her to choose me, it only prevented her from telling anyone that she had."

"So, you're linked with her at all times?" Sara asked.

"To a greater or lesser extent. The link has a privacy mode, like closing a door, but in an emergency, that door could be flung open at any time."

"Then you could swoop in and save her if you needed to?" Jessica wondered.

"Or stand and fight with her. Whatever the situation demands." She shrugged. "I love her. It's as simple as that."

"Wow, that's actually proper romantic!" Jessica grinned.

"If it's true," Sara pointed out, who was less willing to take Dreya's word than was her sister.

"Sara!" Jessica scowled, hands on hips. "Don't be a misery just because you're missing your elf boy. You can't go around asking people to prove they're in a relationship. How's she supposed to do that, anyway?"

"Actually," Dreya ventured, pulling something out of a pocket, blushing as she did so. She didn't usually do things like this. "If it helps, I do have these."

She produced a pair of photographs, taken in the studio in Gaggleswick the last time they were out together, a few days before Catriona went out to investigate Justaria's disappearance and began her adventure with Daelen. They were small and in black and white, hardly up to Earth photography standards of the time, but it was clear what they showed. One was just a portrait shot of Catriona alone. The other was Cat and Dreya together mid-kiss. She'd never shown them to anyone else before. Even the photographer, like everyone else in that town, took it as read that they needed to be the soul of discretion in anything relating to Dreya the Dark. As for Dreya herself, the kinds of feelings she had for Catriona were still new to her, and she hadn't yet worked out how to show them to the world while maintaining her image. With these two, for the first time, she didn't need to worry about that.

"Aww!" Jessica gushed. "Look, sis! Satisfied now? Oh, my gods, Dreya, you two are so cute together!"

Sara's scepticism evaporated. "I'm sorry for doubting you, Dreya," she apologised, holding out a hand.

Dreya shook it. "No apology necessary."

Jessica could barely tear herself away from the photos, but she reluctantly handed them back.

"That's it," she told Dreya, "you two are totally my new top celeb couple."

"Er, Jess," Sara put in. "I just realised."

"Realised what?"

"We tried to kill Catriona's girlfriend."

Her sister's jaw dropped. "So we did," she agreed.

"I won't tell if you don't," Dreya promised.

Jessica flashed a smile and agreed, "Good plan. Well, dearie, what do you say we all have a nice cup of tea and a chat somewhere a bit nicer than this draughty old corridor, eh?"

"That would be lovely, thank you," Dreya acknowledged. "Might I suggest the library? There's something I'd like to show you."

"Show *us*?" Sara frowned in puzzlement. "In *our* library?"

"Oh, yes, I fully intend my visit to be mutually beneficial."

"Well," Jessica declared, "you can colour me intrigued."

Chapter 2

In the library, as Dreya sipped her tea, Sara asked, "So what did you want to show us, Dreya?"

In response, the sorceress pointed to a small ornate box on a table at the far end of the room.

"Catriona noticed Daelen hiding something in that box, using what she calls her special ability of paying attention. She could tell it was a letter or note, obviously for you to read when he thinks the time is right."

Jessica went to examine the box and confirmed it had a time lock.

"Cat didn't say anything because she didn't feel it was her place to interfere. I take a different view: Why does Daelen get to decide what you need to know and when? A pair of bright, independent young women such as yourselves deserve to have all the facts so you can make the best life choices. If the information was important enough to hide, it's too important for you to not know. That's my opinion, so…" she stared at the box and unfolded her power word, "OPEN."

The box obeyed; time lock overridden, and Jessica removed the sealed note.

"What happens now is for you to decide together. It makes no difference to me whether you read it or not. I won't lie and say I care about that. I do this because I want information from you, and this was the only way I could think of to pay my debt, by giving you access to information to which I believe you are entitled."

"And what information do you want in exchange?" Sara asked. Dreya may have mostly won her over, but she was still wary. "We won't tell you anything that would betray Daelen, I don't care what you do to us."

"I've told you, I'm not here to do anything to you," Dreya replied, rolling her eyes, "and what I want to know has nothing to do with Daelen."

"Ignore my sister, Dreya," Jessica told her. "I trust you, even if she doesn't. What can we help you with?"

Dreya sipped her tea some more, before replying, "Tell me everything you know…about dragons."

*****

The two Chetsuans spent the next hour sharing everything they could on the subject, describing different kinds of dragon and their abilities, omitting no detail. When they could think of nothing more, Dreya stood, thanked them for their hospitality and the two girls walked their guest to the portal room.

"Before I go," said Dreya, standing in front of the portals, "I have a couple of small favours to ask." She fished out her photos along with a small parcel, wrapped in brown paper. "First, would you mind keeping these safe for me until I return? This shouldn't take too long, but I don't want to risk them getting lost or damaged."

"Sure, no problem," Sara agreed.

"Is this a present for Cat?" asked her sister, carefully taking the items from their visitor.

"In a way, yes," Dreya confirmed.

"Do you mind if I ask…?" Jessica left the question hanging.

"Have a guess. What would you give the girl who wants to learn everything?"

The two Chetsuans glanced at each other and chorused, "A book!"

"That's it exactly. Just a book. Anyway, second favour, could I borrow a camera, please?"

Jessica pulled a device out of her pocket and handed it to Dreya.

"You're giving her your phone?" Sara wondered, staring in disbelief.

"I told you, I trust her!" she insisted, showing Dreya how to use the camera function. "Besides, what's she going to do, hack my Facebook account? I don't think they have wifi on Tempestria!"

"I'm not going to Tempestria, I'm going to Phitonia."

"Whatever for?" Sara asked.

"Why did you think I was asking about dragons? It was information I needed to do what I'm about to do."

"And what's that?"

"Well," Dreya began, "there's a tradition on my world. Whenever a Dark wizard rises to dominance, they usually try to conquer the world. I've always resisted that particular tradition, but now I've decided that maybe the idea does have merit, after all. But I'm not going to conquer my world," she continued, "I'm going to conquer yours."

With that, she stepped through the portal to Phitonia.

"Dear gods, what have we unleashed?" Sara wondered.

"Something awesome," her sister answered with a grim smile. "An avenging Angel."

"Avenging Faery," Sara corrected.

"Even better."

*****

Making her way out of Daelen's hidden facility on the other side, the first thing Dreya did was open a micro-portal directly to the Black Tower on Tempestria. She didn't know if she was as susceptible to the effects of being cut off from her world as Cat was, but it was possible. After all, there was a reason she'd chosen to make her home right on the border with the Faery lands of Sylfrania. Either way, she couldn't afford to take stupid risks. Also, widening a pre-existing portal was faster than creating one from scratch in an emergency. The third reason for the portal was that she could establish a link with the power of her elite guards. They had absorbed higher planar energy from her battle with Aden, the same as she. Through that link, she could get a top-up at any time without needing to wait for it to recharge. The information the two young Chetsuan women had given her had been invaluable, but there was no way for them to assess the effectiveness of her various forms of magic against these dragons. The only way to establish that was through experimentation. Whatever their individual resistances, it was all the dragons of Phitonia versus one Faery sorceress from Tempestria.

She allowed a small smile to escape her control at the thrill of it all.

"Finally," she whispered to herself. "A decent challenge."

*****

Apart from the two moons and the lack of void storms in the night sky, the most distinctive feature of the world of Phitonia, or at least the bit Dreya could see, was the prevalence of grass and leaves that were blue, rather than green. She knew this suggested the light emitted by their sun must be different and she was vaguely curious about what that would look like come daytime, but she wasn't here for sightseeing. She wasn't a tourist – she was a dragon hunter.

She stepped up to the perimeter of Daelen's containment field. It was curious technology, but it was simple enough for a wizard of her ability to teleport through it. She saw the broken remains of Chetsuan culture that had existed just a few decades ago, Phitonian time. It was a sobering lesson in the fragility of civilisation to see how quickly it could fall.

Dreya began scanning the sky as she walked. It was imperative that she remain vigilant so that she could get the first strike in. She had ways of shrouding herself, but such laziness would cost her energy that would be better used in the battles to come.

It didn't take her long to spot her first dragon in the distance. Its dark scales aided camouflage against the blackness of the night, but then Dreya's robes did much the same for her. The dragon began to swoop down, and following its trajectory, the sorceress saw what it had spotted: a pair of Chetsuan children, young boys, desperately scavenging for food.

"Well, lads," Dreya murmured to herself, "looks like today's your lucky day."

In an instant, she chose her opening gambit. According to Jessica and Sara, black scaled dragons were vulnerable to fire, so a simple, mid-power Firestrike aimed at its head seemed like a reasonable place to start. She could quickly escalate to higher forms of magic, if necessary. Blood magic was available with a quick prick of her finger on the dagger she carried up her sleeve, but she wanted to see how effectual regular magic could be. No sense in wasting power.

The dragon bellowed in pain as the flames engulfed its head. Dreya could see her magic had done significant damage, but it was still alive. She considered using poison but rejected it immediately as she realised her actions could have a side benefit if the carcass remained untainted.

The dragon seemed confused about what had happened, and Dreya took full advantage, unleashing a second Firestrike at around three quarters of the maximum power for that spell. She was pretty confident that full power would finish it off, but if three quarters would do, then so much the better. This wasn't really a battle to her – she could kill the big lizard at any time – it was an experiment, an exercise in efficiency. As she was casting, the dragon, at last, identified the source of the threat and headed towards her. Too late. The fire damage was too much for it, and it crashed to the ground, sliding to a halt, mere feet from where she stood, unmoved, as the two Chetsuan boys looked on in amazement.

"Stop showing off, Dreya," she admonished herself, with a half-smile. "Cat's supposed to be the one with the dramatic touch, not you."

Next thing she knew, the two Chetsuan boys ran to her and flung themselves at her, hugging her and thanking her. Dreya flushed at their adulation. She could only imagine what this would do to her reputation if people back home could see her.

The question of having children was something that did occur to her, from time to time. She hadn't spoken to Catriona about it – it had always seemed a bit soon in their relationship for that conversation, to say nothing of the obvious biological practicalities. Still, who knew what the future might bring?

Further groups of Chetsuans emerged from hiding, then, and approached her. As they did so, one of the boys tugged her right sleeve and with the bluntness of youth, asked, "What are you?"

"Micah, that's rude!" one of the adults rebuked him. To Dreya, she offered, "I'm sure what he meant to say was, '*Who* are you'? Sorry."

"Not at all," Dreya assured her, shaking her head. "I think both are perfectly fair questions, under the circumstances. My people are called Faery, and my name is Dreya the Dark."

"Well, Dreya the Dark of the Faery," the woman acknowledged, "you are a stranger to us, yet you saved my sons and provided our starving community with enough meat for a month."

Dreya had hoped that dragon meat would be digestible for Chetsuans, that was why she hadn't used poison. It was one question neither Jessica nor Sara had been able to answer. They'd never had the chance to find out – dead dragons were something of a rarity.

Dreya planned to change that, and if killing dragons had the side benefit of feeding starving Chetsuan communities, then that was excellent.

The woman's other son tugged Dreya's left sleeve, "Are you a hero?" he asked, hopefully. "Have you come to save the world?"

Dreya laughed and shook her head. "No, I'm not a hero, and I'm not here to save the world. I'm here to conquer it."

"Does conquering the world involve slaying more dragons?" asked the mother.

Dreya confirmed that it did.

"Then, from where I'm standing, whether you call it conquering or saving, I can see little distinction."

*****

Dreya was soon on the move, finding a stray horse to cover the ground more quickly and hunt more dragons.

Word of a disturbance was obviously spreading because dragons were coming to investigate in twos and threes. Other species of the reptiles proved more of a challenge than the black she had first encountered, and she escalated her magic proportionally. Some had magic themselves, some even breathed fire, but Dreya's shields were up to the challenge of their every attack.

With dawn's light, dragons continued to come at her, but their numbers were still no threat to a sorceress of Dreya's power. Frankly, she was beginning to feel quite insulted.

When at last a quartet appeared, she decided to try something new. She made a show of killing three of them in particularly agonising ways. In one she burst its heart, in another she cooked its brain, and in a third she created tiny air bubbles in its bloodstream, causing death by embolism. The fourth dragon panicked and flew away, and Dreya allowed it to escape to warn others. It went against the grain, but maybe a different world warranted a different approach. At the moment, she supposed, the dragons had only vague reports of a disturbance. If word spread that they were under attack from a strange and powerful alien creature, that should induce a greater response. There could only be so many dragons in range, so the more she faced on the journey, the fewer there would be at her final destination. Dreya knew she had no chance of a stealthy approach, no matter what she did. Therefore, she might as well make as much noise as possible to try and draw the garrison out into the open where she could see them and deal with them.

After a while, a wing of five dragons showed up with another, more numerous, group on the distant horizon.

"Taking me seriously, at last, are we?" Dreya called up.

The sorceress knew it was time to take things up a notch with blood magic. It was also an opportunity to advance her plan.

Feeling her power flow through her veins, she dismounted her horse and sent it away. A pair of electrical bolts flowed from each hand, each stopping the heart of a dragon. For the one in the middle, she had something else in mind. This one had magic, and she was curious about how dragon magic worked in this world. Careful experiments with draining a magic-wielding dragon of its power would test whether it was compatible and therefore useful to her. She also knew from the two Chetsuans on Earth that the main dragon headquarters were across the sea. To get there, she was going to need a lift.

Focussing her will on that single dragon, she unfolded her power word, "STUN," and suddenly, it was unable to fly. It fell to the ground, physically unharmed, but unable to move.

"Just wait there a moment, would you?" Dreya remarked, not that it had a choice. "I'm busy."

Chapter 3

The next wing of dragons was now close enough for her Faery eyes to count individuals: a dozen. She also thought she could make out a few curious Chetsuans peeking out from their underground hidey-holes. Dreya the Dark was about to provide them with a feast. It wouldn't be the most varied diet, but at least starvation would no longer be a worry.

"Time to show you lot what I can really do," she told the dragon on the ground.

She waited until all twelve dragons were in range and then fired her beam of focussed energy like a deadly searchlight, blasting straight through the lot of them.

Dreya was no expert on dragon facial expressions, but she flattered herself that the emotion she was seeing displayed before her on the face of the dragon on the ground – now stunned figuratively as well as literally – was fear.

"I didn't actually need to use that much power against a mere dozen of your kind, but I thought it would be a useful demonstration of the fate that awaits you, should you fail to do everything I say from this moment on. In fact, compared to what I will do to you if you disobey, that was mercy."

"What are you?" the dragon gasped.

"I'm y—" she stopped herself. "Sorry, for a moment there, I was actually going to say, 'I'm your worst nightmare'. Can you believe that? What is it about conquering the world that makes it so easy to slip into melodrama? Let me try again: I'm your ruler, now. Actually, I'm not sure if that's less melodramatic or more. Whatever. My name is Dreya the Dark. Mistress Dreya is the most acceptable way for you to address me. Basically, I'm in charge, now, and any dragons out there who think otherwise, you're going to help me convince them.

"In a moment, I'm going to release you. I've already covered what happens if you disobey, so you're obviously not going to do that. Instead, let me tell you what you *are* going to do. You're going to let me ride on your back across the sea to where your soon-to-be-ex-ruler Mallax is based. You know the place, I presume?"

"Yes, Mistress Dreya."

"Excellent, and does it have a name?"

"It is called the Citadel of Doom, Mistress Dreya."

The sorceress gave the dragon a look of pure incredulity.

"You have got to be kidding me!" she demanded, though it was clear he was serious. "There we are again: melodrama. Maybe there's something in the air, here. Mind you, I suppose I'm in no position to criticise. My home is called 'The Black Tower'. That's not exactly subtle, either, is it? Still, it's hardly my fault. I didn't choose the name. Unfortunately, I can make no such excuses about my next line." She climbed onto the dragon's back and cancelled the stun. The dragon rose, carefully and tested his wings. "You see, while I've been talking," Dreya continued, "I've been trying to think of a better way to say this, but I can't find one, so I'm afraid I'm going to have to just go with it."

She closed her eyes against what she was about to say, but there was just no avoiding it.

"Take me to your leader," she ordered, finally, and the dragon took to the sky. "You see? Melodrama. Try as I might, I just can't get away from it."

*****

An hour's flight later, and she'd really caught someone's attention. As they flew, they were frequently assailed by larger groups of dragons. Ten, a dozen, fifteen, twenty. Fighting on dragonback was a new experience for the Faery woman, but it didn't make much difference in practical terms. Some of the assaults she faced were at last powerful enough to be a significant threat, forcing her to invent the technique of short-range teleportation for both herself and her steed to avoid many directed attacks. Every time she used a power word, she immediately compartmentalised a section of her brain to work on refolding it so that it would be ready to use again a few minutes later.

Sara and Jessica's intelligence proved consistently invaluable and unerringly accurate. Thanks to them, she knew exactly what each type of dragon was capable of and could be prepared to counter their threat before they were even in range. Without their help, she would likely have died at least twice already.

One species of dragon had a particular talent for telepathic attacks. Half a dozen of those assaulting her mind at the same time was putting a severe strain on her mental resistance, even with her sympathic link through Catriona to the Ysirian, Pyrah. Without that link, she knew she probably would have succumbed long since. As it was, she had to make them primary targets. Cutting down their numbers was her top priority, even allowing herself to get slightly singed from minor penetration of her shields against physical magic and fire breath.

At one stage, more than two dozen of the creatures closed in on them from all sides. Blood magic combined with higher planar energy turned the sky to liquid flame, and after that, the two that survived, thanks to being immune to fire, were easy pickings.

As they flew closer to the citadel, Dreya was prepared to pull more power from her guards back home. Never one to allow arrogance or conceit over her abilities to cloud her assessment of any situation, the sorceress knew that when she got to the heart of the matter against Mallax and his elite guards, she was going to need all the power she could get.

Conveniently, the so-called Citadel of Doom was also a Citadel of Dome, covered by a dragon-sized domed roof made of glass. According to Sara, this building had once been the seat of Chetsuan government on this continent before Mallax rose to power and wrested it from them. It was about twice the size of the Council building in Walminster whose lofty halls Dreya frequented back home.

She made a mental note to give Cat the news about official things that had happened there, next time she saw her. She was sure she'd be pleased. But that was for later.

In the here and now, from her position high above, Dreya could already see the enormous red dragon that lay inside that building, on what appeared to be all the world's treasure in one decadent golden mountain. Mallax, surrounded by his elite guard of twelve.

It was almost time to make an entrance, but there was one final piece of business to take care of, first: her dragon mount.

"Listen," she began. "You've given me not a bit of trouble the entire journey, and I haven't needed to waste a single drop of power on keeping you in line. I appreciate that, just as I realise that I

15

couldn't have come so far without a ride. That means I owe you, and I always pay my debts. The way I'm going to repay this one is by giving you one chance to keep on living. For your final service, when I say 'dive', I want you to nosedive towards that glass dome. As soon as I'm in range, I will break it apart, jump off your back and levitate the rest of the way down. That is your one chance to fly away. You've seen what I can do, and believe me I've been holding back, so if you even think of trying anything, you will be dead before you ever finish the thought. Do we understand each other?"

"Yes, Mistress Dreya," the dragon replied.

"Excellent. Now, dive."

As the dragon accelerated downwards, Dreya gathered her will, focussed on the glass and said, "SHATTER," causing the glass to break into a million tiny fragments. True to her word, Dreya dismounted and began to float down. As she descended, she created a conduit of power through her micro-portal, connecting with her elite guards and the magic that powered all the defences of the Black Tower's grounds.

Her chief death knight sent a telepathic message that all was ready. There was just one slight wrinkle in the plan, however: Laethyn, the Black robe Triumvirate representative, was approaching her Tower, clearly on the warpath. It was not unexpected, after what she'd stolen from him. It was just inconvenient timing. Still, there would be time to deal with that, later. Right now, she was rather more interested in the scene before her, and she needed to have access to every drop of power at her disposal, even though that would leave the Black Tower defenceless. If all went well, even if her Black Tower were to fall, she would have the resources of this whole world to help her take it back. If things went badly, she wouldn't live long enough to care.

She was prepared to prick her finger on her dagger, but it proved unnecessary as a stray shard of glass grazed her left cheek and did the job for her. As she floated down, everything seemed to happen in slow motion. She prepared to draw on all of her power, leaving nothing to chance, because this was where the intelligence provided by Jessica and Sara ended. Understandably, they knew practically nothing about Mallax himself, beyond his general distaste for Chetsuans. Nothing of strategic value. Dreya the Dark would simply have to be prepared for anything.

Even as she drifted down, the tiny hairs on the back of her neck began to tingle in subconscious warning: something was wrong. She didn't know what it was, but she trusted her instincts. At the last possible moment, she telepathically told her guards to stand down and await further instructions. Then, instead of unleashing her beam of higher planar energy, she sent out a simple torchlight at negligible power. The light immediately shone back in her face, forcing her to close her eyes. It must have been some kind of power reflection field, she realised, not unlike Catriona's Nature's Mirror. If she had unleashed her full power as she had planned, she would have killed herself instantly. She had to concede it was a clever ploy and she had very nearly fallen for it.

As her feet touched the floor, she opened her eyes and realised something else: her feet should not be touching the floor. She should have landed on top of the dragon. Except he had vanished.

The scene changed before her eyes. She found herself in the middle of the vast chamber, as she intended, but there was no mountain of treasure. Instead, the spot in which she was standing was a small, empty space, surrounded by a cylinder of glass. She was inside, and the dragons were on the outside looking in. Mallax deftly picked up a disc-shaped object in his claws, placed it on top of the glass cylinder and screwed it on tight. With horror, Dreya realised that from the dragons' perspectives, she was a fascinating specimen they had caught in a jam jar.

Moreover, as the lid closed, she felt cut off from all of her magic. Even her micro-portal had closed because she was inside an anti-magic field. The dragons rumbled with what she took to be their equivalent of laughter.

"You've been causing my dragons quite a bit of trouble," thundered Mallax.

"I'm delighted to hear it," Dreya replied, acidly. If he was planning to talk her to death, so much the better for her. It gave her what she needed: time. Maybe she'd talk him to death, instead.

"What manner of creature are you?" Mallax wondered.

"Why don't you let me out of this cage so you can examine me more closely and find out for yourself?"

Again came the laughter.

"Oh, there's no rush," he replied. "You belong to Mallax now. You're going to be in there for a very long time, or at least as long as you're entertaining. So, I suggest you learn to enjoy your new life as Mallax' plaything!"

"No," Dreya stated, flatly, holding up a warning finger, as if scolding him.

"What do you mean, no?"

"I mean no!" she insisted. "No, no, no! I won't have it. Not on my world, not on this one, not anywhere. I mean, I'm an open-minded kind of girl, tolerant like you wouldn't believe. I even dabbled with melodrama myself, earlier, but at some point, you've just got to draw a line and say no.

"OK, I admit, you've caught me, and that gives you the right to gloat, no question. Threaten me, taunt me, even torture me, that's fine, but never ever talk about yourself in the third person. That is going too far, I'm against it, and I'm saying no."

"You talk too much, plaything," Mallax growled.

"Really? I thought you wanted me to be entertaining. Well, this is me entertaining you. And I'll tell you something else," she continued. "If you'd got me in this position only a week ago, I have to confess I would have been in a bit of trouble, but it's not a week ago, it's now.

"You see, back home, I have a girlfriend, Catriona. Oh, she's magnificent! Really funny, totally gorgeous, and so, so smart. Seriously, she has an absolute genius talent for magic, and I don't throw the g-word around lightly because I'm in the room. The reason I mention this is that she recently figured out something important about anti-magic fields. Would you like to know what it is?"

"Astound us."

"They're useless. An anti-magic field is itself a form of magic. So, if Cat were here, she'd adapt her magical frequency to run off the field itself. The thing is, though, Cat and I do things differently when it comes to magic. I've learned to drain power, syphon it off and add it to my own. On the way here, I met a very helpful dragon. He gave me a ride, and on that journey, I analysed his magic. Through that, I was able to drain many more of the dragons I killed on the way, and pretty soon, I got a handle on how your dragon magic works.

"Anyway, I'm sure you don't want to know all the technical stuff. The point is, you think you've trapped me in an anti-magic field, but in reality, you've just made me stronger!"

Draining power from the surrounding field, she drew it into herself and fed it her blood. Even as she had been talking, she had been attuning her magic, reaching beyond the glass walls, and quietly reversing the reflection field. As the power grew, the air began to vibrate and hum with energy. It was too much power for her to absorb, but she didn't need to absorb it, just ignite it where it lay. The looks on the faces of all the dragons in that place – the twelve elite guards, and Mallax himself – switched from arrogance to terror in an instant.

The time was now; her power word was ready once more. Focusing on the glass jar, she said, "SHATTER," and the glass blew outwards. She levitated high into the air so that she was level with Mallax' great head.

"What manner of creature am I?" Dreya taunted him. "Oh, to hell with it, just this once, I'm actually going to say it…" She gave a chilling smile, and told him, "I'm your worst nightmare!"

She unleashed a devastating beam of energy straight at Mallax, blasting a hole right through him and coming out the other side. He was in agony, but still alive.

"Kill it!" he gasped, and his guards turned to fight, but it was too late. Far too late. Everything they threw at her reflected back at them, while Dreya shielded like never before and drew the power in close, letting it build for a second or two, before unleashing it. The blast flew out in a ring of fire, pushing outwards, engulfing everything in its path. A moment later, the Citadel of Doom was gone, replaced by a crater in the ground, with a lone Faery woman in the centre of the devastation. Mallax' guards and all dragons in a one-mile radius were incinerated. Only Mallax remained. Focusing her will on him, knowing he was sufficiently weakened, she unfolded her power word, "DIE," killing him on the spot.

When more dragons flew to the scene, she levitated up high to intercept them. "I am Mistress Dreya the Dark," she declared. "Let it be known that Mallax is dead, and his regime dies with him. I am now the ruler of Phitonia. If any of you want to dispute that, come over here, and I'll quite happily kill you." There were no takers. "Alright then," she continued, returning to the ground, "let us begin changing your world."

Chapter 4

Dreya sat down on the foreleg of the dead Mallax, reinforcing the message that she was now their new ruler, and they were to obey her as they had him. According to the Chetsuans, dragons respected strength and power, Dreya now needed to consolidate hers.

"First, a question," she began, "about these Chetsuans of yours, which of you here has killed the most?"

"We don't keep score!" a green dragon scoffed.

"Maybe not," Dreya allowed, "but I bet you still know. Surely there must be someone around here who likes to brag! Feel free to talk amongst yourselves, but none of you is leaving here until I get an answer, and if I don't get an answer quickly, I'm going to get upset."

After a quick discussion, the original green spoke up again, addressing his peers.

"Come on, it's me! You all know it! I've exterminated way more vermin than you lot!"

Dreya was not surprised. She suspected that despite his initial remark, he did keep score. He would serve her purposes very nicely.

"Come down here and tell me your name," she commanded, "I have a special assignment in mind for you."

The dragon thanked her and introduced himself as Madroit, Champion of the Green, while the others made room for him to land. Climbing onto his back, she asked him to fly her a short distance away, while she fished Jessica's phone device out of a pocket, selected the camera app and tried to get Mallax's carcass in shot. When they were at the optimum distance, she asked Madroit to hover while she took a few shots.

Job done, she opened a Prismatic Sphere portal to her Black Tower home on Tempestria.

"You lot wait here," she told the assembled dragons. "I'll be back shortly." Without further ado, she urged Madroit to fly through the portal. "It should be safe while you're with me," she reassured him, planting the idea in the other dragons' minds that it might be dangerous for them to use her portals without her. It didn't even break her self-imposed rule against lying: For all she knew, it might be dangerous – she'd never tried to portal a dragon before.

She materialised over her Tower, just as Laethyn entered her grounds. His furious expression quickly changed to a mixture of surprise, shock, fear and utter astonishment at the sight of Dreya the Dark on dragonback.

She ordered Madroit to land.

As soon as she dismounted, she focussed her will on the dragon, and said, "STUN," paralysing him completely. Then, calling for her elite guards, she ordered them to fetch something she'd had made for her in Gaggleswick. It was similar to a saddle and tack one might routinely use on a horse but imbued with magic and much bigger because it was intended to control a dragon.

While her death knights attached it to the protesting Madroit and made the necessary adjustments, Dreya levitated herself back through the portal to the waiting dragons. The sorceress decreed that there were going to be some new rules regarding Chetsuans on Phitonia.

"Chetsuans are not vermin. Chetsuans are not food. You will not harm Chetsuans." She considered qualifying the last rule with 'except in self-defence', but frankly, they would have to work very hard to convince her that Chetsuans were any threat to the life of a dragon. "Leave them be. Allow them to come out of hiding and start rebuilding their communities. I'm giving you five days to spread the word so that every dragon understands the rules and Chetsuans everywhere know about the regime change that's happened here today."

"But that's not enough time!" complained one blue scaled dragon.

"Thank you so much for your opinion," Dreya replied, following up with her power word, "PAIN."

The dragon bellowed in agony. After a moment, she cancelled her power word. "Anyone else agree with that assessment?" she asked. None did. "Excellent. Let me be clear: when I say to do something, you will do it. I will discuss practical ideas of how it may be accomplished but don't ever tell me it can't be done. Now stop wasting time. I'll be back here in five days to inspect your progress, and if I'm not satisfied, I'm going to get upset again."

Without further comment, Dreya returned to Tempestria and went to greet Laethyn.

*****

"Welcome to my Black Tower, Master Laethyn," she greeted him, formally.

"Dreya, what the hell is that?" asked the leader of the black robes, pointing to the monster in her grounds.

"That is Madroit, Champion of the Green, apparently," she replied, pleasantly, taking his arm as they strolled together back towards her Tower. "He's a dragon, my prisoner and my gift to you."

"A gift?"

Dreya nodded, saying, "I'm hoping that transferring my prisoner to you might buy your silence for a while. I had good reasons for doing what I did, reasons that will be revealed soon, but if my theft came to light now, it could disrupt the plans we've made. How are they progressing, by the way?"

"Everything will be ready when you give the signal," he promised. "As for your gift, you have a deal. My silence in exchange for your dragon as my prisoner."

Madroit protested, "But Mistress Dreya! You can't just hand me over like this! You told me you had an assignment!"

"Yes, I'm assigning you to be Laethyn's transport, guard, or whatever job he might have for you."

"But you can't keep me trapped in this alien world – I have a mate, a family!"

"And how many Chetsuan families have you destroyed?"

"What do those vermin have to do with anything?"

Dreya told him the new rules regarding Chetsuans on Phitonia and explained further, "Since I can't realistically kill every dragon that's ever killed a Chetsuan, and because you confessed to killing more than any of your peers, I'm making an example of you. The only reason you're still alive is that I owe Laethyn here a favour."

"But that's not fair!" Madroit objected. "I only killed Chetsuans because Mallax said we had to exterminate them, because they were vermin. It's not my fault – I was just following orders."

"Oh well, that's different," Dreya accepted. "In that case, you're right. It wouldn't be fair to voluntarily hand you over." To

22

Laethyn, she added, "But of course, despite our little arrangement, you are still my superior on the Council, are you not, Master Laethyn?"

"Yes, absolutely," Laethyn agreed with a crooked smile. He could see where this was going.

"So, is there anything you'd like me to do for you?"

"As a matter of fact, there is," Laethyn affirmed. "Dreya, as Master of the Black Robes of Dark Magic and under the authority of the Triumvirate, I officially order you to hand over that dragon to me."

Dreya bowed, respectfully. "Very well, Master Laethyn, the dragon is yours, with my compliments." As an aside to Madroit, she concluded, "You see? It's not my fault – I'm just following orders."

Since Laethyn was satisfied with the deal, Dreya transferred the control magic in the dragon harness to him. The two Dark mages shook hands and parted ways. Laethyn mounted the dragon and flew away, while Dreya entered her home.

*****

She spent a full day and night there, eating, resting, sleeping, relaxing. By her calculations, a day on Tempestria was about four days on Phitonia or Earth. That gave her one Earth day to check in with Sara and Jessica.

She didn't want to spook them by opening a portal herself, so instead, she teleported to StormClaw and used Daelen's portal system. The two Earth-based Chetsuans were alerted by the unauthorised intrusion, but immediately stood down and greeted her warmly when they saw it was her.

They shared another cup of tea and a chat, although this time Sara thought she might enjoy the beauty of Catriona's Meadow, rather than the dusty old library.

As they stepped outside, Dreya gasped in astonishment, "Catriona did all this?"

Catriona had once taken Dreya to visit Quarthonia, her childhood home among the Faery. It was a strange experience for her girlfriend because even as she was showing Dreya some of the places she'd liked to play as a child, Cat had realised that it wasn't exactly true. All those places had been destroyed in the devastating attack that had robbed her of her parents. What existed there now had been recreated by what she referred to as her Angel.

She had even asked Dreya, "Can it still be my childhood home, if it's just a recreation? Are these still the places I used to play if they were destroyed and brought back?"

For a long moment, Dreya had no idea how to answer that. In the end, she told her, "I think it's all a question of belief. If you believe it's truly your childhood home, then it's true for you, and maybe that's all that matters."

Some of the places Cat had shown her that day, Dreya could see were perfectly replicated here. The sorceress could only imagine what had been going through Cat's mind as she created the place in which Dreya now stood. If not for the lack of void storms, the sorceress could easily believe she had taken a wrong turn with her portals and ended up in the heart of Quarthonia on Tempestria. It was almost as if the same place somehow existed in two worlds, simultaneously.

In answer to her partially rhetorical question, Jessica nodded, "Got mad with Daelen, ripped his training centre apart and created all this in one afternoon. Never seen anything like it."

Sara returned the book and photos that Dreya had left with her for safekeeping, and Dreya returned Jessica's phone, in exchange, absently advising her to check the last few pictures.

Jessica gasped when she saw them.

"That's Mallax! You did it – you killed him! Look, Sara!" she exclaimed, showing her sister.

"So, does this mean you rule the world now?" Sara wondered.

"I'm doing what I can." When the sorceress revealed the new status of Chetsuans on Phitonia, Jessica threw her arms around her and declared, "Dreya, love, you're my hero!"

"I'm no hero," Dreya insisted, but Jessica dismissed the sentiment.

"That's what heroes always say," she returned. "I mean, I know we still can't ever go there again, but never mind us, you've only gone and saved our people!"

Sara seemed to be in shock. "Why?" she whispered. "We barely even know you. Why would you do this for us?"

"I didn't. I did it for myself, but I couldn't have done it without your help, so it's only right that you should benefit from it, too. I always pay my debts."

"Who cares why?" Jessica asked her sister. "She did it, that's what counts."

"If helping myself helps your people, then I'm happy to do it," Dreya stated, simply. "It cost me nothing. But I have to warn you: I can't guarantee your people will be safe from any further dragon attacks forevermore."

"Of course you can't, dearie," Jessica replied, dismissively. "You can't guarantee I won't get run over by a bus tomorrow, either. That's life."

Dreya didn't know what a bus was, but she understood the point she was making, all the same.

Sara nodded her agreement. "You've given our people a chance, so whether you think you're a hero or not, I'm grateful, and I'll tell you another thing: I think you've helped us make up our minds about something." She glanced at her sister for confirmation, who answered her unspoken question with a nod. Sara showed the Faery sorceress Daelen's note.

Dear Sara and Jessica

If I've set the timer properly, then by the time you read this, I will be on Tempestria on the eve of my ultimate final battle against Kullos. I've enjoyed the time I've spent with you, and I'm sorry if I didn't always treat you as well as I should, but I won't be seeing you again, so I'm taking this last chance to keep you safe. At the last possible moment, I will bring Kullos to my secret island, there to destroy us both. It is a shame to die when I've just found a new reason to live, but I have to keep Catriona safe. I have to save her world so she can keep on living her extraordinary life.

But I also need to keep you two safe. That is why I'm writing this. You have to leave, and you have to go now because there is every chance that all my bases will be destroyed. I'm sorry I didn't tell you sooner, but I know you'd have wanted to come and help me. You can't. In the end, I have to do this alone. This is not your fight. Forget about me, choose a world and live your lives. You can pick any world you wish, of course, but I think your best options are to stay on Earth or come to Tempestria. In either case, take as much money and supplies as you need – it's all yours.

In the case of Tempestria, I am attaching directions to a small boat on the Eastern shoreline that can easily take you to Esca – it's only a short hop. Once there, I suggest you go to a place called Calin's Tower. You will be safe there, and I will ask Cat and Mandalee to come and find you. If you're not there, they will know you've chosen Earth, and I'm sure they'll understand.

Thank you for everything and have a great life, both of you.
Your friend
Daelen StormTiger

"Thanks to you," Sara continued, when Dreya looked up from the note, "we've got advance warning, and we've had a chance to talk about it while you were fighting dragons."

"The thing is, love, I'll be sad to leave Earth. I've got used to it here – heck, I've practically gone native – but nobody really knows us here. We have to lie all the time."

Sara nodded. "There's a boy I've been seeing—"

"—And snogging!" Jessica put in.

"Yes, and snogging," her sister admitted, "but the only time he saw the real me, he thought it was a costume when, in reality, the human girl he thinks I am – *that's* my costume. What kind of basis is that for a relationship? Still, we weren't too sure what to do, were we Jess?"

"No, but now we are," Jessica continued. "We want to take a chance on Tempestria. At least there we've got three real mates, but the way we see it, if we want to live on your world, we can't just sit here twiddling our thumbs while you guys try and save it from that Kullos bloke."

"If we're going to live there, then we have a stake in what happens. That's where Daelen's wrong," Sara insisted. "If we're choosing Tempestria, then it absolutely is our fight. So, will you help us to help you? This big battle that's coming, can you take us to where we need to be? I know you kicked our arses, but I still reckon against anybody else, we can make a difference."

"I agree. Please don't judge yourselves based on losing to me – the only person who's got the better of me since I was a child is Catriona. She's annoying like that."

"In a good way?" Sara smiled.

Dreya matched her smile with her own. "In the best way."

"Oh, my gosh!" Jessica gushed. "I can't wait to see you two lovebirds together! But seriously, we're in your hands, Dreya love. Whatever plan you've got cooking in that head of yours, we want in."

Dreya considered their words, thinking how best to incorporate the Chetsuans into her schemes. At length, an idea formed in her head that appealed to her enormously. It was just a question of whether they would go for it. It was asking a lot.

"What if," she began, "there was a way for you to fight for Tempestria, get some personal revenge against the dragons, and just briefly see a bit of your world without risk to your people, all as part of the same plan?"

"Well," Sara replied, "as my sister would say, 'you can colour me intrigued'."

Once the plan was agreed, Dreya found she had some time to kill, so she asked her new friends if they could show her some of this Earth city they were in, including the shopping mall.

After some tests, she confirmed that as long as she had her micro-portal open to Tempestria, she could ward off any ill-effects from synthetic fabrics. Sara immediately had the perfect outfit in mind: the black velvet dress Mandalee had bought for Cat on their first night there. Dreya agreed it was an impeccable choice. Stopping just a couple of inches above the knee, the dress was a lot shorter than anything she was used to, but she found she rather liked it. The colour was almost identical to her usual robes, although the fabric wasn't quite as luxurious. The heels took a bit of getting used to, but Faery were known for their grace, so it didn't take her long to adjust. Her Faery markings were no issue – people would simply take them for tattoos. That left one problem: the tiny straps of the dress did nothing at all to hide her winglets. But Jessica gave her a loose black shrug, and that sorted that out. Now, all anyone would see was a beautiful, slightly petite young woman with some rather elegant tattoo spots. All the two Chetsuans needed was to grab their perception filters on the way out and they were all ready.

When they reached the mall, Jessica asked, "Well, you asked to come here, love, so does that mean you're looking for something in particular?"

"Actually, yes," Dreya confirmed.

When she told them what she wanted, they both started singing a tune that she naturally didn't recognise but presumably meant something to them.

After a few hours of shopping and sightseeing, they shared a meal and some conversation at a restaurant before returning to Daelen's place. Dreya couldn't remember the last time she had enjoyed herself so much without using or even thinking about magic at all. But as she changed back into her customary Tempestrian robes, she knew the time for that was passed. She had just received a very important sympathic call.

Chapter 5

The remainder of the sea voyage to the continent of Northern Alloria had been uneventful – mercifully so, as it had allowed the two young women and one leopard time to recover and adjust their body clocks back to their homeworld.

In general, it was good to be home, but Mandalee did express one regret at leaving Earth so suddenly: After all the shopping she had done, she'd left all of her Earth clothes behind. All except a pair of blue sapphire earrings that she'd barely taken off since buying them. Meagre souvenirs, but at least she had something.

They had left Earth about a week early, Earth time, which on Tempestria was just a couple of days ahead of schedule. That meant they should reach the temple ruins no more than a day either side of when Michael and his team arrived.

Mandalee offered to begin teaching Catriona to speak the language of leopards, telepathically, so her two friends could communicate more easily, and Cat jumped at the offer. Before the lesson, though, Daelen told them it was time to fill them in on his battle plans.

*****

What he told them, gentle reader, he had implied before, so it wasn't entirely new, only a fleshing out of details. Michael would not be turning up alone. Far from it. There was a group, an organisation, dedicated to him – Jessica would no doubt describe it as a 'fan club'. Where Mandalee and Cat were from, on Elvaria, it had never really caught on as much, so it was understandable that they didn't know about it. Throughout Alloria, however, it was almost a religion built around what they saw as a tragic, legendary hero. Many of them were capable fighters, clerics, wizards – a diverse group who most likely wouldn't have anything in common, were it not for Michael. As for the demigod himself, he appreciated what they stood for, even if it made him uncomfortable being idolised. They also had the irksome habit of referring to him as 'Mickey'. They may be fans of Michael's, but he was not a fan of that name. Still, if he turned up at one of their meetings and asked for their help in fighting Kullos' army, they would pledge themselves in a heartbeat. It was difficult to estimate numbers, but every little helped.

*****

When they approached Corolis Harbour, the port that served visitors to the forest of the same name, Daelen dived overboard and swam the rest of the way while Cat changed to seagull form – well out of sight of Shyleen, just in case she was hungry – and flew ashore, indistinguishable from the flock of such birds that flew around the bay. That left Mandalee on board with Shyleen. The assassin had registered the *Dolphin* in her name so, in the unlikely event that anyone checked, the records would show that she chartered the ship to sail there alone from Kingsville Piers on Elvaria.

It was late, so after meeting up they didn't travel far before finding a place to camp for the night.

*****

The next morning, Cat awoke to the sounds of two tigers play-fighting. One of them was quite obviously Daelen. She watched for a little while – it was good to see her friend having fun. She supposed it might be his last chance before the real fighting started. After a while, the real tiger grew either tired or bored – she wasn't sure which – and wandered off. Daelen changed back into his human form, wished her a good morning and asked if she would take a walk with him so he could talk to her about something alone before Mandalee woke up.

"It won't take long," he assured her. "We'll be back before she starts to worry that we've been kidnapped or something."

Cat shook her head. That wouldn't be an issue. "She'll be able to tell from our tracks that we've just gone for a stroll."

"Well then," Daelen offered his arm, "shall we?"

The druidess laid her hand gently on his arm and began to walk with him. Seeing that he wasn't going to speak immediately, she tried to break the ice.

"You seem to be a little out of practice with your tiger form, Daelen," she offered, good-naturedly.

"It was a perfectly convincing tiger," he objected.

"To most people, perhaps," Cat allowed.

"But not to you?"

"Not to that tiger, either," she continued. "He found you quite funny."

"You know this from what Mandalee's been teaching you?"

"Partly," Cat allowed. "Mandalee told me that the languages of all big cats have a common root structure and knowing one gives the essence of another. Tigers aren't great conversationalists anyway, so I find them relatively easy to understand with the aid of my sympathic skills. More than that, though, I learned long ago that just taking on the form of an animal is a long way from actually becoming that animal. Remember I told you that when I went flying as an owl on Earth, I was harassed by another owl?"

Daelen smiled. "I remember your ruffled feathers."

Cat returned the smile. "Yes, well, my point is, convincing humans that you're a tiger is easy. Convincing other tigers is the real test. Think of it this way: suppose Shyleen had morphogenic abilities and she took the form of a human woman. She might convince other animals she was human, but if she didn't know how to speak the human language, act or think like a human, she wouldn't fool us for long. Why do you think I limit the number of animals I change into? In principle, I can take the form of any animal I like, but I won't do it in public until I learn how to truly become that animal. That takes time, study and practice."

After a moment, she cut the small talk and pressed, "So, Daelen, what is so important that you can tell only me and not Mandalee?"

"Well, I've been thinking about a lot of things, like this battle with Kullos, and the thing is, Cat, I want you to let me do it alone, even though I won't be coming back."

From her conversation with the Chetsuans, Cat already had an inkling that he was thinking along those lines.

From her expression, Daelen could tell she wasn't in favour of the idea, but he rushed headlong to explain before she could get a word in.

"I realise I'm asking that you stand by and let me kill myself, but that's how it must be. Taking care of his army is the best thing you can do to help – it will ensure I'm at peak power levels when I confront Kullos – but if what I'm thinking will happen comes true, then I need you to give me your word that you won't interfere with my battle with him. Please, Cat, I need to know that you – and Mandalee of course – are safe. I want you to be able to live a full and happy life. If I destroy Kullos, then there will be some peace for all of you." She opened her mouth, but he cut her off. "Yes, I know that you'll miss me, and I'm sorry about that, but it's for the best. Please, Cat, promise me."

Seeing he was at last done, Catriona took a deep breath and let it out slowly, collecting her thoughts and taking her sweet time before answering.

"No, Daelen, I cannot promise that. I have listened patiently to your reasoning, but it changes nothing. You will not face Kullos alone, and that is the end of it. I will not allow it, and no power you possess will prevent me from fighting by your side. It is not for you to protect me – I reject that utterly – and it's not just your fight; it's mine, too."

"Please, Cat—"

"Daelen!" she interrupted, her tone warning him to be quiet. He'd had his say. It was her turn, now. "There is great danger, not only from Kullos, but also from you. Yes, he has great power, but so do you, and that is precisely the reason I must be with you. All power can be defeated and, if necessary, I will find a way to defeat yours as well as his."

"But even Michael won't be with me this time," Daelen pointed out. "Keeping him out of it at the end should break his Curse and allow him to live his own free life at long last."

Catriona remembered the demigod telling her that he was cursed to die permanently during the final war of the shadow warriors.

"Good for him," she acknowledged.

"Alycia's barrier will prevent anyone else from my plane coming here ever again, so your world – all mortal worlds – will be free from our interference, as it should be."

"Sometimes, your interference is a good thing," Cat countered. "Just ask Sara and Jessica."

"That's another thing," he put in.

He went on to explain about the letter he had hidden in his library. Through her link with Dreya, of course, Cat already knew that his plans for the Chetsuans had been superseded but didn't tell him so.

"Enough!" she cut him off, eyes flashing. "What Sara and Jessica choose to do is up to them. As for me, I have given you my answer, Daelen, and the subject is closed. Now, if you will excuse me, I think I'll go and see if Mandalee's awake."

With that, she walked away.

"That went well," Daelen grumbled to himself when she'd gone.

When she was alone, Cat communicated with Dreya, sympathetically. The time was fast approaching when she was going to need her, and she wanted to check if she was ready. She wasn't. Not quite. Dreya just needed a little more time to finish off what she was doing; she'd been busy. They agreed on a time to put their plan into action and ended their communication.

*****

Two days later, having picked up horses from a stable at the harbour, Daelen and his two friends reached the edge of the Corolis Wood. They found the ancient temple ruins and made camp there to wait for 'Mickey' and his 'fan club' to arrive. Already they could see the foliage had thinned markedly. Less than one more day's ride and they would officially be in the Rhynas Desert, a stone's throw from where Kullos' hidden army was based.

Once they had consolidated their strength, they would begin careful scouting and lay some plans. In three days, they would attack.

Since reaching the temple ruins, Catriona had become distant for a while. Daelen was wondering if she was thinking more about their conversation, the other day. He hoped he could find a way to get her to change her mind. If necessary, there were other ways to keep her out of things, but he'd rather have her agreement, if possible.

As night fell and the last of the sun's glowing embers faded, judging by Catriona's expression, she seemed to reach a decision.

Almost as if she had been counting down to some event – he knew not what – and that countdown had finally reached zero.

"So, this is it, then," she noted, approaching him. "We're almost at the end of our quest. We've come a long way together, and I don't just mean in terms of distance travelled."

"Yes," Daelen agreed, "I know what you mean. It's a shame it has to end at all, in a way. I haven't enjoyed myself this much in a long time. Soon, though, it will be time to strike. Once Michael and the others arrive, all our forces will be in place."

"Ah, not quite all," Cat disagreed. "There is one more who is yet to take their place among us."

"Who's that?" Mandalee asked, wandering over to join them.

"Someone who is key to so much more than you yet know about. Now the time has come to reveal what I've been hiding from you both." Before either friend could respond, she suddenly asked, "Daelen, do you trust me?" She didn't need to ask Mandalee that question.

"Yes, of course I trust you, Cat. What's this about?"

"I need you to hold on to that trust now and try to understand that there are things that circumstances compelled me to do. You may not like it, but I hope your faith in me will be enough to see beyond that and accept that it was necessary and for the best.

"Also, regarding our feelings for each other, we both know where we stand, don't we?"

"Yes, Cat, I do, although I confess, I also wish you would tell me why you won't return my affections."

Catriona smiled apprehensively, "Yes, well, the time has arrived when I can finally tell you. The truth is simple, Daelen. I do care for you, but I cannot love you the way you would wish, because I am already in love with someone else. I'm sorry."

The pain Daelen experienced felt as if an old scar over his heart had freshly torn open. It was irrational, he knew. What difference did it make? A few more days and he would be dead. Still, there was something he wanted to know.

"Why, Cat? Why couldn't you have just told me that instead of…"

"…Leading you on? I swear I never meant to do that. I wanted to explain, but I literally couldn't."

"This is your magically backed promise, isn't it?" Mandalee realised.

Cat confirmed it. "You see, I promised that my lover would remain secret and hidden until the moment was right, and I agreed to enforce my promise with magic. That's why I couldn't explain my feelings to you until now."

"So, who is this lover of yours?" Daelen asked.

"That's the part I can't tell you." It was such a natural question; it was almost inevitable that he would ask it. Since she was blocked from answering, she had always felt it best to say nothing at all. "But now that the time is right, I can show you."

Chapter 6

Taking a deep breath, she closed her eyes, opened a Prismatic Sphere portal and began to focus her sympathic senses, reaching out to nature to enhance her link with another. Help her communicate better with someone perhaps half a world away, or on another world, entirely. They would each open a portal, and as long as their link was strong enough, she was sure their magic and their love would guide their portals to find each other, forming a conduit between them.

Of course, that idea was merely a product of Catriona's romantic nature. In reality, she had Dreya's co-ordinates.

"Come forth, my love," she declared. "The time is right; the stage is set. It is time for you to take your place among us at this crucial time. Come to us, O Shadow in the Night. Reveal your glory and your power in my time of need. My journey is almost complete, and you must fulfil your end. Keep your promise; pay your debt. Come, my Dark Angel, come!"

Daelen found his attention drawn to the shadows around the portal in the trees, and before his eyes, the darkness seemed to grow darker. It was as if something had materialised in the shade of those trees. Something darker even than darkness itself. Catriona smiled and opened her eyes, matching the direction of Daelen's gaze.

"My love," she whispered once more, as out of the shadows stepped…another shadow. A shadow with a humanoid shape.

The shadow spoke with quiet humour, in a voice that filled the night, "A simple 'come here' would have sufficed."

The shadow gained substance, somehow growing darker still in the process, until a figure was standing there, Black robes concealing every inch of skin. The figure radiated a power that gave even the mighty Daelen reason to initiate a few precautionary defences. But it wasn't just her power, it was the way the power surrounded her. Her robes looked like they were woven from the fabric of the night, as if the very essence of Dark magic itself were a lover, caressing the young woman in its velvet embrace. Everything about her spoke of control and mastery. She was not a person to be taken lightly.

When the figure spoke again, this time, the voice was sharper.

"But then, you always did have a flair for the dramatic, Cat. That is one of your many attractive features."

As she finished speaking, she untucked her hands from the sleeves of her robes and threw off her hood. Daelen let out a sharp breath when he saw her face – he knew her. Or at least part of him did. That part of him that was once the dark clone, Aden, recognised this individual as the sorceress known as Dreya the Dark. She was the only mortal mage the dark clone had ever considered worthy of notice. The one he had tried to recruit to his side. The one who had bested him; almost killed him.

Long, shiny, midnight black hair framed Dreya's face and flowed down her back. Her sapphire eyes, deep as the ocean, sparkling with a cool light of their own, were the only splashes of colour to offset the black of her robes and the marble white skin of her face and slender hands. She was undeniably beautiful, but not as Catriona or Mandalee were beautiful. In Catriona Redfletching, he saw the beauty of nature; in Mandalee, he saw the fiery beauty of a heart that was ready to fight to preserve life and goodness in the world. Faery were said to glow with the light of the sun, and that light was there in this one, too – Daelen could see it in her eyes, especially when she looked at Catriona. But the way she shrouded her light, reminded him alarmingly of how he had described the shadow warriors to Catriona: light in a box. He didn't know what that might mean for her future, but she was unquestionably one to be watched at all times.

Catriona didn't seem to mind, though, the way she embraced her girlfriend. Once separate again, Dreya invoked her arcane magic and a bunch of roses appeared in her hand – a mixture of white and black, interspersed with the traditional red. It was a romantic gift that symbolised the balance in which Catriona believed. Cat was delighted and kissed Dreya full on the lips.

Mandalee leaned close to the shadow warrior at that moment and whispered, "How come you never gave her flowers? She gave you an entire garden, and you never thought to give her a single flower? Seriously, Daelen, if you haven't learned that women like flowers in all the centuries you've been coming to this world, there truly is no hope for you."

Folding her arms and turning her back on him, she continued to watch Catriona and Dreya. She was impressed by the chemistry between them and very happy for her friend.

"Doesn't it bother you?" Daelen asked, softly. "Her choice of partner, I mean."

Mandalee turned and glared at him. "I hope that's not a reference to my friend's sexuality, Daelen."

"No, I didn't mean it like that," he assured her, shaking his head emphatically. "I mean, this Dreya specifically – she's devoted to evil and darkness."

"The latter, certainly. The former, I'm not so sure. I'll admit I was sceptical about their association myself, at first. Now I can see I was wrong. Although to be fair to myself, I was hurt and angry at the time. No doubt that coloured my perception."

"Wait – you knew about this?"

The assassin shrugged. "I knew they'd started an association, maybe even a friendship, but that was over two years ago. Cat and I parted ways for a time – long story, doesn't matter – and since I met her again, I guess she had her magically backed promise in effect. Come to think of it, the rumour about those two came up while we were at Calin's Tower, but it never occurred to me to take it seriously."

"So, you don't see any problems with this?" Daelen pressed.

'*Love strikes where it will*,' Shyleen considered, philosophically.

Mandalee repeated that aloud for Daelen's benefit, adding, "but Cat's a sensible girl. She knows what she's getting herself into, and if she trusts Dreya, that's good enough for me."

Deciding it was time to back up her words with actions, she wandered over to the smooching couple.

"Hey," she called out. "Mind if I break up the party?"

Cat smiled and welcomed her, reintroducing the two most important women in her life to each other.

"Dreya, you remember Mandalee, don't you? You met, briefly, just once."

"Of course," Dreya replied, "under most unfortunate circumstances, as I recall."

"Greetings, Mistress Dreya," Mandalee offered, adopting a formal style of address, for though they were of different orders, it was proper to acknowledge Dreya's high rank and position in the Council of Wizards.

The sorceress, however, assured her there was no need to use titles, insisting, "Just Dreya will be fine, thank you, White Assassin."

"Please," she protested with a grin, "I'll admit I am warming to that title, but it's still pretty new and squeaks when you use it. Best to stick to Mandalee, I think."

"Mandalee it is, then," Dreya agreed, offering her hand.

"Screw the handshake," Mandalee declared, then seeing the frowns on Dreya and Cat's faces, she clarified, "I mean, I've just found out you're my best friend's girlfriend. I think we can do a bit better than shaking hands." She held her arms wide. "May I?"

Dreya smiled. "Of course," she replied, embracing her. "By the way," she remarked, when they moved apart, "I saw what you did on StormClaw Island. More than fifty enemies with two small knives? That was impressive even by my standards."

Mandalee smiled grimly. "What can I say? I was upset at the time."

Dreya arched her perfectly plucked eyebrows. "Remind me never to upset you."

"Keep making Cat happy, and you don't need to worry about me. Hurt her, and I'll kill you myself."

"Completely fair," Dreya agreed.

*****

This was indeed a momentous occasion, gentle reader. At the time, they knew only that this was the first time a Dark wizard had ever hugged a cleric of Light, but the true significance was far more profound than that, as they would soon discover.

*****

"So, are you First Wizard of the Order of Dark Magic yet, or perhaps Mistress of the entire Council of Wizards?" the assassin asked, by way of conversation.

Dreya smiled and shook her head. "There is no Mistress of the Council, as you well know – there's a Triumvirate, and I have no desire to change that, although changes are afoot. As for my Order of Dark Magic, I am content with being Black Secondmage. Anything higher would take too much time away from my magic research. Although, just between us," she dropped her voice to a conspiratorial whisper, "I do have the head of my order firmly in my pocket."

"Of course you do," Mandalee nodded, not the least bit surprised.

"Oh, and Cat," Dreya added, "you will be pleased to learn the name has now changed to Council of Mages. They agreed that 'Wizards' discriminated against druids and, arguably, women."

"That's great!"

"There are even moves to invite clerics to join the new Council," the sorceress continued. "Diversity is strength and anything that increases the power of magic gets my vote."

Mandalee shook her head in disbelief. "Clerics of Light, Dark and Balance sitting in council in the same room without that room exploding? I don't think the world has changed that much yet, Dreya."

It had happened once, she knew, but it led to the Demon Apocalypse, and the experiment had not been repeated.

"Perhaps not, but the door is open to any who wish to join."

"If I joined, could I still use physical weapons as well as clerical magic? I value my clerical powers, but I don't want to give up my weapons. Oh, and Daelen gave me this cool new body armour. Don't want to lose...that..."

Mandalee trailed off as, belatedly, her brain linked her body armour, Catriona's initial allergic reaction, and the obvious fact that Dreya was full Faery.

"Dreya!" she gasped. "I'm so sorry, are you OK? I didn't think."

The sorceress frowned, puzzled.

"I mean the synthetic fabric," she clarified.

Dreya nodded her understanding.

"Don't worry, Mandalee," Cat reassured her, "nothing gets through Dreya's shields."

"Except for you, Cat," Dreya countered.

Catriona smiled, broadly, and kissed her again.

Mandalee was surprised to hear Dreya say such a beautiful thing while someone else was standing right there. It was unconventional, but she could see what it meant to her best friend, and with that, she began to understand their relationship better.

Shattering her introspection, Dreya answered her previous question. "Until the clerical Orders join as a whole, the terms are open. The restrictions will continue to apply only to wizard magic and druid magic; you can do as you please with your clerical powers. It may not be strictly fair, and that's one of many things we'll have to look at long term, but for now, that's as far as we've got. It takes time, but I'll knock this world's magic into shape eventually."

"In that case, on a personal level, I formally request full membership of the Council of Mages, in the Order of Light," Mandalee declared.

"As a Druid Mage of the Order of Balance, I sponsor and support the membership of Mandalee the White Assassin and Cleric of Nature," Catriona quickly added.

"Then, by the powers vested in me by the Council, as Secondmage of the Order of Darkness, I hereby recognise the full membership of Mandalee the White Assassin and Cleric of Nature."

Catriona's eyes suddenly glazed over, and she almost fell, but Dreya caught her arm and supported her easily, with a strength that Mandalee was surprised the sorceress possessed.

"Mandalee, you're the healer!" she cried. "Do something!"

If her mind still entertained any doubts about how much Dreya cared for her friend, they were snuffed out in that instant, but Catriona seemed to recover almost immediately.

"It's OK," she assured them. "I'm fine, honestly. Just staff business. Dreya, I'll need to talk to you before too long, but right now, you'd better go make yourself known to Daelen."

Dreya hesitated. "Well, if you're sure you're alright."

"Look, if it makes you happy, I'll go with Mandalee, and she can check me over thoroughly."

Dreya accepted that, and Cat allowed her friend to lead her away.

Mandalee whispered, "Dreya knows about your staff and everything, doesn't she?"

Cat nodded, "Sorry I couldn't tell you about her."

"That's OK. Being completely honest, I'm not sure I would have understood if you had. Seeing you together like this is much better, and I'm really happy for you."

"I know I keep saying this," Cat said as she hugged her, "but you really are the best."

"So," Mandalee smirked, breaking the hug and linking arms as she walked with her best friend, "my initiation was important, somehow, was it?"

"Very important, I'd say, judging by the jolt it gave me."

Mandalee grinned, "That good, huh?"

Cat's eyes glazed over, "By the gods, you have no idea!"

"As Sara and Jessica would say, 'Blimey'!"

Chapter 7

As Mandalee led Catriona away, Dreya stepped up to Daelen, who had turned his back on the proceedings.

"So, you are the mighty Daelen StormTiger," she observed.

When the shadow warrior turned around, she bowed her head in reverence. At first, the shadow warrior thought she was mocking him, but she gave no indication that she was anything other than genuine.

With an icy cool voice, the sorceress continued, "I have long admired your power. You could even say that you are my inspiration. It's funny how life works, sometimes, isn't it? I mean, here I am preparing to fight by your side when I've been looking forward to killing you for so long."

That was just about all Daelen could stand in his current mood. With a roar, he flew into the air, and without further warning, he powered up and fired his beam cannon straight at the brazen witch.

His power flared around the sorceress, but when he could see again, Daelen was amazed to see her standing there, apparently untouched.

She stretched luxuriously with feline grace. "Why thank you, Daelen, it was very nice of you to give me so much power to absorb." In truth, anticipating such a response, she was maintaining an active link with her guards through a micro-portal. That meant she was able to share the power when it was too much to absorb herself. "Mmmm," she purred, "that felt good…I wonder if it works as well for you."

A blast of energy hit the unprepared shadow warrior full in the chest, knocking him from the sky.

Getting to his feet, he demanded, "Where did you learn that?"

"Don't you remember? It's how I beat your dark clone."

"I guess 'Aden' must have compartmentalised that bit. I knew you beat him. I didn't know how."

Dreya gave a facial shrug. "Now you do, although I've improved it since then. I've even experimented with adding a bit of dragon magic to see if it might give the power a slight edge."

"How could you possibly know about dragon magic?"

"I learned about it while I was conquering Phitonia."

"And how did you manage that?"

"Well, I like a challenge, and I can find precious little here, so for years, I've been working on magical transport to other worlds. I was so close! I could open portals, but they were unstable and unusable. Then, by working my magic through Catriona's sympathic link, I got the chance to examine your Prismatic Sphere portals. That's all I needed to see where I was going wrong – though I would have figured it out myself before long.

"The conquest itself wasn't as difficult as I expected, although a lot of the credit for that must go to those delightful sisters, Sara and Jessica. They told me everything I needed to know to conquer their world. Wasn't that nice of them?"

"You've been to my facility on Earth?" The shadow warrior felt himself go cold at the thought of Dreya the Dark bursting in on the Chetsuans. They could defend themselves and their home against most threats, but against this one, he knew they'd be out of their league.

Daelen's eyes narrowed dangerously. "You didn't—"

"—Harm them?" Dreya finished for him. "Please, Daelen, give me some credit. They're fine. I don't do random violence; it's a waste of energy. I only kill those whom I consider a threat. They were hardly that. We sat together and had a pleasant chat. I had no desire to harm them, and I have no intention of harming you, either. You are a renegade and killing you would earn me a great deal of power and prestige, but the situation has changed."

"How so?"

"Heaven's Surrender."

"What could you possibly know about that?"

"Very little," Dreya freely admitted. "That's why you're still alive. I agree with your assessment of the situation: that weapon will be used, and as much as I enjoy power, I know better than to bite off more than I can chew. I have no way of controlling a weapon about which I know nothing. Given the available options, then, between Kullos and yourself, I would prefer it was your hand on the trigger."

Just then, the other two returned.

"Is there some kind of problem here?" Mandalee asked, lightly, seeing the two scorch marks on the ground from their exchange of power. Dreya immediately turned her back on the shadow warrior and quickly checked Cat was feeling OK. She didn't return her attention to Daelen until Mandalee assured her that her girlfriend was perfectly fine. The Cleric of Nature found that endearing and added it to the growing list of reasons why she believed their match to be officially 'A Good Thing.'

She kept the observation to herself, however, as Dreya answered her question, "Don't worry, Mandalee. We're just getting to know one another. Isn't that right, Great One?"

Ignoring that, Daelen declared, "The black witch says she wants to fight alongside us. Is it just me, or does anyone else have a problem accepting the concept of Dreya the Dark trying to save the world?"

Dreya laughed, coldly, "Save the world? Who said anything about me saving the world? I am doing this for the power and prestige I will earn."

"Personal ambition – you heard her, Cat. Doesn't that bother you?"

"Not at all," the druidess replied. "Power isn't everything, but it has its place, and it can be very attractive in its own way. In case you've forgotten, I'm not here to save the world, either. I'm here to gain knowledge, unlock the power of my staff and perhaps avenge my parents' deaths. Are these things any purer than Dreya's motives? Who am I to judge that? Dreya has every right to represent her Order, and her motives are her own business."

Mandalee held up a hand and volunteered, "I'm here to save the world, if that's any consolation. I never thought I'd hear myself say that – I'm an assassin for hell's sake – but it's true. Still not sure whether I'm saving the world *with* you or *from* you, but I'm saving it either way."

"You see, Daelen?" Catriona offered. "We are balanced."

"But it's obvious she's been using you to spy on me all this time, don't you see that?"

"No, Daelen," Cat shook her head, "she did not use me, and spy is a very pejorative word. All along, I told you I wanted to learn about you. What was the point of that knowledge if I didn't share it?"

"You should be pleased, Daelen," Dreya put in. "Everything Catriona learned, I brought to the Council. Thanks to Cat's knowledge and my influence, the Council made a ruling: If there are two dangerous and powerful renegades, and killing both is not an option, then I am authorised to aid one to kill the other. The Council of Mages has declared Kullos a greater threat than you. Therefore, you are granted amnesty for the time being."

"Plus, there's the small matter of the army that's out there," Mandalee put in. "Don't you think it would be a good idea to have the support of the Council of Mages in the coming battle? Maybe even, thanks to the new rules, throw some clerics in there for good measure?"

Daelen had to admit that if they were going to fight an army of wizards, it would help to have a magical army of their own.

"None of this would have been possible," Mandalee continued, "without Catriona and her link with Dreya."

"Or you, Mandalee," Dreya insisted. "Your transition from trying to kill him to saving him and working alongside him did much to persuade Maia and her faction of Light."

Trying to lighten the mood, Cat grinned at Daelen and asked, "What is it with you, anyway? Every time I introduce you to my friends, you try to kill them. First Mandalee, now Dreya. Remind me never to take you home to Quarthonia. I still know a few Faery there, and frankly, they don't need the hassle."

Daelen relaxed enough to smile back. "Sorry, Cat, but it seems to me your friends always start by trying to kill me. Or at least threatening to."

"You know that with Mandalee, it was just a misunderstanding, why can't you accept the same with Dreya?"

"Of course it's a misunderstanding, Great One," the sorceress agreed, still never raising her voice, maintaining control at all times. "If I'd actually tried to kill you, you'd be dead."

"OK, enough, Dreya!" Cat frowned with obvious irritation. "That's not helping."

Dreya raised her eyebrows and demanded, "Have you no respect for the powers arrayed before you here?"

"Not particularly, no."

"Is she like this with you, too?" she asked Daelen.

Smiling in spite of himself, he answered, "All the time."

Turning back to Catriona, she wondered, "So, girlfriend, what would you propose to do if we decided to fight out our differences?"

"Probably just stand in the middle and shout 'stop'," Mandalee put in, reprising her role as assassin peacemaker. All eyes turned to her, but she faced them down and added, "It worked with me, anyway."

"You and Daelen?" Dreya's eyes widened. "She really did that?" She burst out laughing. "Oh Cat, that is so you! I wish I'd been there!"

Everyone joined in with her laughter, then calming down, Mandalee asked, "So, does this mean we're all friends now? A team, Daelen?"

"Maybe," the shadow warrior allowed, "if she and I can talk alone a bit more."

Catriona was unsure of the wisdom of that.

"Cat, I give you my word that I will not attack her in any way, and while we're talking, I'd like you two to do something for me. I'm worried about Michael and his group. They should have been here by now. Could you go and look for them, please?"

"It's a sound strategy," Dreya concurred. "You two are the trackers, not us."

"Mandalee," Cat marvelled, "did those two just agree on something?"

"I believe they did," Mandalee nodded.

Without another word passing between them, they both looked up at the sky, as if searching for something.

"What are you looking for?" Daelen asked.

"A blue moon!" they answered together.

"OK, I walked into that one."

Mandalee mentally called for Shyleen and linked arms with her friend. "Come on, Cat, it will give me a chance to continue teaching you how to speak leopard. You really are learning fast. You'll be as good as me before long."

"Thanks, Mandalee." Turning back to Daelen and Dreya for a moment, Cat raised a warning finger and scolded them, "You two behave, OK? Don't make me come back there and split you up!" With that, the two girls left with Shyleen.

A short way in the distance, Catriona reached back with her sympathic senses, while she pulled a vase out of her pocket dimension. She used her magic to fill it with water and placed

Dreya's roses into it before putting it safely back in her pocket dimension.

"At least, so far, those two haven't killed each other," she remarked to her cleric friend.

'So far *are the keywords*,' Shyleen offered.

"What was that she said, Mandalee?" Cat asked with a challenging raised eyebrow. "I didn't quite catch it."

"Uh…nothing important, Cat," she replied and then in leopard, added, '*I don't need any more problems right now, Shyleen*.' Turning back to Cat with a smile, she said, "But clearly your leopard speak still needs work. Where did we leave off?"

*****

When they had disappeared into the trees, Dreya remarked, "Well, that told us, eh, Great One?"

"I do wish you'd stop that," the shadow warrior grumbled.

"Why? I am merely showing respect for your power. I would have thought you would appreciate it after being surrounded by 'power isn't everything' for so long."

"The trouble is, Dreya, I can't quite tell with you, whether you're serious or making fun."

"Yes," she conceded, without confirming either way, "I can see how that might be confusing."

Putting that aside, Daelen continued the conversation from what seemed to be common ground.

"So, 'power isn't everything'. She does that with you, too, then, does she?"

"All the time," Dreya nodded. "Infuriating, isn't it?"

"Yes, it is," Daelen agreed. "Of course, what's even more infuriating is that she's usually right."

"It's also one of the things that makes her so attractive. That sharp mind that can find a way around the most complex of problems using nothing more than…"

"…two sticks of celery and a shoelace?" Daelen suggested.

Dreya snorted, "And the celery's just something to eat afterwards."

"Exactly!" Daelen laughed.

"Alright then, Dreya the Dark," the shadow warrior began, after a pause, "while we're walking, I would like you to do something: block her from your mind. What I have to say is strictly between you and me. For once, I'd like to have a private conversation."

"Our sympathic connection does have privacy settings," Dreya assured him, "so doubtless you've had many private conversations, but if you'd rather I block her completely, I have no objection."

"Please do so."

Dreya paused for a moment, then told him, "I've just sent Catriona a final sympathic message, for the time being, so she doesn't worry that there's something wrong. Now I've blocked the connection. Nothing can get through." Stepping forward, she laid a hand gently but firmly on Daelen's arm. In answer to the shadow warrior's questioning look, she asked, "Don't you know a gentleman is supposed to offer a lady his arm when they walk together?"

"I know the custom, but we're hardly lovers out for a stroll or even friends."

"That's no reason to be rude," she countered. They walked in silence for a few moments before the sorceress spoke again. "My, isn't this all terribly civilised?"

"Very," Daelen agreed.

"Now, what shall we talk about?" she wondered.

Chapter 8

"I need to know if I can trust you, Dreya," Daelen began as they walked along together.

"Catriona trusts me. She loves me. Isn't that enough?"

"Catriona is young, inexperienced."

"Catriona is only a couple of years younger than me, and she has more experience in affairs of the heart than I do," Dreya countered.

"Perhaps she is blinded by love," Daelen suggested.

"Perhaps you are blinded by jealousy."

"You know I have feelings for her, then?"

"I know she returns them."

"That doesn't seem to bother you."

Dreya shrugged, unconcerned. "It is no crime to love two people at the same time, Daelen; it's all a question of what she does about it. I trust her to be faithful."

"And you, Dreya?"

"I am always faithful to her," she insisted. "In my own way."

"What's that supposed to mean?"

"It means that the magic will always come first, my love a close second, though I cannot imagine a situation where the two would be in conflict."

"And you would never betray her?"

"I cannot promise that. All I can say is what I once told Mandalee when she said something similar: It would have to be the advantage of a lifetime. Cat accepts that."

"Maybe, but don't you think she deserves someone who would put her first?"

"What I think, Daelen, is that it is her choice and, since she currently loves only two people, your suggested option is not available at this time."

"You're saying I wouldn't put her first?"

"I am saying you would put the world first."

Daelen found he couldn't honestly counter that, so he tried to shift the focus of the conversation. "We seem to be drifting from the point here, Dreya."

The sorceress' look was innocence itself. "You have a point? I thought we were just making polite conversation, getting to know each other. Is that not what we're doing?"

Daelen chose not to dignify that with a response, so Dreya continued, "If I *were* concerned with making a point, then I would simply say this: You cannot have it both ways."

"What's that supposed to mean?" Daelen asked, not understanding.

"It means that either I am in a relationship with a mature and sensible young woman who knows her own mind, or you have been trying to take advantage of an impressionable girl who is confused about her feelings. Which one is it? You cannot have it both ways."

Daelen could see he was not going to win these word games, so he decided to just give it to her straight.

"Listen Dreya, if you do anything to hurt Catriona, I'll—"

"—I don't think you want to finish that sentence, Daelen," she interrupted in a mildly threatening tone. It was the first emotion he had really heard in her voice. "After all, you are hardly qualified."

"Not qualified?" Daelen wasn't prepared for that.

"I'm not the one who fired a beam cannon blast at full power at her unprotected back in a fit of pique," she pointed out, pleasantly.

"That wasn't the real Cat," Daelen argued, somewhat desperately.

Dreya was having none of it. "You didn't know that at the time."

"Even if it had been the real Cat, she has proven she could have defended herself."

"Ah, I see, so it's OK for me to use destructive magic against Catriona, as long as she has a reasonable chance of defending herself, is that it?"

"That's not what I'm saying. I just lost control; it won't happen again."

"It should never have happened in the first place; once is all it takes. Fortunately for Cat, I don't lose control, so she will always be safe with me."

"Dreya, you're twisting things," Daelen objected.

"No, Daelen," she returned. "You are making excuses. Tell me: if I were to try to harm Catriona, would you accept my excuses? Any excuses?"

"No," he answered simply.

"Then you will understand if I am not particularly interested in yours. The simple truth of the matter is that you have already tried to kill Catriona, while I have never so much as raised my voice to her. On that evidence, do you still think you have the right to start issuing warnings and threats? Would it not be more appropriate if I were the one warning you?"

Daelen realised he had completely lost control of their conversation, and at his silence, Dreya the Dark continued in the mild tone she had adopted almost throughout, "But threats are such unpleasant things when we're getting along so well."

"I still need a reason to trust you, Dreya."

"I have already given you one," she insisted. "Catriona trusts me. For you to trust me requires only that you have faith in her judgement. After all, you expect me to trust you not to lose control and attack her again. The only way I can do that is through my faith in my girlfriend's judgement. If she trusts you, that is good enough for me. If you cannot demonstrate that same level of faith, then I would suggest that says more about you than it does about me. Trust is a choice, Daelen, so let us simply choose to trust one another, for her sake."

At that point, Daelen gave up, revising his earlier thought. He had not 'lost' control of this conversation because he never had it in the first place. Dreya had been in complete control before they spoke a single word. He never stood a chance.

"Alright," he agreed. "Please just remember, when it comes to the final battle, when you fire that energy beam of yours, you are aiming at Kullos' forces."

Dreya smiled, "I'll try to keep that in mind," she promised.

"If you are as skilled with magic as you are with words, our enemies would do well to run away now."

"When I was a child," Dreya offered, "before I grew in the magic, words were the only weapons I had, and I learned to use them with precision. I now use my magic with that same precision."

Daelen stared at her in pure astonishment. He never would have expected Dreya the Dark to volunteer such personal information, but he knew she had chosen her words carefully. With two simple sentences, she had told him everything he needed to know about her. This was what set her above and beyond any mortal wizard he had ever encountered in his long life. It wasn't just her power; it was the precision and control with which she wielded it.

Daelen decided to change the subject entirely.

"So, you say you conquered Phitonia. How did that go?"

The sorceress was quite content to share the details as they continued to walk together. However, she did not tell him about the plans she had made with Sara and Jessica. He would find out soon enough.

*****

The two trackers quickly picked out the route Michael and the others were supposed to take to the rendezvous site. As they walked, Mandalee continued her instruction to help Cat learn how to speak the language of leopards.

They had covered quite some distance, and the light was fading when Mandalee told her friend, "You're still relying too much on your sympathic skills, Cat; it's holding you back. You need to have more faith in your leopard speech and just go for it."

"Sorry, but that's the way I've picked up bits of animal languages in the past; a gradual transition from purely sympathic to language."

"In the past, you didn't have me to teach you. Trust me; it's quicker this way. Of course, it could be even quicker if you made the same trade I did."

"Half my soul for complete knowledge of wild things? No, I don't think so."

In leopard, she added, '*No offence, Shyleen, but I can't imagine talking to you is worth half my soul.*'

In response, the leopard remarked, '*Humans and Faery are diverse creatures. What one considers a good trade, another does not. Perhaps that is why you fight each other so much. Indeed, it is a wonder any of you get along at all.*'

Switching off her sympathic abilities, Cat smiled and said, '*I must admit, though, I am tempted by the offer. Discussing the finer points of philosophy with you is a truly fascinating experience.*' Turning to her cleric friend, she asked, "Did I say it right?"

"Almost…although, I'm not sure leopards have much interest in taking pictures." Catriona looked blank, so she clarified, "You said you wanted to discuss photography."

"Did I seriously say that?" Cat looked disappointed. "I thought I'd got it that time."

"Don't worry," her friend reassured her, "philosophy is a difficult word to say in leopard. It was a good show of confidence that you even tried."

'*Your accent could use a little tightening, too, if I may say so,*' Shyleen added.

"It's a minor thing," Mandalee agreed, "and many wouldn't notice, but if you pay close attention, you still sound a little too human in places."

"Shut up!" Catriona hissed.

"Come on, Cat," Mandalee objected, feeling a little hurt, "there's no need for that, we're only trying to help."

"No, Mandalee, I meant 'shut up' because I think I heard something," Cat clarified.

"Oh, that's OK, then. What did you hear?"

Cat rolled her eyes, "If you'd shut up for a minute, you might just hear it for yourself."

Mandalee listened. At first, she didn't hear anything out of the ordinary. Just the sounds of nature. Then came a brief ringing sound, way in the distance…a sound no animal had ever made…the sound of steel against steel. "A battle!"

Cat nodded. "Now consider that Michael and his group are supposed to be on this route and have been held up for some reason."

Mandalee could see where her friend was going.

"You think this battle has something to do with them. They've run into trouble."

The two women and one leopard increased their pace toward the battle site. They each knew how to blend in with the sounds of nature, to make their approach swift and silent.

"This isn't the first time they've been attacked I'll wager," Mandalee speculated, keeping her voice low.

"You think so?"

"Yes, think about it: that's why they're so late. It would make perfect sense. Most of the time, we've been either gone from this world or sailing on a ship that you couldn't pick out in a fleet."

"That's true," Cat accepted, "so I guess it's hardly surprising we've only had that one encounter with Kullos' forces."

"StormClaw was well hidden, so it took them a while to find us."

"You're right," Cat agreed. "So, while he couldn't find us…"

"…Kullos has sent his forces after the others – that's what I'd do in his place." As an assassin, Mandalee was more used to military situations than her friend, so she continued to share her expertise. "But the attack on StormClaw tells us something more about his strategy."

"What's that?"

"They were there specifically to kill me."

"Taking things a bit personally, aren't we?"

"Don't worry, Cat. I'm sure they would have got around to you eventually," Mandalee quipped.

"Oh, well, that's alright then!" her friend shot back, acidly.

"But I know they were after me, because why else attack Shyleen? I saw no evidence that they had injured or killed any other animals, did you?"

Cat agreed that she hadn't.

"So why target a random leopard? Unless they knew she wasn't a random leopard."

"They attacked Shyleen to draw you out," Cat understood. "More fool them."

"Yes, but it tells me that Kullos is intent on removing Daelen's support – us – and he'll be just as keen to get rid of Michael's group. Then the army can focus on Michael, forcing Daelen to either expend energy on fighting his army or face Kullos alone. Either one gives Kullos the advantage."

Cat agreed that all made sense.

"Just one thing," she added. "Why haven't we been attacked since we left StormClaw?"

"Kullos may not even know we're here yet. As I said, he probably couldn't pick out our ship among all the others heading this way. His resources are limited, and he's committed to fighting Michael and the others. He can't pull back his troops unless he's certain there's a bigger prize within reach. If he suspected, he would have to send spies, and I can't imagine any spies being able to hide from the three of us. Even if they did, they would have to send a message back to Kullos, and he would have to either send out a message of his own or risk further weakening his garrison by sending out more of his forces. Both would take time."

"I see, so in either case, whoever is attacking our friends out there won't be expecting us."

Mandalee smiled dangerously. "I'm sure they'll be delighted to see us."

The pair slowed as they approached the battle scene and crouched in the bushes at the edge of the clearing, with Shyleen, to plan their attack. Catriona recognised the Champion of the Gods, Michael, from their brief meeting when this whole adventure started. The members of his 'fan club' were not hard to pick out: they each wore a short tabard showing an image of the demigod's face. The warriors and mercenaries of Kullos' forces had them severely outnumbered.

It seemed that Mandalee was right about this being the latest of several attacks, judging by the torn leather, patched robes and damaged armour. Even Michael himself appeared to be limping slightly. At first, it seemed the one thing going for them was that there were no enemy wizards, but the sight of four dark shapes, directing the attackers from the edge of the battlefield, shattered that belief: four death knights. They reminded Cat of the similar quartet that served as Dreya's servants and guards. They gave off similar, levels of magic and higher planar energy. She surmised that they probably served as Kullos' commanders.

Cat fervently wished that she had pressed Daelen for more information on what powers Kullos' forces possessed. She didn't like operating in the dark, but the issue had always seemed distant until now. She said as much to Mandalee, but she was less concerned.

"As an assassin," she explained, "I rarely have the luxury of having all the answers. Operating in the dark is nothing new to me. Understand enough to know my enemy truly is my enemy – which I know I failed to do with Daelen – and then decide that I am not going to die today. That's often all I can rely on."

Cat didn't like that. "I'm used to studying and analysing any potential threat so I can decide how best to fight it. How do you lay plans if you don't know what you're up against?"

"Who said anything about plans?" Mandalee shrugged, grabbing a bottle of beer out of a pocket and taking a good, long swig. "I just get drunk, armed to the teeth and sort of make it up as I go, improvise. Besides, there's no other choice at this point."

'*I smell fear*', Shyleen put in.

"That's the other facet of the plan, isn't it?" Cat suggested. "Kill Michael's support and demoralise him to make it easier to kill him, too."

"Yes," Mandalee agreed, knocking back more beer, "but in the more immediate term, if we don't do something soon, they're all going to die. They're hiding it well, but I can see the signs of exhaustion – perhaps mental more than physical. They simply don't believe they're ever going to make it to the rendezvous. They need something to give them hope. That alone could make all the difference."

"Mandalee, you've just given me a ridiculous radical idea. That fear spell of yours, can you affect a large group like this at the same time?"

"I don't see why not, though I probably won't be able to sustain it for long."

"I don't need long; I just need it to work. Would it affect our new friends?"

Mandalee finished the beer and pocketed the empty bottle. With a shake of her head, she replied, "Fear spells don't really work on people who are scared already."

Cat nodded. That's what she had thought. "If you were in that situation, what would be your greatest hope? Or, to put it another way, what do you suppose the enemy fear most?"

"That Daelen StormTiger himself will appear and pull out their insides," she stated.

"And what does Daelen always bring with him when he turns up to fight?"

"A storm," Mandalee replied. She could see where this was going.

"One storm coming right up," Cat declared.

Chapter 9

It was already overcast, but Catriona's storm plunged the area into even deeper darkness. Heavy rain and strong wings put out all lamps and fires. Mandalee's clerical magic did the trick of heightening the fears of the enemy; they were so afraid of the storm that they stopped fighting. Michael and the others also believed Daelen was coming, which inspired them to a swift and deadly fightback. Then a figure appeared amid the storm, invisible in the darkness except for an array of weapons, which seemed to be glowing with their own light. In reality, it was just Mandalee, standing on Catriona's Windy Steps. Cat was using her steel-light magic to make all her various weapons glow. She was rather proud of that little addition: Mandalee wasn't the only one who could improvise.

Many of the enemy mercenaries decided their pay wasn't enough at that point and tried to flee, cutting the numbers by about a quarter. Catriona made sure they didn't get far, asking the forest to snare them until they could deal with them. The remaining forces began to realise this wasn't Daelen they were facing, but several arrows from the trees made sure that was, in several cases, the last thought they would ever have in this life. The death knights directed a quad of warriors to seek out and kill the hidden archer, but when the four reached the edge of the clearing, they found no archer, but a leopard and a wolf. Neither animal was inclined to stop and explain their presence; they just attacked. Two of the warriors lost their throats before they even had time to scream. Any resistance the other two might have offered was ended before it had begun, thanks to their hesitation at the sudden transformation of the wolf into a second leopard.

'*Nice touch,*' Shyleen offered, '*but your spots don't look real.*'

'*What's unreal about them?*' the Catriona leopard objected.

'*They are too symmetrical, not random enough.*'

'*I thought symmetrical spots were the height of fashion among leopards, these days.*'

'*That is true,*' Shyleen allowed, '*but more random spots are considered more radical.*'

'*Well, I like my spots, radical or not. But if they don't meet your high standards, that's fine; I'm going to change back anyway. They're going to need my magic.*'

As Cat shifted back, Shyleen rolled her eyes – quite an achievement for a leopard. '*Oh, joy, more humans to bite. It takes a whole moon cycle to get the taste out of one's mouth.*'

'*Maybe you won't need to bite them,*' Cat remarked, acidly. '*Maybe they will simply faint away after you dazzle them with your markings.*'

Cat had tried hard to convey sarcasm, but Shyleen seemed to consider the comment quite seriously.

'*There is always that chance, I suppose. One can only hope.*'

Cat had several rude responses in mind but did not know how they would translate into leopard, so she let it lie.

Meanwhile, Mandalee had returned to the ground to join the fight, enjoying the chance to use her returning blade in one hand for ranged shots and her Pureblade sword in the other for melee fighting.

She fought her way through to Michael, who observed, "You are not Daelen."

Mandalee grinned and remarked, "Don't tell me, my boots gave it away!"

"Amongst other things," he agreed, smiling back.

"I'm Mandalee. A friend." She sliced open the throats of a pair of mercenaries who got too close. "Fight now, chat later, yes?"

"Good plan," Michael concurred, shattering all the bones in three more bodies.

Next thing Michael knew, the sun came out, and Catriona appeared, standing on a rainbow in the sky. Striking her staff to generate a static spark, she fried a couple of warriors with a lightning bolt.

"Remember me?" she called down.

"Catriona, of course I do!" he replied. "You are working for Daelen."

"Working *with*," she corrected, "not working *for*."

"She's spent most of our journey marking out that distinction for him," Mandalee offered without losing her fighting rhythm. "They've even come to blows about it once or twice."

"Either way makes little difference to me," Michael shrugged, "you are both a very welcome sight."

"Michael," Cat spoke up, "how come your friends aren't using magic?" She had noticed that the warriors were protecting wizards that seemed to be doing very little.

"Let me show you," a wizard offered, overhearing.

He tied to cast a fireball, but it fizzled out. Cat was surprised, though not as much as when her Rainbow Road vanished from under her feet, and she fell toward the ground. Fortunately, she had the presence of mind to change to her falcon form to stop her fall and glide down.

"Land next to me!" Mandalee called out. "I'll defend you if you can't use your magic."

So saying, the assassin switched to her dragonclaw daggers, penetrating with ease the heavy armour of one individual, almost severing his sword hand with one blade and stepping forwards to disembowel him.

'*Magic is all very well,*' she sent to Shyleen, '*but there's still nothing like the direct claws-on approach.*'

When Cat shifted back, she replied, "Thanks, but I can fight as a leopard or wolf, if necessary. I would like to get my magic working, though."

Michael explained, "At first, we fought with magic, but whenever we tried, the knights set up a powerful anti-magic field that we can't break."

Now that he mentioned it, she could feel its interference. It wasn't designed to prevent shapeshifting, though, which was understandable since as far as she knew, she was the only one who could do it. The other thing that struck her was, "It wasn't there before."

A trio of warriors fought their way over to protect what they thought was another vulnerable wizard.

"They didn't have it active before you appeared," one of them explained, "because they know we understand it's pointless attempting magic. We've learned that lesson well by now."

"Pointless, is it?" Cat mused. "Well, we'll just have to see about that."

Mandalee grinned, knowing what was coming. "Oh, wait 'til you see what my friend can do!"

Catriona concentrated, forcing herself to keep calm even though she'd never attempted this in a real battle before. She used her sympathic senses to analyse the anti-magic field until she could feel the resonance it created. All she had to do then was adjust her magic, adapt it to run off the field itself.

"OK, let's start with something simple, like this…"

She threw her waterskin a few feet away and concentrated on the liquid that spilt out, multiplying it to form a waterfall. Three warriors, who decided to step through it, suddenly found themselves encased in a wall of ice as the waterfall froze. Elsewhere on the battlefield, it began to rain fire, while others ran into pockets of dense air. Still others were washed over by immense waves of boiling mud that sprang up from small puddles.

Mandalee was the only person on the battlefield who wasn't surprised.

"Your magics won't work," she told the others, "but at least we'll have Cat's powers working for us, plus I can still use mine thanks to Shyleen."

With that, knowing Catriona could once again take care of herself perfectly well, she used her super-speed to slice open a few more enemies. They died without ever knowing what hit them.

The pair made all the difference. They knew each other's fighting styles as well as their own. Now that they could combine magic and steel, the balance shifted in their favour. Catriona's trickery confounded the enemy and gave her allies a reason to laugh – something Michael and the others hadn't done for quite a while. That injection of hope and inspiration gave them a much-needed lift.

Mandalee found the enemy warriors to be considerably lacking in skill – relying on strength of numbers alone – and she was happy to demonstrate some of the finer points. Unfortunately for them, her points were invariably lethal, so they were never going to get any better.

At one stage in the battle, as she was slicing her way through her enemies, Mandalee was aware of one trying to sneak into position from behind her left side, from where she knew he would think to rush her when she had her hands full. What he didn't realise was that thanks to her link with Shyleen, she effectively had a second pair of eyes out there. His stealth attack would do nothing more than move him up her 'to kill' list. When he rushed forward, however, she found she didn't need to do anything about him, as a spear embedded itself in his head.

61

Through Shyleen, she knew the path the spear had taken, threading cleanly through the fighting mass. Mandalee shifted her angle of attack so she could see the warrior who had made the shot. He had now reverted to some rather impressive sword fighting, although his weapon had seen better days.

"I know you'd have had him," he called out, "but I needed the throwing practice!"

"Not judging by that shot, you didn't," she called back, "but thanks anyway!"

"Just got lucky," he returned.

Mandalee doubted that very much. "Got a name?" she asked, fighting closer to him.

"Windell."

"Mandalee," she returned. Looking pointedly at his chipped and tarnished weapon, she asked, "Fancy a new sword, Windell?" She had a couple of spare ones in her arsenal that she didn't use anymore.

"I never refuse a gift from a Lady," he replied with a wolfish grin. "Especially one armed with such a vicious pair of knives."

Mandalee was used to mocking remarks about her gender. She could sense the smallest hint of sarcasm, as a shark could detect a single drop of blood in the water. When this warrior called her a Lady, there was not the tiniest trace. While the comment was cheeky, it was also a sincere compliment. She could count on one hand the number of times that had happened.

"Just for that, noble sir, I'll keep my knives to myself, and you've earned yourself an upgrade."

Using her super-speed, she ran over and placed her Pureblade in his hands. He immediately saluted her with it and swung it into action, putting it to good use.

While Mandalee, Windell, Michael and the others took the fight to the enemy, Cat used her magic mostly for crowd control, splitting the enemy, holding them back, creating choke points, anything to nullify their advantage of numbers. Some enemies tried to shoot her with arrows or spears, but the wind was always her friend, blowing them off course. Others made the mistake of trying their luck on her Rainbow Road. She removed most of it, reverting to her old invisible Windy Steps, either letting her enemies plunge to their deaths, or leaving them stranded on a few remaining bits of the rainbow with no way off except straight down. A couple of times, their enemies thought they'd got her, but thanks to her Mirror Image magic, all they did was waste their energy killing a mirage.

Shyleen remained on the fringes, concealed by the undergrowth, but whenever a warrior strayed too close, that was the last mistake he ever made. After each kill, she retreated, and next time attacked from a different location. The enemy didn't know whether they were being struck down by one leopard or several.

*****

The battle lasted into the night until the bodies of the enemy littered the ground.

Seeing that magic was no longer so important, Cat suggested, "How about I see what I can do about those death knights?" She looked around and asked, "OK, where did they go?"

The others looked, too, and realised they had gone. But gone where? Everyone had been too busy to notice.

The remaining enemy warriors took the opportunity of the momentary lull in the fighting to retreat. Catriona volunteered to snare them, though she couldn't guarantee to get them all.

"Let them go," Michael boomed in command, "it's not worth chasing them, we'd be risking another ambush. We need to make our rendezvous. Just let them go."

Cat had other ideas, however. "Not all of them, I think."

She scanned the fleeing masses and picked one out. "That one could be useful." She then called for Shyleen, who stepped out of the shadows. Cat pointed and told her, '*That one there – stop him but don't kill.*'

Shyleen sprang into action and had no trouble trapping the terrified warrior.

Catriona asked to borrow a water bottle from someone. Windell gave her his. She poured some of its contents over the enemy warrior's feet and froze it into a block of ice. The ice began to rise slowly upward to encase his legs.

"You are some kind of warrior commander, I think, is that right?" He nodded. "Then you will be able to help me. Here's the deal: I have only one question, and you have only one chance to answer me truthfully. That sounds fair, doesn't it?" The warrior

63

nodded again. "Good, now tell me: where did the death knights go?" When the warrior hesitated, the ice began to grow faster, reaching his waist. "Oh, did I mention the time limit?" Cat wondered.

The warrior quickly decided to talk. "Please don't kill me!" he begged. "I can't be sure what their plans were!"

"Best guess," Cat prompted. The ice was now moving up his chest, making breathing difficult, in addition to the effects of the extreme cold.

"Alright! They're probably following the trail of your unique magics back to Daelen," he replied, speaking rapidly, desperate to get the words out before he froze to death. "They will attack him, seek to catch him by surprise, weaken him while he's alone. I think those were Kullos' standing orders for them if you two appeared without him."

Catriona considered that and agreed, "Your answer makes sense. Congratulations, you get to live."

With that, she melted the ice just as it reached his neck. He wouldn't have had much longer. Once Mandalee had relieved him of the excess weight of his weapons, they sent him away.

The druidess tried to contact Dreya sympathically but found she was still blocked. After a quick group discussion, they decided it wasn't a good idea to split up again. So, the cleric and druidess set about healing the most severe injuries, before accepting guard duty, dividing the watch between themselves and Shyleen, while the others got some rest – they hadn't had much chance for that, recently.

The group would set out for the temple ruins in the morning. There seemed little point in rushing – whatever battle might have taken place between Daelen and the death knights would be well over already. They simply had to trust in Daelen's ability to look after himself. Besides, there was the advantage that the knights thought Daelen would be alone – they wouldn't be expecting to face Dreya the Dark as well.

*****

"Dreya," Daelen began, preparing to broach a delicate topic when there was a lull in their conversation. "I must tell you what I told Cat: I do not want any of you to interfere with my battle with Kullos."

"I can imagine how my girlfriend reacted to that," Dreya remarked.

"Do you need to imagine?" Daelen wondered. "Don't you know every detail of what I said to her?"

Dreya shook her head. "Doesn't work like that. Like I told you before, our sympathic link has privacy settings. We don't read each other's every thought any more than we would read each other's diaries. We share what we choose to share and conceal what we choose to conceal."

The shadow warrior pounced on that. "Ah, so you admit you hide things from her?"

"Those green eyes of yours are showing again, Daelen," she shot back. "You seem determined to find a weakness in our relationship that you can attack, but you won't find one. Yes, of course I keep things from her. Earlier today, when I saw the woman I love for the first time in weeks, I gave her flowers from my garden; roses from the same bushes that she planted there when we first met. It was a symbolic gesture of love. Had she already seen my intentions in my mind, that would have greatly diminished the effect, so I kept them from her. On a professional level, as Secondmage in the Black Order on the Council, I am privy to confidential proceedings that Cat is simply not authorised to know about. On Catriona's side of things, I'm certain Mandalee, as her best friend, will have told Catriona personal things, confidential things. She has not shared them with me. Nor should she. I do not invade my girlfriend's privacy. Plus, there are all the million day-to-day trivial things that happen in a person's life that simply aren't important enough to mention." She fixed him with a penetrating gaze as she added one more example. "Then there's this entire conversation that I'm keeping from her because you specifically asked me to block her out."

Daelen held up his hands in surrender. "You're right. I spoke before I thought. I'm sorry." He then repeated his original request, adding, "and you must convince Catriona to agree, too. I need to know she is safe when I drive Kullos back to the darkness from which he came."

"I will try not to take offence at that," Dreya remarked.

Daelen realised what she meant and tried to clarify. "I know that you are fond of the darkness and yet I'm beginning to accept

65

that there's more to you than that. I can see it in your eyes now that I'm looking properly."

She thought carefully before speaking, as she always did.

Finally, she insisted, "You've got a few things wrong, Daelen. I am wholly aligned with Dark magic for the power it gives me. Let there be no doubt about that. Where Kullos and I differ is that the darkness serves me, while for him it is the other way around. Kullos is weak – powerful, but weak. You see, at the extreme edge of Darkness lurks chaos, just as it lurks at the extreme edge of the Light. That is why we mortal mages believe in the Council. We are free to devote ourselves to Light, Darkness or Balance, or even choose to be unaligned if we wish, but on one thing we all agree: there must be order. Magic is powerful and that power, all power, must be controlled – not limited, but controlled. This is why we have such a strict policy on renegades – they disrupt order and give chaos a foothold. That cannot be allowed. Kullos has given in to chaos, whereas I am strong enough to resist. Therefore, I would appreciate it if you would speak of sending Kullos back into chaos, rather than darkness.

"As for the issue of you fighting Kullos alone," she continued, "I cannot convince Catriona to agree, because I share her views. You will not fight him alone. Cat will be with you, I will be with you, and in the interests of order and balance, Mandalee will be there, too. Sorry, Daelen, but that's the way it—" she broke off and shouted, "Daelen, look out!"

Four death knights shot powerful energy bolts towards the shadow warrior, but Dreya was faster. She had already pushed Daelen out of the way and activated her Power Absorb as the bolts struck her. She had never tried to absorb so much energy at once by herself before, and instantly realised it was too much. She prided herself on her self-control, which meant that, despite her ambition, she wasn't greedy. She knew how much power she could safely take in one go and would not be tempted to risk crossing that line. At the precise moment she reached her limit, she adjusted her magic to Power Protect. Her magic shielded her from the remaining power well enough, but the sheer force knocked her to the ground where her head struck a rock. Darkness embraced her, and she lay still.

Chapter 10

"Dreya!" Daelen cried out, powering up and rushing to her side.

Fuelled by rage, his first instinct was to flatten a few acres of forest and his attackers along with it, but Catriona had had a considerable effect on him. As he had been trying to train her, she had been training him. She accused him of being predictable and at that moment, he realised she was right. Thinking to catch him off guard, the death knights had channelled much of their power into their blast. Now they were relatively weak and defenceless. Using his powers against them now would be a waste of energy. Instead, in a rare moment of restraint, he stopped before dealing the killing strike. Sending them back now would force Kullos to waste power recharging them.

"Go back to your Master," Daelen growled. "Tell him how you failed and also tell him this: If he wants to finally destroy me, he's going to have to look me in the eye while he does it. Otherwise, he'll always be wondering if I escaped, ready to take my revenge the moment he lets his guard down. Tell him he needs wait but a little while longer. Soon we will meet for the last time, and I'll send him back into the maelstrom of chaos. Now go before I forget about the message and destroy you right here."

The death knights didn't hang around.

*****

Some distance away, Catriona was awakened from her sleep, when her Crystal Mage Staff glowed in her face. Out of the air, she heard a by-now-familiar voice:

Black faction second attempt gone. One attempt remains.

*****

A few hours later, Mandalee, Cat and the others arrived. Cat took one look at the unconscious Dreya and ran to her side.

"I think she's OK," Daelen reassured her. "I just thought it best not to move her until you arrived. I gather you ran into some trouble of your own out there."

He stepped aside with Michael, who told him everything they had been through. Meanwhile, Cat and Mandalee looked the sorceress over and healed her. Even so, she still woke up with a splitting headache.

"That's what you get for headbutting rocks," Mandalee quipped.

"Thanks, you're all heart," Dreya replied, with a half-smile.

"What can I say?" the White Assassin shrugged. "Sometimes, nature's a bitch."

Once Cat was sure her girlfriend was fine, she excused herself, saying that she and Mandalee still needed to tend to the injuries sustained by a few of Michael's group.

When they had moved away, Daelen approached the sorceress.

"Dreya, I just want to say—" he began, but she held up a hand to cut him off.

"Don't thank me, Daelen, I didn't do it for you. I did it to gain power."

"Of course, I should have realised." The shadow warrior hid a smile. He was beginning to understand Dreya's pride, and it was the least he could do to play along. "Although if you wanted power, you could have helped them kill me, and then taken mine."

"Thought about it," she admitted with total honesty. "Decided against it."

The shadow warrior dropped his voice, making sure no-one else could hear. "Shame you didn't include the rock in your thinking."

Dreya offered a facial shrug. "Nobody's perfect."

"I see," he pondered, continuing to speak quietly. "So, Dreya the Dark takes the Black Tower in five minutes, brings my dark clone to his knees in under an hour, and conquers Phitonia in a spare afternoon. Yet, when attacked by a quartet of death knights that she could destroy in her sleep, she falls and hits her head on a rock, thereby making herself vulnerable before the power of a shadow warrior who she knows doesn't trust her."

Dreya raised her eyebrows. "When you put it like that, it sounds ridiculous, so I would deem it a favour if you didn't spread that version around. Even to a certain mutual love interest."

Daelen agreed. "Just one other thing," he added. "I can't imagine why, but all of a sudden, I'm prepared to trust you."

"Excellent. I suppose it must be our conversation that convinced you."

"Must be," Daelen concurred, "although they do say that actions speak louder than words."

"Where do they say that?" Dreya wondered.

"It's an Earth expression."

"How fascinating. Anyway, how come I don't see any corpses?"

The shadow warrior explained what happened, leaving out only the part about the message.

"Promise me something, Daelen," demanded the sorceress. "In the final battle, those death knights are mine. I can't have people thinking they can take pot-shots at Dreya the Dark and get away with it!"

"Your reputation is important to you; I can understand that. If you want the knights to yourself, that's fine with me."

"Dammit!" Dreya swore suddenly. "I must have hit my head harder than I thought. I always promised myself I'd never do it, but I finally did, didn't I?" Answering Daelen's blank look, the annoyed sorceress explained, "I just referred to myself in the third person."

*****

The full company traversed the remaining distance to the temple ruins, arriving early afternoon. There, they set up a defensive perimeter. Cat and Mandalee did their rounds over the next couple of hours to treat any remaining injuries. Once this was done, Catriona soon had her nose back in her books, studying some more until, about an hour before sunset, she called her girlfriend and two friends together.

She informed them that she planned to do some scouting in owl form that night, to see what she could learn about the army that awaited them.

"Is that safe?" Daelen wondered.

69

He was worried that she might be detected, but Dreya assured him that in tests, whenever Catriona took the form of an animal, every scanning technique the sorceress knew – including some she'd invented herself – registered her as that animal and nothing more. While that wasn't definitive proof, they were bound to have to take some risks at some point, and the rewards were compelling enough to be worth this one. She had every confidence in her girlfriend's ability to take care of herself.

Before that, however, Cat told them there was one more thing she needed to do, for which she needed their help. Something that was highly sensitive, and not for anyone else to know. Therefore, as soon as it grew dark enough to clearly see the stars – and Cat could, of course, ensure it was a clear night, at least where they were – they would leave the camp in Michael's capable hands while they slipped away. Until then, she would say no more.

*****

A couple of hours later, Catriona sent a sympathic, '*Now*' to the others and they all complied: Daelen, Dreya and Mandalee with Shyleen, leaving the camp together, accompanying Catriona back into the forest, the way they had come. As soon as the druidess was satisfied that they were sufficiently isolated, she decided they could stop walking.

"Dreya, did you bring the book I asked you to get for me?" she asked.

Dreya suddenly looked uncomfortable – no, Daelen realised, not just uncomfortable but afraid. That grabbed his full attention instantly. She had faced down his power without flinching, yet the mere mention of this book had her scared.

"Dreya," Catriona enunciated, "did you bring the book?"

"Cat, are you sure about this?"

"What is it, what's this all about?" Mandalee demanded, picking up on Dreya's tension.

Using her natural sleight of hand, the sorceress produced, from some hidden pocket in her robes, a small parcel covered in brown paper. Removing the protective wrapping, revealed a book bound in nightblue leather with silver markings that were apparently

70

more than just decoration. It was the *Nameless Book*, believed to be the work of the first wizard, Magias.

"This book is so ancient," she explained, "no-one can translate the writing on the cover, so we don't even know its name. What we do know is that it is the most heavily fortified magical installation ever constructed. No one knows for certain who wrote it or what is written in it. It is protected by layer upon layer of magical traps, shields, warding, defence, attack…in short, it is impenetrable without the specific set of magical keys, and no-one knows what they might be."

"I do," Cat stated. "They're the same as for my staff. As of today, I have broken through every barrier between me and the power I am trying to understand and possibly release. All bar one. I'm assuming this book will tell me everything I need to know about the power I am dealing with: How it was created, why it was trapped, what it does and ultimately present a case for its release. Then I will simply have to learn the final key and using it will be my choice. Look, I appreciate everyone's concern, but I know what I'm doing. If I were not certain beyond all reasonable doubt, I would not attempt this. Trust me, this is not one of my ridiculous radical plans. Now Dreya, for the last time, please, give me the book."

With a sigh of resignation, Dreya handed it over. After all the trouble she'd gone to, stealing it from the home of Laethyn, Master of Dark Magic himself, she supposed they might as well put it to good use.

Daelen and Mandalee shared a look – they weren't happy about their dear friend taking such a risk, but she had asked for their trust, and they couldn't deny her. The Cleric of Nature stepped forward, took Catriona's hands in hers, and looked deep into her eyes.

"You're my best friend, Cat, and I love you, so you know I'll support you no matter what. Just tell me you're sure this is the right thing to do."

With a look of fierce determination, Cat attested, "Everything I've done since the Day of the Angel has been about this moment, so yes, I'm sure."

"Then whatever you need from me, it's yours." With that, Mandalee released her friend and stepped back to rejoin Shyleen.

The leopard, sitting by Mandalee's side, sent, '*I don't like it either. None of us is happy about it. But though none of us can say why, I believe we all know it must be done.*'

'*Cat believes this is the path our lives should take, so I'm ready to follow wherever it leads. For her.*'

'*The path of life is often anything but a path,*' suggested the philosophical leopard, 'but *rather a tangled, and delicate spider web.*'

'*Ugh, Shyleen,*' Mandalee shuddered, '*do you have to use spider analogies?*' But she knew the great leopard was right. They turned back to watch Catriona open the ancient book, but they were about to find out that it wasn't that simple.

Choosing a comfortable spot in the grassy clearing, Catriona told her friends, "I have a number of instructions I need you to carry out for me. I'm going to need absolute concentration for this, so I cannot risk being disturbed. No matter what happens, no matter what strange things you may witness, you must not interfere. Even if you think I am in danger, there is nothing you can do to help me once I have begun. But you can help now. I need one person close by, and I choose Daelen. Nobody else is allowed within ten feet."

"Why Daelen?" Mandalee asked. She wasn't sure which fact was more surprising: that Cat hadn't chosen Dreya or that Dreya hadn't voiced the question herself.

"Because I suspect higher planar energy might be required, and while Dreya can now wield such power, Daelen is still more familiar with it."

"Your logic is undeniable, Cat," Dreya agreed, then she turned to the shadow warrior.

"It's like we were saying, Daelen, about choosing to trust one another. I'm placing the life of the woman I love in your hands, shadow warrior," she implored him. "Please be worthy of that trust."

"I will, Dreya," he vowed. "I swear, I will."

Catriona sat down cross-legged on the grass and invited Daelen to sit opposite, but not so close that he might accidentally touch her and disturb her concentration. Next, she made the grass and plants grow to form a circle, roughly ten feet in diameter. It didn't need to be high. It just had to serve to mark a clear boundary. Once finished, she asked Mandalee to impart her clerical blessing on that ring and place Daelen and herself in her very best demon trap.

"Won't that cut you off from your magic?" she asked, remembering how they first met.

Cat shook her head. "For this, I can only use the magic from within."

Mandalee agreed but suggested that before she did so, Cat might want to ask the tree branches to grow overhead, "Just to shield us from any aerial recon by Kullos and his minions."

"Good thinking," her friend commended her and did so, though not enough to block their view of the stars. "Now, Dreya, I need guards to make sure no-one crosses the boundary we've created. They must be impossible to bribe or threaten, absolutely lethal and able to carry out instructions to the letter, killing, if necessary, without compassion or remorse. This is too important to risk using human guards who might hesitate at the crucial moment."

"I know just what you're looking for," the sorceress understood. "I was going to leave them to guard the Black Tower, but if you need them here, then here is where they shall be."

She closed her eyes and began to work her wizard magic.

The shadows deepened and out of the darkness stepped a quad of knights; each dressed in black armour with a skull breastplate and massive double-handed broadsword. Red eyes gleamed in the depths of their helms. The Knight leader moved closer still, dropped to one knee, and rumbled, "I await thy commands, my Lady."

Dreya continued weaving her magic until the knights were accompanied by three floating, shadowy shapes, each with a pair of ethereal white eyes – ghouls. The trio approached Dreya as she opened her eyes to look upon her soldiers. The lead ghoul's eyes lowered in reverence and whispered, "How may we serve you, Mistress?"

"Listen carefully to my instructions. My lover, Catriona, is going to be working some powerful magic and must not be disturbed for any reason. The ring formed by the plants form the boundary she has specified, and no one but Daelen and Catriona herself is allowed within the circle. If any living being should try to cross, you are to kill them – even me. There are enemies arrayed against us that could attack at any time. If that happens, you are to protect Catriona even at the cost of your own undead existences, even above me. I can take care of myself. You will take further instructions from Daelen. He will tell you when the magic is complete. Then you may resume your regular guard duty under the standard terms." Turning to her girlfriend, she asked, "Does that cover it, Cat?"

"Almost," she replied. "One last thing: besides preventing entry into the circle from the outside, you also must kill any living being who attempts to leave the circle from the inside – even myself – before Daelen tells you to stand down. Now your instructions are complete."

The undead guards bowed respectfully and took up positions around the perimeter of the circle.

"I recommend you stay well back," she cautioned those on the outside, "and also, could you do me a favour and watch the sky? Just in case the stars decide to shift or anything."

Mandalee, Dreya and Shyleen all moved away, leaving Catriona alone with Daelen inside the circle. Catriona prepared herself, and then quietly gave Daelen one final instruction. Something she knew he wouldn't like but was absolutely necessary.

"Daelen, if things go wrong, you have to promise to do something."

"Anything," he asserted. "What is it?"

"Kill me."

Chapter 11

"What!" Daelen demanded.

He couldn't believe what he was hearing, but Cat persisted.

"I was only partially honest with the others about my reasons for choosing to have you with me. You see, if I unleash this power and things go wrong, I do not know what will happen. If I'm lucky, the power will simply kill me."

"And if you're unlucky?" Daelen asked, not liking this one bit.

"Let's just say there are many things worse than death. Forms of existence that would make me jealous of how good Dreya's undead guards have it. If that happens, I don't know what powers I might possess. Dreya's guards have been commanded to kill me if things go wrong, but they may not be able to do so alone. What I'm saying is, if I do this and things go wrong, and I still live…if you love me…you must kill me. You may be the only one with the power to do it. Stop at nothing if it comes down to it; hit me with everything you've got and destroy whatever body I have left.

"Swear you will do it, Daelen, or I will be forced to change my mind and have Dreya in here instead – she would agree to it, but I'm afraid I might kill her. Please, Daelen, you must swear, because if things go wrong and I live…well, if it's any consolation, it won't be me you're killing. It will be something else, and if that were released…" she trailed off before concluding, "it would be far better if Kullos were to win."

She softened and tried to reassure the shadow warrior with a smile. "Look, it's just a precaution. This whole scenario is one big precaution. Nothing's going to go wrong. If I weren't as certain as I could possibly be, I wouldn't attempt this. It's just that I can never be completely sure until I've done it, so I need to make sure I've covered every angle."

Daelen let out a long, slow breath before finally answering, "Alright, I swear. If it comes down to it, I would rather kill you than let some vile creature take control of some twisted form of your body. As long as you're absolutely certain that this is really necessary."

"It's vital. The letter under your training centre told me so and I trust the messenger. From what information I already have, I get

75

the impression that all this has happened before, somehow. But I didn't have this book. Not yet. Not until it was too late. There's more at work here than just the fight against Kullos. That's one part of something bigger. I don't really understand what that means, yet, but hopefully, the book will tell me more. Now, if there are no further questions, I'll ask for silence, and I'll begin."

Daelen nodded. He remembered his lover, Rose, long ago, telling him that among the Faery, trade was based on giving freely, in the name of love, that which was precious. If his unyielding support was what Catriona needed from him, then he would give it freely, in the name of love. No question.

*****

They settled down, Catriona calmed her nerves, and taking a deep breath, she began to work her way through the security of the book.

It took all of Daelen's self-control to avoid moving to defend the mortal woman he loved, as he felt the incredible power rush from the book. A power that made him feel suddenly very small. For the first time in centuries, he was forced to concede that there might be forces in the mortal plane beyond his own power. Against this power, he felt, his beam cannon would look like nothing more threatening than a torchlight. The thought of Catriona sitting in the centre of such power brought him no comfort, but he knew it was essential that he let Cat deal with it herself. If he did something wrong, he could kill her or worse. On the plus side, the inner strength Catriona must possess to do this was a wonder to behold, and the look of intense concentration on her face, he found, made her all the more attractive.

Over the next few hours, Daelen and the others saw, heard and felt powerful magic that was both wondrous and terrifying. Monsters appeared to try and devour the vulnerable-looking druidess. Beam cannon-like energy blasts fired into, through and out of her body. There were explosions; aurorae flew around within the circle, crackling with power. Handsome men and seductive women stepped out of the book, trying to persuade Catriona to give up this magic and do something more pleasurable. Even the tiniest wavering, the briefest loss of concentration would be fatal, but these outside distractions were nothing compared to the things that entered Catriona's mind and soul.

Powerful, insidious magic tried to convince her that it was all useless…hopeless. Death would require less effort. Why not give in and end the painful struggle? She was infected with convincing illusions of poison and disease, trying to make her waste energy trying to heal herself instead of breaking down the magic itself. Sometimes, she was almost lulled to sleep before catching herself and fighting back. The book knew her Balanced alignment and tempted her with promises of gifts from each of the three angles: Perhaps a quiet, peaceful place in the Light, surrounded forever by the beauty of nature and all that is pure and good – no pain and no death. She could choose the Darkness and gain the power to reshape Creation according to her own design, or summon and command the Keeper of the Underworld. How about immortality here in this world? Think of the knowledge that she could gain! She could share these gifts, too. They need not be hers alone.

All these things and more challenged her concentration as she tried to visualise the magical keys that she had committed to memory and fit them into the locks. The task seemed endless, like peeling an onion – remove one layer, and all you find is another layer.

"I can't remember," she thought suddenly. Had she said that out loud? She wasn't sure. "The last key…it's gone…what was it? I can't hold the defences back much longer…what am I going to do? I'm going to die…gods help me…I'm lost!"

One of the voices in her head grew louder; assailing her with magic unlike anything she had faced before. Magic not of wizard, druid or cleric, not of Light, Balance or Darkness, not of order but of chaos. Magic with its own rules, operating in a way that was anathema to all Creation. A power known only as *IT*.

'*You are nothing*', *IT* whispered, '*nothing. You don't exist; you're just an illusion. Remember the last time you ended your Mirror Image spell…? You got it wrong…destroyed the real you instead of the copy…You are the copy…just a copy…illusion…nothing.*'

Cat gasped in horror at the idea. Could it be true, she wondered? When she thought she'd cancelled her copy, did she get it wrong? She couldn't remember! How could she be sure? Maybe she destroyed the real Catriona. If so, then she was just an illusion, a facsimile of life! But Cat wanted to exist. She wanted to live so badly.

'*And you* can *exist*', *IT* soothed. '*You can! IT has the power to make you real. All you have to do is say the words...you are nothing...Tell IT!*' *IT* commanded.

Cat felt a wave of relief and gratitude wash over her. Was that really all *IT* needed her to do? Just say those words? That was so easy. "I—" she began, but something was holding her back. She couldn't imagine what it was.

IT almost had her...she was weakening. In moments, *IT* would feel her sweet life draining away. '*You will never be real until you accept that you are nothing.*'

"I—I am—"

IT hated life. Life was the ultimate triumph of Creation and order and structure. Life was an aberration, an abomination. Life was wrong. This one was the worst of the lot, doing something especially abhorrent and she didn't even know it. But she was also *ITs* way in. All she had to do was say she was nothing, believe the ultimate contradiction. If *IT* could get her to admit she didn't really exist, deny her own reality, her life would become a gateway for *IT*. *IT* had other plans in motion, but in moments, they would be unnecessary.

"I—I am n—"

So close, just one more little push would do it. Soon *IT* would drain her...but not utterly – that would destroy *ITs* gateway. No, *IT* would not grant her death, but a new cursed half-life that would last forever. Hers would be a new soul for *IT* to enjoy tormenting in its chaotic realm; a spirit for *IT* to torture for eternity...but not before she had killed all her friends and ripped apart their souls.

Oh yes, she would do all that at *IT's* command; beg to do it, in fact. She would do anything to please *IT* and she, too, would take pleasure in the act. She would lose all control of her new chaotic form as she gave this world to *IT*. From this world, through her, *IT* could consume everything, the whole of Creation. All would belong to *IT*.

IT would leave her with just a small pool of her former conscience. That would add to her torture, as she watched herself smile while the people she cared about died slowly at her touch. Rending their souls would bring her exquisite delight and her conscience would be forced to witness it all. She would laugh in joy and exhilaration as every world, every plane of reality ceased to be. That would be the last feeling of pleasure she would ever experience. After that, for eternity, *IT* would make sure that she was the only semblance of life that remained in existence, and all she would know was pain…pain far beyond anything mortals could ever experience. Moreover, her conscience would forever tell her she deserved her fate for unleashing *IT* upon the cosmos and bringing a final end to life.

'Don't you want to be real? You can wish yourself into existence, IT can make you real. Just say that you are nothing. Believe you are nothing. Why do you hesitate?'

Yes, why was she hesitating? Cat couldn't understand why she hadn't said it already. Why couldn't she think? In fact, wasn't that proof? She remembered how much the real Catriona liked to think, to learn, to understand. If she couldn't do that, wasn't that proof that she wasn't the real Cat?

'Say the words, my little broken doll! You will know no release until you do. Speak them and believe,' *IT* encouraged her. *'Tell IT what you know in your soul to be true. You are nothing, little girl, nothing.'*

"I—I am not—" Cat began, then something stuck in her throat, and she coughed. She swallowed, took a deep breath and prepared to accept the truth: she was nothing. Tears streamed down her cheeks as she realised how obvious it was. She was nothing. She couldn't imagine how she ever could have believed otherwise.

So why was it so damned hard to say?

IT knew *IT* had won; in mere seconds, the next time she spoke, she would deny her existence and she would belong to *IT*. In a moment, Catriona would be like *IT* and *IT* would be unleashed upon Creation. Then the feast would begin. Those undead guards would not prevent *IT*. They had been instructed to kill any 'living being' that crossed the line, but *IT* was not alive in any sense they would recognise. Those other fleshy things outside the circle concerned *IT* not at all. Even this shadow warrior thing, powerful though he was, by mortal standards, would fall before *IT*. *IT* just needed the power of Catriona's belief to bridge the gap to this world from *ITs* strange realm.

Just as Catriona opened her mouth for what would surely be the last time, faces flashed across her mind: Sara, Jessica, Daelen,

Dreya, Mandalee, Shyleen, Jacob, childhood friends, Pyrah, her father, and her mother. The last face filled her mind. The mother who, at least in her mind, fought for her daughter's life right up until the end.

That tiny part of Catriona that was still fighting suddenly knew the final key. It was the greatest magic, the ultimate power in the universe...Love.

Romantic, family, friendship, even just the concept of the ultimate value of people, of life itself – they were all aspects of the same thing: Love. With the last of her strength, she took all the love from those around her, added it to her love for them and directed every last drop into the book. It wasn't enough to simply say the word in her mind. Love was much more than a word. It was a concept, an idea. Calling on her years of experience with sympathic communication, she projected everything that love was, into the Nameless Book.

IT roared, '*No! You are too late! You belong to IT now. You are nothing, little girl! Nothing!*'

Forcing out the words, she screamed, "I...am...not...a little girl! I am Catriona Redfletching, and by the power of love, I defy you, for while people have love, we can never be nothing. In the name of love and of life, I claim the right of access to this Book and all that it contains!"

But even as she spoke the words, she knew it wasn't that simple. Now that the book was open, the fortifications were gone. *IT* might not be free of *ITs* prison, but *IT* was out of *ITs* cell, and there was no putting *IT* back because all the locks were broken. She had smashed them – that made *IT* her responsibility, but she couldn't stand guard forever. She needed somewhere to safely lock *IT* away again. But where?

Then she remembered her trip to Earth. All that technology. All those devices. Those mobile phone things that Sara and Jessica had. A single tool that could contain so much power, and all those different...what were they called again? Apps. Applications. One device, many functions. And because they could do so much, they had to be protected by security. A powerful, secure, multi-functional tool. It was a concept that hadn't really appeared on Tempestria yet...or had it?

It came to her in a flash. She had such a thing: something that could store different forms of power and keep it secure. It was her most precious possession, the gift of an Angel. Entrusted to her. She called it her Crystal Mage Staff, but it was much more than that. Just as the people of Earth called those devices 'phones' when they were clearly so much more. She looked again at the security on the staff, and while they were indeed the same keys as the book, they were designed to be re-lockable, where the book had been intended to be a one-time-only release. And her staff could store so much more than it already contained. Even giving the power within it room to grow, there was plenty of storage space for a second partition. Just as Daelen had created the Tower of Dreams in his temple on the edge of the Elvarian Peninsula, to keep Michael safe, in a separate partition to the Wishing Well. She could do the same with her staff.

Concentrating as never before, she created a dimensional conduit between book and staff – like her pocket dimension, except it opened at both ends. Then she forced the essence of *IT* into the staff and locked *IT* away with all the security that had been present on the Day of the Angel.

If ever she wanted to unlock the original power of the staff, she could do so with just the final key: love. But even if she did, *IT* would remain trapped in this separate partition. Perhaps one day she, or someone who came after her, would find a way to safely dispose of *IT*. Until then, in her staff is where *IT* would remain.

At last, the Book's final security lock fell away, and there was a brilliant white light as the circle exploded.

*****

When Daelen came around, he saw Dreya arguing with one of the ghouls.

"Stand aside and let me in!" she demanded. "I am your Mistress, and you will obey."

"I am sorry, Mistress," the ghoul whispered, "but I cannot comply. Your instructions were specific: no living being may enter, and if you do not step back, I will be forced to kill you."

Its eyes glowed menacingly, and Dreya was forced to take a prudent step backwards. By the look on her face, she was preparing to use magic to fight her own guards to gain entry. Mandalee was ready, weapons in hand, primed to fight at her side, while Shyleen growled threateningly.

Daelen took a moment to bathe in the wonder of that: a Dark sorceress and a cleric of Light, side-by-side, united by their love for one truly remarkable individual. Of course, he could add a leopard god and a shadow warrior from the higher planes to that list and even a pair of Chetsuans from Phitonia, had they been there. Michael, Champion of the Gods, had taken a shine to her, too. Cat had a way of bonding such diverse people to her, just by being herself. He knew Catriona didn't see herself as particularly remarkable or extraordinary. To her, she was just a simple half-Faery druid girl. But everyone else around her knew she was so much more.

Daelen shook his head, to clear it of distractions.

"It's OK!" he called out. "It's over. Guards, you may step down now and allow free access in and out of the circle."

The undead guards bowed their compliance and moved away. Mandalee rushed to Catriona's side and declared, "She's fine, just exhausted. Don't disturb her, don't even try to move her. Let her sleep."

There was no question of taking turns to keep watch. One shadow warrior, one Faery sorceress, one human assassin and one leopard god – they would all guard her together. Nothing and no-one was getting at Catriona tonight, without going through each and every one of them.

Chapter 12

A couple of hours later, the druidess stirred and sat up, rubbing the sleep from her eyes.

"I'm alive!" she breathed. "It worked!" Her friends gathered around her, all making sure she was all right. "I'm fine," she laughed, "honestly! I thought I'd lost it there for a moment, but I pulled through. Now, where's that book? After all the trouble I've been through, I think it's time I read it."

Dreya told her she had been unsure if it would be safe for any single one of them to hold it, so she had entrusted it to one of her death knights with strict instructions to give it only to Cat.

He handed it to her upon her request.

"Why thank you, Sir Knight," she offered politely.

"You are most welcome, my Lady," he replied.

Catriona blushed and giggled girlishly, then responded to her friends' strange looks, saying, "Sorry, it's just that archaic 'My Lady'…and he's really quite handsome in his own way."

Nobody elected to comment on that.

The others were wary when Catriona opened the volume, slowly, carefully, but nothing out of the ordinary happened – the defences were gone.

She read the title aloud: "*Guardians of Time & Magic – the Chronicles of Magias.*"

"Magias? The legendary first wizard?" Dreya breathed in awe. "The mythical founder of magical society?"

"Not so mythical, apparently," Cat replied absently, already absorbed in the text, "although, more correctly, Magias was the legendary first *sorceress*. It's quite clear from the text that Magias was female."

"How come everyone's always assumed the first wizard must be male?" Daelen wondered.

Putting on her very best Jessica voice, Mandalee pointedly replied, "I think it's called sexism, love!"

"Touché," he conceded.

It was a long time before Catriona spoke again. When she did, she summarised what she'd learned.

*****

At the beginning of the world, the gods discovered they could use inter-planar forces for a power they called magic. They kept the power for themselves, except for leaking it out to mortals in exchange for worship and even then, only if they felt like it. The force grew and evolved until it gained a kind of intelligence – even sentience. It gave itself a name: Magias. The gods realised their mistake; Magias would provide mortals with power over magic. The gods grew jealous and resolved to destroy Magias, but another power intervened: nature. Having created something, destroying it was forbidden by rules of the cosmos that could not be tampered with by mere gods.

"What do you mean, destruction is forbidden?" Daelen objected. "I've destroyed plenty of enemies in my time." To illustrate his point, he blasted a cluster of trees into dust with a small beam cannon blast.

Dreya shook her head. "No, mighty shadow warrior. That's not what she means. You have disintegrated those trees, and you have killed your enemies, but you have not destroyed anything."

Catriona nodded. "What you have done is change living matter into dead matter, and because my magic has a temporal element, I can fix that." So saying, she used her druid magic to restore the trees to their former condition.

Mandalee agreed, "Death is a part of life; if you burn a forest, you change it into ashes and smoke."

Catriona concluded, "Changing things from one state to another is what magic and nature are all about."

*****

Though it may seem as if wielders of wizard and clerical magic can create something from nothing, gentle reader, the truth is, they are merely giving magic shape and form. There has only ever been one true Act of Creation – the Cataclysm that began the cosmos. One may attribute that Act to a Creator and in some sense that may be true. That is unknowable and beside the point. The point is Creation happened. Time simply allows that which was initially Created to change. Everything that exists changes. Everything that lives dies, but it remains a fact of Creation that they lived, they existed. Nothing within the rules of the cosmos can deny that. Nothing unreal exists. Nothing that exists can be made unreal.

*****

"The gods were trying to command magic itself to cease to exist. They knew there was a power outside the walls of Creation, the power we call *IT*. That is the only power that can truly destroy. 'Uncreate' or 'unmake' might be better words," Cat suggested. "To make something cease to exist. Not just in what we think of as the present and future, but in the past as well, as if it were never created in the first place. There is an excellent reason for this rule: even the gods could not foresee the consequences of true destruction. It's not just about the object itself; it's everything it interacted with."

"I understand," Daelen agreed, "by uncreating one object, you'd set off a chain of events that might change the whole of reality."

"Well, not just any object," Dreya countered. "I mean, it's unlikely that the cosmos would unravel because you unmade my favourite teacup. Some objects are more important than others."

"Even if the effect were not so extreme, it could still be a terrible weapon," Mandalee pointed out. "Imagine if someone tried to unmake people. Not just murder them – terrible as that is – make them unreal, make them cease to exist…" she trailed off. Then those old, familiar feelings of insecurity rose up. "Don't mind me. I'm probably not making any sense, as usual."

Cat and Dreya refuted that.

Daelen, too, thought she was making a great deal of sense and tried to imagine such a weapon, before quickly deciding he didn't want to think about it. "But still the gods tried it?" he wondered.

Cat confirmed it. "They thought they could limit the effect to only unmake the kinds of frequencies that wizards use, leaving those the gods pass on to their clerics intact, but once *IT* gained a foothold, *IT* wouldn't stop until the whole of reality unravelled.

"What Magias did was what I had to do tonight: reject and resist the chaotic power of *IT* and claim the right to her own life, her own agency. As a result of that, *IT* was banished once more, and magic could be withheld no longer. Mortal achievement didn't need to be at the whim of fickle gods – they could achieve anything they wanted by their own agency."

"All my life," Mandalee offered, "I've always believed that magic is a gift of the gods. Now it seems it was a gift they never wanted us to have. If they'd had their way, they would have kept it from us forever."

'*Not all of us,*' Shyleen told her. '*That kind of attitude is partly why I left.*'

'*I know, Shyleen,*' Mandalee returned. '*Just as I know you've never withheld your magic from me.*'

'*All I have is yours, Mandalee. Always.*'

At that, the Cleric of Nature began stroking her feline friend.

"Obviously," Catriona continued, resuming her lecture, "this is a creation myth, and not to be taken literally, but the essence of the story is true. However, there was one form of magic of which even Magias was wary: Time magic. It was available to clerics in a small way, expressing itself in the form of healing. Druids could do it, too, in a different way. But wizard magic was much more attractive to people for the overt power it offered, and so druid magic became something of a niche art, largely forgotten in the scheme of things as their founder, Alycia, Mother of Nature, slept."

Catriona broke off from the script to add, "Until, that is, one brilliant, resourceful and, let's be honest, stunningly beautiful half-Faery pioneer came along: me!" Nobody seemed terribly impressed, so she just shrugged. "Suit yourselves."

"But true Time magic is more than that, isn't it?" Mandalee asked.

Dreya already had the answer. "What Cat is talking about is nothing less than total mastery of time and space. The very fabric of reality. This world. All worlds. With such power, I could truly be the Greatest Mage Who Ever Lived…and need not worry about any who come after." Her eyes had taken on a dangerous glow, though her smile was sweet and her voice dripping with honey. "Tell me, Cat, my love, how is this power released?"

"It's all right here in the Chronicles," Catriona replied absently.

"I see. And is it all written in that secret language of yours?"

"Oh, no!" Cat laughed. "That's just the cover. Now that the security seals are open, the whole point of the book is to make Time

86

magic accessible. It wouldn't be able to do that very well if I were the only person who could read it, would it?"

"No, it wouldn't," Dreya agreed. Then her voice became hard and cold. "In that case, 'my love,' I have no further use for you." Before anyone could react, Dreya snatched the book from Catriona's grasp, stood and focussed her will on her girlfriend, unleashing her ultimate power word, "DIE."

Mandalee and Daelen cried out as one, but it was too late; Catriona flopped lifeless to the ground. One of the ghouls floated forward, grabbed the staff and handed it to its mistress, who spoke again, "TORCH." Catriona's body went up in flames, turning it to ash and smoke, blowing away on the breeze until there was nothing left but a patch of scorched grass. The others were too stunned to leap to the fight as Dreya's undead guards prepared to defend their dark mistress.

"You killed her!" Daelen cried in despair. "She trusted you – you even got me trusting you – and you betrayed her!"

With a misty-eyed look at the place where Catriona had been a moment ago, Dreya sighed, regretfully, "If it's any consolation, I really did love her, but I told you the magic would always come first and now that they're unlocked, these," she held up the book and staff, "represent the advantage of a lifetime."

The others were over their shock, now, and advanced on the sorceress. Shyleen growled and prepared to strike at the killer of her half-Faery friend, but Dreya warned them off.

"Together, the three of you might – just might – be able to stop me, but I doubt it, and I can be long gone before you can call Mickey and his gang. If you come after me, then what? What about Kullos? After fighting me, even if you won, you'd be too drained to fight him. You know he won't wait forever. Pick your target, shadow warrior: me or him – you can't kill us both."

"If Kullos wins, he'll destroy the world!" Daelen reminded her. "The world you're standing on!"

Dreya shrugged, unconcerned. "That's OK. I conquered another one just in case!" She laughed. "Sara and Jessica love me! They think I'm some kind of hero, the Saviour of Phitonia. They've no idea I only did it to give myself a second power base. If Kullos kills you and decides to come after me, I'll have the resources of that entire world behind me – dragons and Chetsuans alike. Before he can strike at me, I will have learned all I need to be the Mistress of Time and Space – trust me, I'm a quick study.

"Do what you want, shadow warrior, but whatever you do, I win! Pray that Kullos kills you, Daelen, for if he doesn't, I will make you my favourite toy. I have many interesting games to play with you, although I don't expect you'll find them too much fun. Dreya the Dark has a bad habit of breaking her best toys!"

To Mandalee, she simply offered, "My condolences."

"Go to hell!" she spat back.

"Now there's a challenge I hadn't considered," Dreya remarked, raising her eyebrows. "Enough!" she declared at last. "Guards, we're done here. We won't return to the Black Tower. That's the first place Kullos would come looking for me. I'll commandeer that ship, the *Dolphin* – it evaded his gaze once, why not twice? Back to StormClaw and then to Phitonia. Consolidate my power base there." With a final "Farewell," she and her guards became one with the shadows and drifted away.

*****

When she was gone, Mandalee collapsed in a heap on the ground and wept for her lost friend.

"Dammit!" Daelen swore. "I should have killed her the moment I met her."

"Too late for that, I'm afraid, Daelen," Mandalee sniffled. "We need to decide what we're going to do now."

"Do?" Daelen wondered. "We stop Dreya, avenge Cat. That's what we do!"

"I'm not so sure," Mandalee disputed, drying her tears. "I think we need to talk about that."

"Talk?" Daelen demanded. "We should be racing after Dreya!"

"Stay calm, Daelen."

"Calm? Catriona is dead, and you want me to be calm?"

"Yes, stay calm and think: what about Kullos?"

"Kullos? Well right at this moment, I don't ca—"

"What are you, Daelen, my echo?" Mandalee wondered with a quizzical look. "You seem to be repeating the keyword in everything I say."

"Mandalee, I know you're grieving, but this is no time for…jokes…"

His voice trailed off as Dreya and Catriona walked into the clearing, arm in arm, laughing.

"I'm afraid the joke's on you, Daelen," Mandalee smirked.

Daelen was so shocked, he would have collapsed if Mandalee hadn't stood and propped him up. "What's going on?"

"Just a little deception," Cat answered with a grin.

"The beauty of a sympathic link," Mandalee added. "As you know, I have a special relationship with nature. In a place like this, I hear animals talking all the time. Through them, I became aware of a pack of wolves hiding in the bushes. They seemed odd somehow, so I used my link with Cat to ask her opinion."

"Remember what I told you, Daelen, about morphing into a tiger?" Cat asked.

"You pointed out how it's easier to fool humans than it is a real tiger," Daelen replied.

"Exactly, well I cast Mirror Image, leaving my copy talking to you and checked out the pack in my own wolf form. They never noticed their numbers had suddenly increased by one. Anyway, they may have looked like wolves, but they weren't acting very wolf-like."

Daelen gasped, "Spies! Sent by Kullos!"

"That's what Dreya said. She could use her own magic through me to penetrate their disguise. They weren't really shapeshifters. Just wizards using illusion magic."

"Wizards? The ones who were being taken against their will?"

Cat shook her head and told him, "Not all of them were."

"Renegade wizards," Dreya spat, her words a curse. "The Council suspected there were some working for Kullos and now I knew it was true. They were interested in gaining the *Chronicles of Magias* for their master, so I figured they would follow the bait wherever it went. I cast a copy spell of my own, through which I put on the show of betraying you."

"Nice job, by the way," Mandalee commended her. "I loved the 'Dreya the Dark has a bad habit of breaking her best toys' bit. I got chills!"

"Really? I was worried it was a bit much."

"No, pitched it just right, for me."

"Thanks, and speaking of performances, what about you? Crying on cue like that. I was impressed. Really sold it, I thought."

"Aww, thanks, Dreya. I just had to get myself in that space, you know? Imagine how I'd feel if Cat really had just died, and channel that."

Dreya nodded appreciatively.

"You did refer to yourself in the third person, though, Dreya," Cat pointed out. "I thought you had a rule against that."

"I was in character. It doesn't count," Dreya insisted.

"OK, I'll let you off."

"If you three have finished with drama club," Daelen grumbled, "could somebody please explain what just happened?"

"Oh, yes, sorry," Mandalee apologised. "Well, I stayed to ensure the 'wolves' followed Dreya's copy and to keep you in check, so you didn't ruin everything. We couldn't risk telling you, and besides, your reaction helped to make it more convincing."

"The book Dreya's copy stole was actually my grandmother's recipe book for herbal remedies," Cat explained.

"One of my guards will give it back shortly," Dreya promised.

Cat smiled in acknowledgement. "As for my staff…" she held out her hand, and it appeared obediently out of her pocket dimension. "That was a fake, too. I thought a decoy might be a sensible idea. I shaped the wooden part while we were on the Dolphin. As for the blue crystal…"

Mandalee indicated her left earlobe, which was now bare.

"Had to sacrifice an earring," she sighed.

Daelen boomed with laughter, allowing waves of relief to wash over him. "I am way out of my depth with you three! I apologise for doubting you, Dreya."

The sorceress waved the apology aside. "Your doubts also helped to convince our enemies. If you believed my betrayal was real, so would Kullos' spies."

"So, what does your copy have planned for them?"

Before Dreya could answer, her undead guards returned. The Knight commander bowed and reported, "Nine renegade wizards destroyed."

"Good," Daelen approved.

"Nine?" Mandalee put in. "There were ten wolves."

At that, the lead ghoul shimmered closer to Dreya and explained, "If it pleases you, Mistress, before you cancelled your copy, she ordered me to keep one alive as a prisoner."

"Interesting," Dreya remarked. "Did she say why?"

"He claims to have a message for Lady Catriona, Mistress."

"I'll deal with that later," Catriona decided, dismissing the issue for the moment. "Now that we're alone, we can finish what we were doing."

Chapter 13

Catriona made it clear that even if Dreya had really betrayed them, it wouldn't have done her any good.

"You see, all along I've been wondering, if I can unlock the staff, why hasn't anyone done it before? As I've said, I'm not that conceited. Same goes for the *Nameless Book*. Well, it's all explained in this passage here."

She produced the *Chronicles* and showed her friends the page that read:

CONDITIONS
: Only one who does not seek power may unlock it.
: It requires the willing, unselfish co-operation of three mortals bound together – one given to the light, one shrouded in darkness and one forever balanced between them.
: All flavours of magic must be represented in the Three: wizard, druid and cleric.
: If any of the Three seeks to gain this power over the others, or if any one of them desires its release less than the others, Time Magic shall not be released.
: In addition to the Three, there must be one long-lived being from the higher planes, one of both light and dark, and yet of neither, who would wish to stand against the one with the power to strike at the home of the Angels. One whose essence is bound to the staff bearer.
: Even if all these conditions are met, the release shall be impossible in the absence of the greatest magic that exists in the world.

"What does all that mean?" Daelen asked.

"It means us," Mandalee stated.

"We fulfil the conditions," Dreya agreed.

"I do not seek power," Cat checked off the first condition. "The three of us represent Light, Dark and Balance, but we're co-operating fully and freely." Check two. "Dreya is a wizard, I am a druid and Mandalee is a cleric." Check three. "Dreya betraying us to gain this power for herself was an act, so it doesn't count against us.

None of us is seeking this power at the expense of the other two, and we all want it to be released." Check four. "The being from the higher planes is you, Daelen. You were split when we first met – light and dark clones, but now you are one being of both, but you are a renegade, so you are recognised as neither. The 'power to strike at the home of the Angels' is a cryptic way of saying 'Heaven's Surrender', and you intend to use your 'Wish' barrier to protect our world against it." Check five.

"One whose essence is bound to the staff bearer?" the shadow warrior wondered.

"Yeah, not sure about that bit," Cat admitted, frowning in puzzlement. She'd taken some of his essence inside her body for a while, but she'd given it back, so it was hardly bound to her. She dismissed it with a shrug. "Anyway, the final condition refers to the final key needed to unlock the power – the greatest magic that allowed me to open the *Chronicles*: love. We are all bound by love of one form or another." All conditions checked off. "The gods agreed to these conditions only because they believed them impossible to fulfil, but we have proved them wrong, and now we are ready to begin."

She then directed her friends to another page in the Chronicles:

FULFILMENT
: This marks the beginning of a new age of magic.
: Upon the release of the Time magic within, the Three mortals shall become Guardians. One White, one Black, one Red, they shall protect the magical world, magical power and magical knowledge. The presence of the greatest magic that fulfils the final condition (see previous section subtitled 'Conditions') shall prevent them from ever turning against one another. Despite their differing views, they shall all share one sincere devotion to order and magic.
: Magic itself must survive and increase; that is imperative, for Time will bring challenges for which the world must be ready.
: Their other task, no less important, is to protect the integrity of Time. Laws of Time magic shall be created, and the Guardians shall be charged with enforcing them, as well as repairing any damage done by the renegade or the inexperienced. (For further details see section subtitled 'Spacetime Manipulation: A Guide'.)

: While the Guardians will continue to be mortals, by their very nature, they shall possess innate Time Magic through which they exist outside the flow of Time. (Details of specific spells may be found in Appendix 1.)

: They may stay in their post as long as they choose (subject to agreed rules) but be warned: Timelessness is wearying. So, whenever they wish, they may pass on the mantle to another of their order, when they decide to complete their mortal lives in the world.

"That's pretty much all we need to know for now," Cat opined. Turning to Dreya and Mandalee, she asked, formally, "Do you accept the positions of the Guardians of Time and Magic with all the attendant privileges and responsibilities?"

"Absolutely," Dreya declared hungrily.

"Oh well, Shyleen," Mandalee remarked, "Looks like I'm having a change of career for a while." Shyleen just purred. "Yes," she affirmed, "I accept. Sounds exciting."

"OK, you've agreed, now what?" Daelen asked. "Sorry to rush you girls, but there is still the small matter of stopping Kullos."

"This will only take a moment longer," Cat assured him confidently. "Then, as soon as I see what that prisoner wants, I'll go and do the scouting I promised."

Catriona instructed her three companions to each place a hand on the staff that she held. Daelen was wary of this, after what happened last time, but Cat reminded him he was different then, plus with all four of them touching it, she believed there should be a balance and so the staff wouldn't react badly.

"Don't worry, this won't be like unlocking the *Chronicles*," she assured him. "I can put the key in the lock, but I need someone to, how did Jessica put it...blow the bloody doors off?"

"So, this will finally unlock the power of the staff?"

"No, Daelen, keep up!" she admonished him, rolling her eyes. "The staff serves as the final security key to access Time Magic within the Book, but it's not its primary function. I still have no idea what the staff was originally designed to do. I assumed the book would tell me, but it seems an unrelated mystery. Let's finish solving this mystery first, shall we?"

"What do I do?" he asked.

Cat encouraged him to imagine firing his beam cannon into the staff. Project the idea of it.

So, with four hands gripping the staff, he did just that. Cat sent the unlocking sequence into the device, sympathically, mentally surfing on the wave of Daelen's power.

It began like the last time the three would-be Guardians held the staff together. The pull was stronger, but the balance still felt off. Once again, light flared from the crystal, painting a pattern in the sky that seemed to be trying to match the void storms. Symbols appeared, brighter than before, but once again, they flickered and died before achieving full resolution…and with a resounding thud, Cat's mind hit a wall, like a mental block. The final barrier had not opened.

"What happened?" chorused her friends.

Cat flicked frantically through the *Chronicles*. "I don't understand it! We've done everything right. Just like it says." Her disappointment was so great, she collapsed in a heap on the ground.

"All my life I've been working for this moment. So many years of effort, studying, research, risking my soul by opening the *Chronicles*, and it doesn't even work!"

She was almost in tears at her failure. Her friends tried to comfort her, and Dreya read the *Chronicles* for herself, to see if she could find some flaw, but she agreed they had followed the instructions faultlessly.

*****

"I'm sorry, Cat," Daelen murmured gently, after a while, "but we really can't wait any longer. We have to concentrate on our coming battle with Kullos and to do that we need you to scout the army. You're the only one who can do it. We need you."

Cat blinked back her tears, stood up, took a deep breath and agreed, "I'm with you. Forget the Book of Magias; I've still got a book of my own, and it's filled with tricks that are going to tie Kullos' army in knots!"

The shadow warrior smiled and hugged her. "That's my girl."

There being nothing left for him to do, he simply found a comfortable spot and sat down to drink in the atmosphere of the forest for a while.

Cat shared a hug with Mandalee, too, then a slightly longer one with Dreya.

Shyleen pawed her and asked in the language of leopards, '*Do I not get a hug, too?*'

The druidess laughed, '*Of course! How could I leave out the leopard with the finest markings ever?*'

As Catriona crouched down to stroke her, Shyleen asked, '*You really think so? Well, you look very nice, too, whatever form you take, although I'm not keen on the wolf.*'

"Alright," Cat declared, standing once more, filled with a new grim determination. It was time to focus. "I suppose I'd better go and see our prisoner."

She thought he might have information that would help her scouting mission, so it made sense to deal with this small matter first. The druidess found where the wizard was chained up and dismissed Dreya's guards. He might open up a bit more if they were alone. Besides, what was one chained up wizard to a druid of Cat's ability?

*****

As Dreya and Mandalee read the *Chronicles* together, Dreya quickly discovered she had underestimated the cleric's ability to understand arcane matters. In her defence, however, that was mostly because Mandalee continued to underestimate herself.

"It's a pity this failed to work," Dreya told her at length. "I believe you would have blossomed in the role of White Guardian."

Mandalee was surprised to receive such a warm compliment from the legendary Dreya the Dark. She had a reputation as a cool ice queen, but Mandalee could already see that reputation was a pale shadow of the Faery woman herself.

"Maybe there's some way we can work together, anyway, the three of us, once this business with Kullos is over," Mandalee suggested.

Dreya's smile was one of relief. "You don't know how happy I am to hear you say that. This fight will keep Cat occupied for now, but, well, you knew her before I did. If her staff business is basically done and the *Chronicles* is a dead duck, can you imagine her without some kind of project to challenge her mind?"

Mandalee shook her head and agreed, "No, I can't. You're right. She's going to need us to put our heads together and come up with something."

"We will," Dreya promised.

"Dreya," Mandalee ventured, "I know I wasn't keen on you when we first met, but I want you to know I'm happy she's got you."

"Well, she's got you again, now, too, Mandalee, and I'm glad to see it. Just so you know, I've already given my guards new standing orders that you are welcome at my Black Tower any time. My door's always open to my girlfriend's best friend. In particular, I want to make sure you're with us when I give her this."

When she showed Mandalee what she had bought from Earth, the cleric threw her arms around the Faery woman, and any remaining trepidation drifted away on the breeze. If someone from the future had come to her just a few days ago and told her she was going to be friends with Dreya the Dark – real, proper, firm friends – she never would have believed it. Yet here she was.

"Just let me know when, Dreya," she smiled. "I wouldn't miss that for the world. Any world."

Finally abandoning the *Chronicles*, the two young women, White cleric and Black sorceress, found themselves walking together, arm in arm, swapping stories about Cat. Mandalee sharing some of their early adventures, and Dreya telling her, in return, things she'd missed in the two years she'd been away.

*****

The mismatched friends' conversations were interrupted by a scream coming from where the prisoner was being held.

"Cat!" they cried together, racing to the scene. Shyleen and Daelen sprang up, too, and ran with them.

First to arrive, Mandalee saw that the prisoner's shackles were shattered and broken on the ground, looking for all the world like they'd somehow rusted away. With them lay the broken remains of a vicious-looking weapon. It was designed so that when the hand closed in a fist around the handle, what appeared to be four claw-like blades extended outwards from the knuckles.

Mandalee didn't know how it could be so, but she quickly realised that 'claw-like blades' was describing it backwards: they were really blade-like claws – dragon claws.

To compensate for the loss of the shackles, Catriona was using her magic, asking the surrounding foliage to restrain him, but it was more than that. The vines seemed to be slowly pulling him apart and not content with that, Catriona was causing the air all around him to discharge electricity into his body. This was clearly the reason for the scream they had heard, as the prisoner's body convulsed in agony.

Mandalee and Daelen were clearly shocked by Catriona's actions, while Dreya's reaction was more one of curiosity and interest.

"Cat?" Mandalee called out.

With barely a glance, Cat threw a bottle of water between them and used the spilt contents to create an ice barrier.

"Stay out of this," she warned, "and don't even think of flying over it!"

"What the hell are you doing?" Daelen demanded.

"I'm sure she has her reasons," Dreya insisted.

"What reasons could possibly justify this?" Mandalee wondered.

If the prisoner somehow escaped and tried to hurt her friend, the assassin would have been the first to support Catriona's right to kill to protect her life. But torture?

'*Have you noticed they are not alone?*' Shyleen asked her human friend.

She hadn't, but now that she looked more closely, she realised the leopard was right: there was a figure standing with Cat and the prisoner. Just a white aura glowing softly. Insubstantial. Mandalee found it was stirring vague memories.

"That white figure," she pointed out. "I've seen something like it before." Why was she suddenly thinking about the day she received her contract to kill or otherwise 'stop' Daelen?

The shadow warrior agreed, "So have I." He was sure she was the one who warned him about Kullos taking wizards away to fight this war. The aura wasn't a perfect match, but it was close enough to convince him that they were the same being.

"I once saw something similar," Dreya offered. It had appeared to her at her Black Tower just before Aden escaped.

"No, twice!" she corrected herself. The first time had been as a child living in Sylfrania. She hadn't thought about that for years.

She remembered how the entity had scared away the bullies with their mere presence and told her that one day, if she worked hard in her magic, she would have the power to stand up to all the bullies and monsters in the world. "I'm sure she was the one who planted the idea to kill you, Daelen. She was different, though. She was shrouded in darkness. Almost like she was somehow made of shadow. Still, this brighter one reminds me of her, in a way."

"What the hell is wrong with you?" Cat was yelling at the prisoner. "Why would you want to do something so sick?"

Her expression was a mixture of tears, rage and utter contempt.

"Because it's an Abomination that needs to be destroyed!"

"You keep speaking with someone else's voice. Are you being controlled? Is someone making you do this?"

The prisoner seemed to forget all about the pain and laughed.

"Oh no, darlin'!" sneered a different voice – one that seemed to better match him. "I assure you I'm quite willing. That's why I was chosen – because I'd enjoy it!"

The original voice returned to say, "He has quite the hunger for killing innocents – you could say he's made a career out of it – but this is a whole new level even for him. Given half a chance, once he's through with you, I'm sure he'll do it again, many times."

"No, he won't!" Cat growled. "I'm going to make sure he can't!"

"Do what you want to this body," the voice laughed. "It doesn't matter. My plans are flexible. One way or another, history will change and the Abomination will never come to be."

Chapter 14

As soon as Cat was alone with the prisoner, he had done something to make the shackles corrode away and drop off. Then he pulled the claw weapon out of a pocket dimension. She didn't think anybody else knew how to do that. She backed away and tried to throw her magic at him, but nothing would work. Her pocket dimension was closed to her. Even her shapeshifting abilities were gone. She searched for an anti-magic field, but there wasn't one. That's when she'd first noticed that nature had ceased. The birds in the trees, the animals, even the breeze. The air wasn't just still; it was stopped. Everything was stopped. Time was frozen.

"Hello, you!" the wizard greeted her with a voice that seemed entirely wrong for his body.

"How are you doing this?" she gasped.

"Ah well, that's the thing," he replied. "You'll never know now. Not this time."

He advanced on her with a wicked grin, slashing the air with his claws. She tried to run, but she couldn't move. She called out, but within just a few yards, the sound abruptly stopped.

His laugh chilled her to the bone, but that was as nothing to her reaction when he told her what he was planning to do to her. She was going to die a horrible, painful, pointless death, but that wasn't the half of it. There was more. What he had told her next, she could not comprehend. She refused to tell her friends what it was.

"I can't," she insisted. "I'm sorry, I just can't. It doesn't matter, anyway – he's not going to get the chance to do it, thanks to her." She indicated the white aura.

The white figure had materialised and charged at the wizard. There was a brief struggle until the entity did something that broke the wizard's weapon, which fell uselessly to the ground. Then Time had restarted.

"Your agency and powers are returned to you," the entity had told her with a distant feminine voice.

*****

Back in the present, Cat called out to her girlfriend. "Hey, Dreya, you might be interested in this. You know you've got your power words, well, I've created one of my own."

She reminded Dreya of the time a group of clerics used their congregation to attack her because they believed replicating Holy Water was blasphemy. When she finally tracked down the clerics themselves, she had used her magic to reflect their hatred of her back on themselves. Her power distorted their beliefs so that they would obey her instructions as if they were commands from their gods. She did it, not because they tried to kill her, but because they had violated innocent people and placed them in harm's way to do it. Even children. She'd told the clerics to drown themselves in their precious Holy Water, and they had; compelled by their devotion to her, fuelled by their hatred.

"I remember," Dreya replied. Mandalee and Daelen also knew the story.

"Well, I didn't think anything could sicken me more than what those clerics did, but this one has just found a whole new level to sink to. So, I've created a power word version of that same spell especially for the occasion."

"What did you call it?" asked the sorceress.

"What else could I call a spell that takes unreasoning hate and changes it into unthinking devotion?" She turned her attention back to the renegade wizard, encouraging him to focus on all of his hatred for his 'target'. Then, she cancelled all other magic, directed her will and her gaze upon the prisoner and said, "LOVE."

Immediately, he dropped to his knees and begged. "Command me, Mistress! Let me please you! I'll do anything!"

"First of all, without repeating what you were going to do, please confirm for me: was that your free will? Something you wanted to do?"

"Oh, yes, Mistress!" he affirmed. "I so much wanted to do it!"

"And is it true that you've killed other innocent people before?"

"Many times, Mistress."

"And if given a chance, would you do the same to others?"

"Again and again and again, Mistress," he grinned excitedly.

"Why?"

He looked puzzled for a moment, as if he'd never considered the question before, and then answered, simply, "For fun, Mistress."

"Then there is only one thing you can do for me," Cat commanded with a voice as hard as steel. "Walk away. Walk far away and keep walking. I don't care where you go, as long as it's away. You may stop to drink and rest as often as you need to, but you will be unable to eat. Your vile hunger would continue to cause the deaths of innocents. This way, the only death your hunger will lead to is your own. That will please me very much. Now go."

The wizard leapt up and cried out in joy, "Yes, Mistress! I will go away and die as you command. Thank you for letting me do this for you, Mistress!"

Without another word, then, he simply walked away.

The white aura spoke to Catriona once more, "I have to go, too. Don't worry – they won't understand now, but they will one day. Take care, Catriona."

The aura faded until she vanished altogether.

Cat ignored her friends' horrified looks. Even Dreya had a puzzled frown on her face that told her even she couldn't imagine what had driven such a response. The druidess didn't want to deal with them at the moment, though, so she immediately shifted to owl form and flew away to see to her long-delayed scouting job.

*****

When Catriona found the barrier around Kullos' hidden army, she probed it gently with her magical senses. It seemed safe enough. As she watched, other birds were flying through it without incident, so she tentatively lowered herself through it. It tingled a bit, possibly trying to identify what she was, so she concentrated on being as owl-like as possible. That way, any such detection magic should register her as a bird and remain unconcerned. As she breached the barrier, there appeared to be no call to arms, no sense that anyone thought anything out of the ordinary was happening. Encouraged, she began to fly around, taking in the scene below.

She estimated that Kullos' army must number into the thousands, about half of which were demons. Mostly Lesser ones, but there were several dozen Greater Demons, from the deeper planes. The other half of his army was mostly comprised of humans and Faery, but there were other creatures, too, that Cat did not recognise. They didn't seem to be demons – they didn't have the right magical signature for that. Catriona puzzled over the issue for a moment. If they were neither from Tempestria nor from the higher or lower planes, what did that leave? She quickly reached the only logical conclusion: aliens. They had to be. It made sense – if Daelen could create portals to other worlds, then so could Kullos.

She didn't know whether they were here willingly or whether they had been coerced. Come to that, she didn't know how many Tempestrians were here because they supported Kullos and how many were here against their will. She didn't want to be a party to killing innocent people, no matter what world they were from, but this was war. She and her friends were heavily outnumbered, so there was no fighting this war defensively. Cat could see plenty of opportunities for crowd control: wells provided water, campfires burned for warmth and cooking, and despite being in the middle of the desert, a few hardy plants still grew. All could serve the needs of her druid magic, but it wasn't enough. They had to do what Mandalee had done when she'd been forced to fight more than fifty alone: attack. Hit hard, hit fast, make every strike kill, no hesitation, no mercy. If only there were some non-lethal way to take the mortals out of the fighting, and let justice sort the willing from the unwilling later. She had no qualms about slaughtering demons. Mandalee had been doing it for years, and with no innocents getting in the way, Dreya could unleash mass devastation with blood magic, power words and beam cannon blasts. If their allies grouped around Michael, it would be simple enough to avoid targeting that area. But to facilitate that, Cat needed more information.

Gradually, night gave way to day, as it always does, and Cat was beginning to think a nocturnal owl might start to look suspicious, so she found a secluded spot to quickly shift to falcon form, instead. Taking to the sky once more, the falcon, with her super sharp eyesight spotted the solution: a single Red robe sorceress. She'd met her only once, years ago, but she'd made an impression. She was the reason Cat had embarked on this quest in the first place: Justaria, the missing Triumvirate representative. At last, she'd found her. But how to talk to her without arousing suspicion?

Keeping an eye on her position, Cat stopped worrying about the people and demons, and instead focussed on nature. People tended to think of deserts as barren, lifeless places, but it was still home to many varieties of animal and plant life. There were palm trees, willows, and cacti, as well as flowering plants, including yellow marigolds and white lilies. Once again, Blessed Alycia, Mother of Nature had provided all a skilled druid needed. It was time to plagiarise one of Justaria's ideas.

Remaining in bird form, she subtly used her magic to encourage more lilies and marigolds to grow together near a palm tree on the edge of Kullos' territory, close to the barrier, not far from where Justaria was sitting. Then she bent all the lilies so that they were pointing towards the tree. Just one final component to add. She didn't know how to do it with magic, so that meant the hands-on approach. Trouble was, she knew Kullos and his forces were on the lookout for her, and she couldn't afford to be spotted. But there was another option. She hadn't used it for years – Cat had promised she never would – but under the circumstances, she could see no other way. Being careful not to be seen, Catriona landed behind the tree and shifted into the shape of someone she used to know well: Jacob. Maybe she'd look him up when this was over, she considered. That might be nice. She wasn't sure of the accuracy of the image in her mind, but it didn't have to be perfect. Compartmentalising one part of her mind to keep concentrating on holding this unfamiliar shape, she reached out with her sympathic communication, trying to project something into Justaria's mind: *'Friendship, tree, quiet, care'*.

It wasn't easy trying to get through the mental defences of a sorceress as skilled as Justaria, but she knew she could do it. The key was subtlety. The gentler she was, the less of a threat she seemed. As a side-effect, this meant Justaria was less likely to be startled by the impressions in her mind. It took patience, but after a few moments, Justaria's body language began to change, as if she were getting an idea and trying to make it take shape.

As Cat projected, *'flowers, tree,'* Justaria's expression was one of curiosity, not suspicion. She wasn't sure why she wanted to look at these yellow and white flowers so much but could see no harm in the idea. She was a nature lover, after all, and missed her garden. That thought was the trigger. Suddenly, she could see how the white lilies were bent, even though their yellow marigold neighbours were standing straight. This was just like what she had done with the white daisies and yellow buttercups around that old oak tree at home, back when Kullos came for her. Her hopes elevated, but she was conscious of the need to not draw attention. Rather than approach the tree directly, then, she spent the next five minutes casually wandering around, even calling out greetings to people along the way as she usually would. Her stroll appeared random but was, in fact, a carefully calculated route to take her naturally back to that palm tree.

Waiting for her, was a young lad, probably no more than eighteen, wearing the red robes of a wizard. She thought she knew all the wizards in Kullos' camp, but she didn't recognise this one. She had believed Kullos had stopped 'recruiting' as he was expecting an imminent attack.

"Who are you?" she asked.

"A friend," the wizard answered, pointing to a carving in the tree that read 'CAT'. "Think back a few years to a particular Conclave for a certain young druid girl, facing charges brought by old Renjaf."

"Conclave records are public domain," she scowled, suspiciously. "Anyone could know about the one you're talking about. It doesn't confirm who you are."

"I know," Cat agreed with a nod, "but I also know what happened after that – the private chat you had with that young druid girl." She relayed the entire conversation, as close to word-for-word as she could recall. "In the end," she continued, "you told me that you thought you were doing me a favour by kicking me out of college and letting me learn my own way." She smiled. "You were right."

"Catriona!" Justaria gasped, with a broad smile. Then with a mock frown, she took in how Cat looked and scolded her, "I thought we agreed you weren't going to do this again."

"What can I say? Old habits," Cat quipped.

Justaria grinned. In reality, it wasn't hard to guess why she was disguised this way. Taking the form of another person was illegal, but that law had never been formulated with this situation in mind.

"Still a handful of trouble, I see."

"Oh, two handfuls by now, at least," Cat returned.

"I see you got my message," Justaria remarked, raising a hand to indicate the tree.

Cat nodded. "A whole team of wizards missed it before I got there," she replied, asking nature to carefully remove all trace of her own handiwork. She briefly outlined the circumstances and apologised for making such a mess of her stable and garden, and then stealing her horse. She assured her that he was stabled at Kingsville Piers, where they would no doubt take good care of him.

More illegal actions. More crimes committed in the name of doing the right thing. Justaria promised that Cat would receive a full pardon and a commendation for her resourcefulness.

"Now, for my next trick," Cat quipped, "it's time to get you out of here."

"How?" asked Justaria. "If escaping were that easy, don't you think I would have done it by now?"

"That had occurred to me. I just look at things a bit differently. The barrier allows passage in only one direction, right?"

"You know about that?" Justaria asked raising a questioning eyebrow.

"Well, (a) it makes sense, and (b) I noticed the birds." Specifically, she'd noticed the birds flying *into* Kullos' zone, but none flying out.

"And you came in anyway?"

Cat shrugged. "I've been in way worse traps than this."

Between her attempts to unlock Time Magic and the incident with the prisoner, she'd had a horrible night. Today was a new day and she was damned if a mere barrier of higher planar energy was going to stop her. Two failures were her limit.

Justaria explained that her investigations had begun to reveal a pattern to the abductions, favouring those who had publicly indicated mistrust in Daelen's brand of 'protection'. That made it easier for Kullos to persuade them of Daelen's ill intent – his story fitted with what they already believed was true. To test her hypothesis, Justaria had begun to vocalise her own support for Kullos over Daelen. She assured Cat that that wasn't the case.

"Quite honestly," she admitted, "between Kullos, Daelen and that dark clone of his, I wasn't sure which one to trust, if any. All I wanted was to gather independent information in hopes of sharing it at some crucial moment before any confrontation happened."

"That's why I'm getting you out of here," Cat told her. "I'm on a mission, a quest with some powerful friends. I came here tonight to scout around, but finding you is even better. If you'll come with me, you'll finally get the chance to share your information."

"But how do we get through the barrier?" Justaria asked. "I've never found a weakness."

"Kullos is powerful, but not that smart," Cat opined. "He's done what you wizards do – created a dome shield instead of a bubble. Want to know how I know?" she asked.

Justaria nodded, so Cat pointed out the palm tree by which they stood. Some of the roots were slightly exposed near the trunk before disappearing under the sand. A few of them were heading towards the barrier. She'd seen similar roots on the other side of the shield, snaking out from the interior, still connected to their parent tree, still gathering water from deep underground.

"If the shield prevents living things from passing through from this side, how have those roots not been cut off and died? Conclusion: the barrier doesn't extend that far down, which means a dome shield, not a bubble."

Cat could get herself out at any time by burrowing in mole form, but Justaria was going to need something a bit larger. She could fuse sand into glass for her Nature's Mirror, but for this, she was going to need to shape a tunnel at the same time. That required concentration and time.

"Mistress Justaria," she addressed the Red leader, formally, "while I'm doing this, could you please collect some of those marigold flowers for me?"

"What for?" Justaria asked.

"My friends would call it a ridiculous radical plan because those little flowers are going to help me solve a problem and save a lot of lives."

Asking no further questions, the high-ranking sorceress did as the druid asked until the tunnel was complete – an underpass with walls of glass. Justaria admitted she wouldn't have the first idea how to do that.

"That's OK," Cat assured her, "we all have different strengths. Speaking of which, how are you with illusion magic?"

"Not bad, why?"

"Could you hide the entrance? We don't want anyone to know there's been a breach, and if my plan with the flowers works, I'm afraid you're going to have to come back later."

Chapter 15

When Catriona brought Justaria back to their camp by the ancient temple ruins, she first introduced her to her best friend. Of course, she already knew Dreya the Dark from Council sessions.

"The White Assassin," she greeted Mandalee, shaking her hand. "I've heard of you."

"You have?" she replied, astonished that one of the Triumvirate would think her worthy of notice.

Justaria nodded. "In fact, I was planning to hire you for some Council-sanctioned demon hunting jobs a couple of years back, but you disappeared."

"A bad thing happened, but it's all fine now," she replied simply, giving an embarrassed Catriona a reassuring smile,

Dreya knew the 'bad thing' in question, of course, and decided to move the conversation along.

"It is good to see you alive and well, Mistress Justaria," she offered formally, inclining her head in respect for one of the Triumvirate. Naturally, Justaria's disappearance had led to a replacement being appointed, but after the formality of a Conclave, Justaria would doubtless be exonerated of any wrongdoing and be free to reclaim her seat, should she wish it. Besides, Dreya liked Justaria. Despite their different alignments, she had often been an ally on the Council.

"Dreya," Justaria returned the greeting. "I trust you kept the Council from breaking apart in my absence?"

"More than that, I used the distractions of your disappearance and this business with Kullos to push through reforms almost without them noticing. Changed the name, gave druids equal status and opened our doors to clerics."

"Still the same Dreya the Dark," Justaria remarked, trying to hide an amused smile. "For years, I beg, plead and reason with the Black robes to stop fighting among themselves, without success. You put a knife to Laethyn's throat, tell him to pack it in and bar the odd incident, it stops. I don't even want to know who you manipulated to get the Council dancing to your tune this time, Dreya. Officially, I can't condone your methods. Unofficially, I can't help but admire how you get results. So, have you got around to conquering the world yet?"

Her question was a joke. She was not prepared for an entirely serious, "Yes, I did. I had a spare afternoon." Then after a pause to let that sink in, Dreya qualified her statement. "Not this world – another one. At least, I *intended* to conquer it. Some people seem to think I may have accidentally saved it at the same time."

Justaria laughed. "Like I said, still the same Dreya the Dark: still making excuses for doing good things."

Doing her best to look offended, Dreya objected, "I'm sure I have no idea what you're talking about."

"Of course you don't," Justaria replied, putting on her serious face. "Blame my weeks in captivity."

Moving on, Cat introduced Daelen and Michael, equally casually, momentarily forgetting that to Justaria, these friends of hers were mysterious, legendary beings of awesome power.

Justaria shook her head in disbelief. "When I predicted an exciting future for you, Catriona, all those years ago, even I never imagined all this. For all Dreya's machinations, I suspect you are the glue holding all this together, and if it's not too presumptuous of me, I am unbelievably proud of you."

Blushing, Cat wondered if she would still say the same if she knew what she'd done to the prisoner. Not that she regretted it.

*****

Without further ado, Justaria handed over the marigold flowers and while she told the others everything she had learned, Cat drew Mandalee to one side.

"So, are we going to talk about what you did to that prisoner?" Mandalee asked her friend.

"No, we're going to talk about these." She grabbed a bowl from the food tent and poured the flowers into it. Elaborating on her plan, she explained she knew they were poisonous to sheep and cattle. That made her wonder if, with a little bit of Cleric of Nature magic, they might be toxic to humans and Faery, too. "Not fatal," she assured her. "Just enough to give people a bad bout of stomach cramps for a while, if they happened to ingest some in their water supply."

110

"Cat, you know I don't like using poisons," Mandalee complained.

"Yes, I know you don't like it, Mandalee, but can you do it?" Catriona snapped, irritably. "Think of it this way: we don't know how many of the people in that camp truly are our enemies, and how many are like Justaria. With these flowers, a bit of magic and a pinch of luck, we can take most of them out of the fighting altogether. If you were sitting in that camp, having been abducted, which would you prefer: a bit of sickness, or death in a battle you want no part of?"

Of course, even if her idea worked, they couldn't guarantee it would work on aliens, but they were relatively few compared to the amassed horde. Cat would do her best to look out for them and restrain any who were not sick but seemed to be reluctant to fight. No war could guarantee zero loss of innocent life, but this plan was the best way she could think of to minimise such casualties.

Mandalee pointed out that Kullos had abducted clerics, as well as wizards, so they would have access to healing. But Cat had thought of that.

"Yes, but the healers will get sick themselves, which should delay their response. Even after they heal themselves, the illness will leave them weak for a while. Then every time they heal someone, they expend energy. If we time this right, they won't have much left by the time we attack. That all helps to take more people out of the fighting, which saves their lives. Anyone who doesn't fight doesn't die."

Mandalee had to concede she made a persuasive argument. It was just the kind of ridiculous radical plan her friend would come up with. Deliberately making people sick to save their lives. Despite her initial reluctance, then, Mandalee agreed to do it. Grinding down the flowers, she added water and applied heat to brew a kind of tea. Thanks to her understanding of nature, she knew how the poison affected sheep and cattle. Factoring in how humans differed, she could visualise how the plants would have to evolve to have that same effect on people. She also had to consider how Faery physiology worked a little bit differently to that of humans because it needed to attack both equally. Then, for good measure, she thought about the standard clerical healing spells that she would start with when trying to cure this herself and made the poison resistant to them. Hopefully, that would delay response time even further and help her save more innocent lives.

It was delicate, inventive work – Mandalee wasn't used to using her clerical powers in this way – but after a good hour's work, the poison was ready. She carefully poured it into a drinking flask, which they gave to Justaria, warning her to be careful not to get it mixed up with the safe drinking water they had given her. That water needed to last her only a matter of hours because tomorrow they would attack.

*****

Walking over to the command tent Michael had set up with Daelen, they rejoined the others and shared their strategy. Michael built on the idea, saying he could send a swarm of biting insects into the camp, which would carry an infection with much the same symptoms as Marigold poisoning.

"Since the flies are the more obvious source," he pointed out, "it should take them even longer to realise the water's contaminated, too."

Unfortunately, without his presence to control the flies, he wouldn't be able to protect Justaria from them, but with his help, Mandalee was able to give Justaria the best defence she could: insect repellent.

Cat escorted Justaria back to Kullos' camp and bade her wait while she burrowed under the barrier in mole form to check the way was clear. Once she was satisfied no-one had stumbled across the tunnel, she sent a sympathic message to Justaria. '*Clear*'.

Wishing each other luck, Cat returned the way she came, while Justaria set about the perilous mission of tainting the camp's water supply.

*****

When she returned to the temple ruins, Catriona found herself growing restless. She didn't know what to do with herself. Her research was at a dead end, and the young woman couldn't think of any more druid magic tricks to use in tomorrow's battle that would make any difference. She was avoiding Mandalee because she knew her friend was desperate to understand what she had done to that prisoner. But the druidess couldn't talk about that – it was too soon. Daelen wasn't happy about her actions, either, and she was worried that if she let him look into her eyes, he might see the eyes of a stranger. She didn't think she could bear that. Worse still, while she had no regrets about choosing Dreya, she also loved Daelen, just in a different way, and maybe it was selfish of her, but she'd grown used to seeing his love for her in his eyes. That's why she was avoiding looking at them now – just in case that love wasn't there anymore. Nevertheless, she couldn't explain it to him. She knew people often talked about waiting for the 'right time' to tell somebody something when generally speaking, there was no such thing. Even so, right now, on the eve of war – very possibly a fight to determine whether her world would still exist in a couple of days – this was definitely not the right time.

As much as it pained her that those two wanted an explanation, she was irrationally annoyed that Dreya didn't. To her, it was simple: if Cat had decided that level of response was warranted, that was good enough for her. Cat knew she was trying to be supportive, but she was finding it hard not to snap at her, "You watched me tell a man to go away and kill himself! How can you be OK with that and not demand to know why?" Although, of course, she wouldn't tell Dreya even if she did ask, and Dreya knew that, so what was the point of her asking?

Add to that the fact that she'd come within a hairsbreadth of dying at his hands when her magic deserted her, plus her failure with the *Chronicles* that still made no sense, and Catriona's emotions simply couldn't handle it. So, she made it clear she wanted to be alone for a while. If they needed her, they'd find her sitting under her own personal black cloud, which, for a druid, could be entirely literal.

In the end, she decided an actual raincloud was not necessary...her own tears were quite sufficient.

*****

She sat there alone for over an hour, unable to get a handle on either her mind or her heart until she heard the now-familiar leopard language in her head.

113

'*I am sorry things did not work out for you, Cat,*' Shyleen offered, kindly. Catriona hadn't heard her stealthy approach. '*Life is a great puzzle, especially for you, and sometimes you just don't have all the pieces.*'

Cat thanked the philosophical leopard but otherwise said nothing, so Shyleen slinked away.

*****

Dusk fell, and people began to think about getting some rest, ready for the big day tomorrow. Most headed for tents, but Cat wasn't at all surprised to see Mandalee settling down with Shyleen to sleep under the stars. The Cleric of Nature and her leopard, inseparable as always.

Cat got up – she could at least wish her friends a good night – and froze as realisation struck.

She shouted to the heavens, scaring the entire camp half to death, "I am so thick!"

She ran over to her friends, laughing, "Get up, you two! You can sleep later. I've just figured it out!"

In leopard, she declared, '*Shyleen, you are the smartest person I know!*'

"Seriously, you two, get up!" she insisted, hauling Mandalee to her feet. "We need to get Daelen and Dreya, too!" Cat could barely contain her excitement. It was infectious.

"What's this about, Cat?" Mandalee asked. She had no idea why her friend was acting like this.

"It's about the *Chronicles*! I know what I was missing! Come on!" Refusing to let go of Mandalee's arm, she impatiently pulled her along as she ran through the camp. Shyleen at their heels. She found Daelen first, just stepping out of the command tent and called out to him, "Have you seen Dreya?"

Without him having to answer, her girlfriend popped her head out of the same tent. Letting go of Mandalee's arm, at last, she put her hands on her hips and tried to look annoyed.

"And what have you two been doing together? Should I be getting jealous?"

Daelen looked flustered, but Cat reassured him, "I'm kidding, you fool!"

Turning to her girlfriend, she told her, "You'd better still have the *Chronicles*!"

"Of course," she replied, fishing the book out of her pocket and handing it to her.

"Perfect. Right, you lot come with me. Same as last night, but this time, we're doing it with all the pieces."

*****

They left the camp and returned to the same clearing they had used the night before. This time ensuring there were no pesky spies around before they started.

"I know why it didn't work – it's so obvious!" the druid exclaimed. "But it took a cleverer cat than me to make me see it. It's not that I didn't have all the pieces, I just left one out. Maybe Magias didn't anticipate such a unique variation, or maybe I'm just thick!"

Her friends looked at her like she was losing it, so she forced herself to calm down and explain, "It didn't work because the Three were only Two-and-a-Half. Mandalee, don't you see? Shyleen has half your soul!"

Mandalee gasped, "So the magic saw me as only 'half there', sort of!"

In leopard, she said, '*Shyleen, how about it? Just think, for as long as we want to do this job, I'll age only intermittently, when we enter the time stream to fix things. We can be together for longer than we ever dreamed possible!*'

Cat added, '*I'm so sorry I missed you out last night. I didn't mean to try and separate you; I just didn't think.*'

"Will you join us?" Mandalee asked aloud.

Shyleen considered carefully and answered in her own good time, '*Of course I will join you, Mandalee. It is better this way; you would obviously get it all wrong without me!*'

Catriona laughed, '*You're right, of course!*'

It was Dreya who asked Daelen, "One more try?"

The shadow warrior nodded his assent.

This time, four hands and one paw held the staff. This time, upon Catriona's command – and a good hard push from Daelen's power – the ancient astral doors swung open. This time, the symbols in the sky were clear. She still had no idea what they meant, but that didn't matter. What mattered was that this time, the essence of Time Magic flowed out into the three mortal mages and one leopard, through their bodies and out into the world. Moreover, when the blue crystal sent its lightshow high into the night sky, it was perfectly apparent to everyone that the stars shifted in response.

Even though the magic did not touch Daelen, he could taste the difference in the magic surrounding him.

"It's like I've been stuck inside for centuries, and now I've stepped outside and tasted fresh air for the first time."

Dreya acknowledged his analogy with a deferential bow of the head, appreciating his long experience.

"Now, I suggest a good night's sleep, and then tomorrow, it's time to hit Kullos with some of this fresh magic."

The others agreed – Shyleen growled, too.

"Why wait?" Cat was feeling inspired. In the interests of causing more havoc and disruption, she volunteered to send a thunderstorm over the enemy camp. "Even demons need sleep," she pointed out, "most of them, anyway. I say we make sure they don't get any tonight."

"Won't work," Daelen told her, shaking his head. "Kullos can dispel a storm just like I can."

With a twinkle in her eye, Cat asked, "How many?"

"How many what?"

"How many times is he going to do that in one night?"

Cat explained that if she could add a temporal element to her usual storm magic, she could make it so that every time Kullos got rid of a storm, another would start up, or rather the same storm over and over again all night."

Reusing an idea from when she and Mandalee saved Michael and his group, she thought the army might believe it was Daelen StormTiger, at first. They would quickly realise it wasn't, but then another storm would hit. They would either spend all night jumping at every flash of lightning or become so dulled to it that by the time Daelen did announce his presence, it would take them a while to grasp that it was for real, this time.

Even Dreya looked impressed. "You can do that?"

Cat grinned, feeling invigorated. "A few hours ago, I thought I'd failed in everything I'd ever worked for. Now, after what we just did, I think I can do just about anything I set my mind to!"

Dreya kissed her and insisted, "You always could. You just needed to see it. Go get them!"

With a seductive look into her girlfriend's eyes, the druid purred, "Just for that, you get to sleep in my tent, tonight. If you want."

"Sounds like a magical night to me," the sorceress smiled.

"Hey, Dreya," Mandalee offered, tongue-in-cheek, deliberately interrupting the two lovebirds. "As part of your drive for reforms, will you sponsor Shyleen as a full member of the Council of Mages?"

The sorceress considered that. "I will have to raise the issue of leopard mages at the next general meeting."

"I'll be sure not to miss that one," Cat remarked. "It could get interesting. By the way, Mandalee, when I said I can do anything I like, that includes you."

"What about me?"

"What I promised you the day we met," she replied. "To fix, shall we say, certain biological errors. At last, I can do it."

Mandalee gasped, "Really? I'd given up on that ever happening!"

"Yeah, sorry it's taken so long," Cat grinned. "More complicated than I thought and it'll probably violate half a dozen rules of Time Magic that haven't been written yet, but who cares?"

Laughing in joy, Mandalee swept her friend up in a huge embrace. "You are the best! Thank you!"

"Just one thing," Cat added, breaking the hug, "we'll need to get back to Elvaria to do it, which is a pretty long way, so do you mind if we save the world first?"

Wearing a look of intense concentration, Mandalee considered that for a moment, then agreed, "Oh, go on, then. Might as well. While we're here."

Chapter 16

As I gaze through Time to that moment, gentle reader, I can see that Daelen has agreed that it would be best to camp for one more night and begin the final push to Kullos' fortress at first light. Since there are no more plans to make, while the others head for their tents for the night, the shadow warrior has chosen to go for a walk alone to relax. He knows it will probably be his last chance to enjoy something so simple.

Even with all his power, the great shadow warrior always took pleasure in the smallest things.

The shadow warrior has been walking for close to an hour, when he comes across a female figure standing in the moonlight, dressed in white body armour much like his own, with white boots and a purple mask that conceals the upper part of her face.

"Greetings, Daelen," she offers. "Ah, but it is good to see you like this again; it's been a while."

*****

If that opening seems familiar, gentle reader, then I congratulate you on your memory. My story, or at least this part of it, has, at last, come full circle to where we began.

This is where I've sent Aunt Mandalee to meet up with Daelen and seek his help. Thankfully, he's agreed. But I have much more to write before I can meet with him myself, so I must continue to Freeze Time in a bubble around my house, to prevent the Black and Red Guardians from, well, basically doing their jobs.

However, we are at a point where I can reveal a little more. Specifically, to answer a conundrum that I left you with earlier in my writing. The same one Mandalee and I were faced with when I first came up with this ridiculous radical plan: How to find Daelen at a moment in history when he was (a) friends with Mandalee and Catriona, (b) at the peak of his powers, and (c) alone, yet in a precisely known location.

Clearly, this moment, on the eve of battle against Kullos and his forces, fulfils the first two conditions, but what about the third? Here's how Mandalee and I made our case to the other two

Guardians: Not one person even knew he'd left the camp that night and Daelen StormTiger was indeed alone, in the sense that there were no other people around him. There was, however, one curious leopard, who stealthily followed the shadow warrior without his knowledge. Shyleen is the reason we know about this moment at all. If not for her, I genuinely believe we would not be able to do what we're doing. Which just goes to show you, gentle reader, never underestimate a cat!

The other two Guardians rejected this as 'splitting hairs' or 'using the letter of the law to justify breaking its spirit'. They maintained that taking Daelen out of Time was too dangerous, especially at such a critical time. As you know, Aunt Mandalee and I disagreed, and took matters into our own hands.

So, just before Aunt Mandalee revealed herself to Daelen, she first had a quiet word with Shyleen. Of course, Shyleen is a clever kitty, so it naturally took only a moment for her to realise why her friend suddenly looked ten years older than when she'd seen her a moment ago.

'*This is because of the Time Magic that our mutual friend just unlocked, isn't it? Your eyes have seen much, I think. But you are still my Mandalee.*'

'*As always, Shyleen, your explanations are much better than mine, but I'm afraid I didn't come here just for a chat.*'

'*Of course,*' Shyleen replied. '*How can I help you?*'

'*Actually, you've already helped more than you know simply by being here, but you really need to go back to the camp, now, and share none of this. One day, a long time in the future, I will specifically ask you if you ever saw Daelen when he was completely alone. Then you must share this exact time and place.*'

'*This is an important responsibility, Mandalee,*' Shyleen understood, shifting uncomfortably under the weight of it. '*How can I be sure I will be able to give you what you need?*'

'*I was hoping you would ask me that,*' Mandalee replied with a relieved smile. '*If it's OK with you, I'd like to use the gentlest bit of magic on your mind. It's perfectly safe,*' she promised.

'*Like a mental block, or a magically backed promise?*' the leopard wondered.

Mandalee shook her head. '*It's based on those ideas, but much gentler. Following Daelen tonight will seem like just one of a*

119

million little moments in your life that simply aren't worth mentioning. It's not a secret – just unimportant. Until I specifically ask you. Then you will be able to recall it with perfect clarity. Is that OK?'

'Of course. That sounds perfectly fine, and I trust you completely. Just one thing – I know I should not ask about my own future, but please tell me: am I still part of you, where you are?'

Mandalee knelt down and stroked her friend, who began to purr, as she assured her, *'Always. Even before Catriona, there was you.'* She paused, shedding a tear as she added, *'Even after she...'* She pulled away, shaking her head getting her emotions under control. *'No, sorry, I can't tell you about that. I mustn't.'*

Shyleen placed a gentle paw on her shoulder.

'My fault for asking,' she apologised. *'Now you had better work your magic, then I can go back to the camp and leave you to do whatever you came here to do.'*

Mandalee did so and bade farewell to that version of her friend, who left as silently as she came.

According to the current version of the Timeline, Daelen returned to the camp a few hours later, telling no-one anything of his midnight stroll. After all, it wasn't as if anything significant had happened.

*****

At first light, the warband moved out, heading for Kullos controlled territory, remaining vigilant at all times, for they knew advance forces could attack them at any moment. Dreya walked with Ossian Miach Kaidool, and they used their different forms of magic to extend their sensory perception. Michael found he rather liked this Dark sorceress...though she had picked up the irritating habit of calling him 'Mickey'. It was bad enough his 'fans' using it, without her joining in. Of course, Dreya knew it annoyed him, and that was sufficient reason to use it as often as possible, as far as she was concerned.

Dreya ran over her plans in her head, satisfied that there were sufficient contingencies built in, just in case certain people made different choices to the ones she expected. Everything fitted perfectly, but somehow the picture was incomplete. Or perhaps more accurately, there was something more to the picture than she yet consciously knew. It felt as if her plans were a jigsaw puzzle, and the image was there in front of her, yet there were pieces left over. She didn't understand how that could be. For now, she firmly shoved it in a box in her mind and labelled it as 'Guardian business to be dealt with later'.

Mandalee was receiving constant situation reports from nature, as she spent the journey getting to know Windell a little better. As an assassin, Mandalee didn't often work with other people. However, much as she enjoyed solitude and her unique relationship with Shyleen, it was nice to have the chance to swap battle stories with someone. Being a physical fighter – as she was, predominately, despite her magic – Windell appreciated her stories more than Catriona did. Catriona's response to the technicalities of swordplay was much like the cleric's own response to Cat's intricate explanations of the inner workings of magic.

At the same time, something was buzzing in the back of her brain. Something that seemed Guardian related, though she didn't understand how she could know that. It was almost as if there was somewhere she needed to be and soon. For now, though, the coming battle required her full attention, so she suppressed the feeling lest it distract her.

That left Daelen walking with Catriona when she wasn't patrolling in falcon, wolf or leopard form. When in the latter guise, Shyleen decided to accompany her rather than listen to Windell and suffer what she considered to be very uncouth stories next to those of her friend. For Daelen's part, the shadow warrior had reluctantly agreed that Catriona should be the one to fly. After all, they wanted to have advance warning of the enemy, not give the enemy advance warning of their own approach. A bird in the sky was somewhat less conspicuous than a shadow warrior, and subtlety wasn't exactly Daelen's strong point.

The area surrounding Kullos' fortress was a mini-city, surrounded not only by tents but also by permanent wooden buildings. As if these people believed they were here to stay. In the early morning twilight, Catriona could see how it had changed from when she had been there last.

Smiths no longer worked the forges and timber merchants had abandoned construction and repair to buildings. Where, only the day before, stone masons were starting work on an extension to the fortress itself, today they had downed tools and left. Only a few warriors practised their swordplay, and a scarce handful of wizards and clerics were up and about.

As the morning light spread across the Eastern sky, it was clear that the settlement was in chaos. Justaria had managed to sneak out of the camp so that she could meet up with the attacking group and fill them in on events.

The plan had worked perfectly. Plague and pestilence had beset Kullos' army. Even after the flies had been dealt with, people continued to get sick. It took some time for the contamination to be traced to the already limited water supply. Winds had peaked suddenly, collapsing tents and wrecking the settlement's poorly built structures. Many expected their powerful enemy Daelen StormTiger to appear at that moment. The battle alarm sounded, and those who were still able, ran to take up arms, many of those clutching their stomachs, but the shadow warrior did not appear. The storm was apparently natural. That incident served to embarrass the commanders and weaken the already fragile respect of the lower-ranked warriors. After the third or fourth storm, almost everyone had grown complacent, more annoyed that it was impossible to sleep than fearful. Kullos refused to keep coming out to deal with bad weather, so people, demons and other creatures clamoured to be let into his stable, secure fortress, but were turned away. That led to anger and violence.

Unchanged, however, were the elementals, the undead, the demons, and of course Kullos' four death knights. Justaria had described this in detail, so they were not surprised, but to see it for themselves was quite a heart-stopping sight. The allies were outnumbered about fifty to one.

The allies decided that they should enter the camp using the tunnel Catriona had created, Justaria using illusion magic to make them…not invisible, but unnoticeable to any who were not specifically looking for them – and after last night, vigilance was at an all-time low. There were just two exceptions to this: Daelen, who levitated high above the barrier with his perception filter active, and Catriona herself who passed the barrier with ease in falcon form and was best able to co-ordinate. Cat waited until everyone was ready and in position, then called out sympathically to Daelen, Mandalee and Dreya, simultaneously.

'*Begin.*'

All the small campfires around the settlement suddenly grew into enormous columns of flame that raged around, spreading fire, fear and confusion. It also began to rain molten rocks. A blazing wall was heading for the medical area, where more than ninety per cent of the humans and Faery, along with many aliens, were being treated by clerics who were no better off themselves. Before the flames endangered them, however, a wall of sand rose up high and fused in the heat, protecting them all behind a screen of thick glass.

A trained assassin, side-by-side with a vicious golden leopard, threw herself back into her old demon-hunting career with a vengeance, slashing her way through them at speed. A cry began to ripple through the settlement, as the army realised they were under attack. There was no clarion call, no organised formation, no planned strategy. This was not how it was supposed to be.

At the right moment – orchestrated by Catriona Redfletching, embracing her flair for the dramatic, just as Kullos' army began to assemble – Daelen revealed himself, flying overhead and bringing a fresh trademark storm with him. All eyes turned to him, and the enemy hesitated. That was fatal as Mandalee and Shyleen were forgotten, and the defence ended before it had really begun. Equally unnoticed, was a group of fifty warriors that had slipped in while the enemy was distracted. They cut down two hundred or more before anybody knew what had happened. Elsewhere, a towering giant of a man slashed, hacked and magicked his way through the awe-stricken crowd. A trio of shimmering ghouls appeared in their midst, sucking energy from more demons and sending them tumbling back down to the lower planes. Four undead death knights charged unopposed on ghostly black steeds with red glowing eyes. Even Catriona had no clue where her girlfriend had conjured those undead horses from. She made a mental note to ask later. A Black robe sorceress appeared; her hood pulled low over her head. Silent and deadly as a wraith, she was a lethal shadow.

Her own theatrical entrance helped many of their enemies to believe they were visited by the very embodiment of Dark magic. She tried to focus on the elementals and other supernatural creatures that would cause problems for physical fighters. They were no threat whatsoever to her.

The horde was decimated before any semblance of resistance began to form.

Watching from the sky, still in her falcon form, Catriona was thrilled to see her special effects had worked so well. But there were still too many to face at once, so it was time for some mathematics, namely division. As chief strategist, it was not yet her part to enter the main fighting. Much of her druid magic could function equally well from a distance. Including earthquake creation. This would take significant power by druid standards, she knew, but she could see no other choice. She needed to keep half the remaining active force out of the fighting and a gaping split in the ground, stretching for miles, would do that quite nicely, except for those few with flight magic. Switching to her natural form and standing on her Windy Steps, she concentrated on the line she wanted Nature to draw. It had to be precise so as not to endanger her friends or those in the medical wing. She gently altered the natural movement pattern of the ground, coaxed opposing forces and enhanced them, so the ground ripped apart in a more-or-less straight line halfway between her friends and the fortress. Many fell in and were killed, but far more were left trapped. Sure, there were archers among them, but they were useless – they were more likely to hit one of their own. A thick wall of ice further bisected the enemy and Cat decided it was time to embrace her reputation as a handful of trouble.

Her time spent demon hunting with Mandalee, when she was younger, stood her in good stead. From what her friend had taught her, she knew that many of the species of demon below were not the happiest of bedfellows. It would only take a small push to get them to ignore the invaders and fight each other instead.

Daelen was staying out of the battle for the moment. It was vital that he retain as much power as possible for the real fight against Kullos himself. Cat made her way over to him and told him her plan.

"I'm going to be sending my Mirror Image down there and making her shapeshift, but it's going to take a lot of concentration, which means you get to be my hero and protect me."

"First time for everything," he chuckled. "Don't worry, nothing's going to harm you. Do your thing."

She then proceeded to send out her copy in the form of a blue-scaled Mazroth demon that deliberately wounded a red Yarzoth demon with runes tattooed all over its skin. The Yarzoth lashed out and killed the Mazroth, and another Mazroth killed the Yarzoth in revenge, then another Yarzoth (again, really Cat's copy) killed another Mazroth in further retaliation, escalating the conflict. In moments, all the Yarzoths and Mazroths were fighting each other to the exclusion of all else, until another of Cat's copies enticed a green Vegroth demon to lash out with magic at both. She then spent some time reprising her Trickster form. Even other demons found them annoying and if they weren't careful with their attacks, other demons were quick to retaliate. With just a few more interventions, that entire section of demons forgot who they were meant to be fighting and tore at each other, instead.

Mandalee glanced over at Dreya, even as she cut and sliced her way through the enemy with her blades. Occasionally, she threw in some cleric magic or her returning blade, but mostly she stuck to her knives. Maybe it was her new status as White Guardian, she wasn't sure, but she felt a connection to the Dark sorceress that hadn't been there before. It wasn't just a sympathic connection via Cat, but something more direct. She couldn't read her mind, as such, but she was getting a general sense of what was going on in her head. Her emotions were under tight control, her face impassive, as she continually analysed and calculated a precise response to everything that was around her. Every time she used a power word, she had to compartmentalise part of her brain to reconstruct it, ready to be used again later. Whenever demons came at her with magic, she seemed to make an instant decision about whether that power was compatible with hers and if so, how much she could take for herself, all according to some arcane rules Mandalee knew nothing about. Mandalee thought she must have a thousand spells in her head. How Dreya selected the right one at the right time was beyond her, but she did.

At the same time, this was Dreya's first opportunity to see Mandalee in action, the Cleric of Nature, demon hunter and assassin. In the same way, Dreya was feeling their new connection through the Guardianship and getting the essence of what was going on inside her. Everything about Mandalee was instinct honed by training and experience. Her emotions were ablaze, every nerve in her body sending her a million separate signals that she somehow forged into a single impression of the world around her. She was using her cleric magic without conscious thought, so it seemed to the assassin that she wasn't using it at all. She was. It just wasn't about discrete spells. It was more about enhancing her speed, her agility, her focus, her balance, her grace. Dreya had seen fighters succumb to an unthinking battle frenzy, lost in the lust for fighting. Somehow, Mandalee seemed to dance on the edge of that without ever crossing the line.

Dreya believed magic was more than a tool; it was an art. In the same way, Mandalee's fighting style was a thing of beauty to her. The White Assassin fought not because she enjoyed killing, but because she loved life. These demons, Kullos' army, they would take that precious thing from her and from other innocent people. Mandalee had decided she wasn't going to allow it.

Catriona could feel the two of them sussing each other out, forging a bond between them, even as they fought to keep their lives and everything that they valued. It lifted her heart to witness her girlfriend and her best friend beginning to realise what she saw in each of them. Recognise also that, if one was prepared to look beneath the surface, they were not so different. It was easy to see fire in Mandalee and ice in Dreya, but that was far too simplistic. Many times, Dreya had kept her warm when she was cold, and equally, Mandalee had cooled her down when her temper was running hot. Even the way they fought was similar. Yes, they each used a different set of tools, but Mandalee's knives and Dreya's magic weren't the real weapons – the true weapons were the minds that guided their actions. They both fought with the same precision, wasting no energy, nor giving their enemy a second chance to kill them. Doing no more and no less than what was necessary to eliminate the threat, permanently. They both had the same desire to improve, to be the best at what they did, because the best got to survive.

Chapter 17

Catriona continued to snare, split and frustrate the enemy with walls of ice, rock and fire, and the creative use of cacti. Pebbles rained from above, becoming huge boulders on the way down.

Ossian Miach Kaidool often killed two or three with one sword thrust and a swarm of flies summoned by his magic served to protect him, as well as add to the tally of the dead. His team was doing equally well. Most stayed close to him, but Windell was working valiantly to try to keep up with Mandalee. The fact was he couldn't – no-one could – but that wasn't going to stop him trying. He seemed to have taken quite a shine to her, and while she was trying to hide it, Mandalee was definitely enjoying the attention.

Of course, there was little to stop Dreya's ghouls except for other undead creatures. However, Dreya the Dark did not choose just anybody to be her elite guard. When they were alive, before they attacked the sorceress, they had been the most formidable White clerics among the Faery of Ainderbury. Likewise, the knights had been four of the finest in Gaggleswick, decorated by their order many times. That gave them more than an edge even against others of their kind. They were unstoppable.

Each of them used their own unique methods, but one way or another, the result was the same: death to the enemy. Demons by the dozen began to think better of the whole thing, choosing to Descend back to the planes of hell, rather than face oblivion by staying. Overall, the battle began to turn in the allies' favour, but that was when everything changed.

*****

The gigantic doors to Kullos' vast fortress opened amid a cacophony of sound. The doors squealed and groaned, and great horns heralded a fresh wave of enemies. These were the elite troops. The ones that were most loyal to Kullos, including humans and Faery that had been protected from that night's troubles. Michael's pestilential flies had never penetrated the fortress walls, they had their own independent water supply that was never tainted, and the building was sturdy enough to withstand any storm short of a tornado. Cat had not been prepared to whip up anything that strong for fear of killing the very people she was trying to protect.

Doubtless, Kullos thought this tactical reserve would force Daelen to enter the fray, and every drop of energy he used on lesser forces tipped the odds in Kullos' favour in the final confrontation.

Thanks to Justaria's intelligence, it wasn't going to work because they had a tactical reserve of their own: the Council of Mages, plus knights, warriors and clerics from all over the continent of Elvaria. Imperial Kelna had sent troops from the farthest reaches of Southern Alloria. They were massed and ready, arranged in their efficient, disciplined lines.

Dreya had indicated that she had one more trick up her sleeve but had so far declined to fill in any details.

Cat shifted to falcon form and flew to Dreya's side. Shifting back, she started using her magic more directly to kill the demons, elementals and hellspawn all around them.

"I think it might be time for this secret plan of yours, Dreya," she suggested.

"I think you're right."

The sorceress' change of expression was subtle, but Cat knew it well. She called it Dreya's scheming face.

"You're still not going to tell me what it is, are you?"

The sorceress smiled. "It's a gift for you."

"No offence, Dreya, but now is really not the time for flowers."

"Oh, this is way better than flowers," Dreya returned. The sorceress transferred command of her guards to her girlfriend, with one final instruction. "Every single one of you dies before she comes to harm, understood?"

They all saluted, and she teleported to the tunnel, which she used to get out beyond the perimeter of the barrier. She could have drained the power of the shield and torn it down at any time, but she left it alone because it worked in their favour. It was easier for her girlfriend's magic to contain their enemies and keep her friends and allies from being overwhelmed by numbers. If it were not there, it would be too easy for the enemy to outflank and surround them.

Once outside the barrier, Dreya opened a blue Prismatic Sphere portal, forming a magical tunnel all the way to the Council building in Walminster, where the magically backed army was ready and waiting. Mages with illusion magic expertise entered the portal first, to help disguise the army's assembly all around the perimeter of Kullos' barrier. In moments, the enemy forces were going to find themselves surrounded on all sides...including from above.

Dreya didn't hang around the Council building too long, once she had checked with the White faction leader, Maia, that there was nothing else they needed from her. Maia had been incensed to learn that Kullos was drafting innocent Tempestrians against their will, and the disappearance of Justaria, her Red robe Triumvirate counterpart, had been the last straw. As a White robe, she had not always seen eye to eye with Dreya the Dark, but when she had shared the intelligence gathered by Catriona 'in the field', on this issue, they were of one mind: Kullos had declared war on Tempestria and the only correct response was to fight. Leaving the allied army in Maia's determined and capable hands, Dreya teleported home to the Black Tower. There, waiting for her, was the Black robe leader, Laethyn, along with two purple catlike aliens – the Chetsuans, Jessica and Sara – each with a special surprise for Kullos' forces.

"Ready?" Dreya asked. They each indicated their agreement. "Then let's go!"

*****

Despite all the allied efforts and Catriona's crowd control magic, the arrival of the elite troops had given a definite boost to the enemy. The allies were fighting closer together, now, protecting each other as they fought. Catriona had shifted to the form of a large bear, pounding the enemy all around with great swipes of her forepaws. Daelen was about to intervene himself, but a blue Prismatic Sphere portal opening in the sky above the dome shield gave him reason to pause. Out of that portal came something the shadow warrior had never expected to see on this world: four enormous dragons, each of which had a rider – two Black robe mages and, to his further astonishment, a pair of Chetsuans. The expressions on Sara and Jessica's faces were, in Daelen's estimation, about one part terror and two parts exhilaration.

"Now then, dearie, don't you even think about dropping us," Jessica threatened her dragon, "or you get a laser bolt right between the eyes!"

"And after what you lot have done to our people," Sara told hers, "count yourselves lucky we're not going to do it regardless!"

The dragons bellowed in response and dived to bathe Kullos' elite troops in fire and fry them with electrical bolts. The two Chetsuans fired their laser weapons, Laethyn attacked with powerful Dark magic, and Dreya shot out deadly dark beam cannon blasts, powered by higher planar energy and blood magic.

The dark sorceress even decided the situation warranted a, "Woohoo!"

Cat, shifting back to her natural shape, scowled and called up, "Stop it! You're not impressing anyone!"

"Liar!" Mandalee shot back at her.

Cat glanced over and nodded, admitting, "Yeah, you're right. Who am I kidding?" Gazing up at her girlfriend again, she grinned and admitted, "Seriously, you are amazing!"

Blowing her a kiss, Dreya called down, "This is why I had to slip away, last night. Sorry about that! Had to bring our friends over to play!"

*****

That night, after unlocking Time magic, Cat had been in such a state of exhilaration that she knew she wouldn't be able to sleep straight away. She needed to unwind, and she could think of no more enjoyable way to do that than to make love with Dreya. They'd never been apart this long since they started seeing each other and she'd missed her so much.

Dreya felt just the same and had been delighted when Cat invited her into her tent that night.

"My life's felt so empty without you," Dreya murmured softly. "I had to conquer a whole other world just for something to do."

"Aww," Cat sympathised, between kisses, as they began to remove each other's clothes. "Poor thing. It must have been horrid for you."

"It wasn't easy, but I got through it," Dreya replied.

130

"How do you think I felt?" Cat shot back. "Time moves differently on Earth, so even with your time on Phitonia, I've actually been away from you longer than you've been away from me." She frowned. "I think."

"Yeah, that's weird, the time thing," Dreya agreed. "Tried to analyse it with magic, but I couldn't make heads nor tails of the results."

"Well, never mind that," Cat told her. "There's only one kind of magic I'm interested in right now."

Dreya pulled away for a moment, teasing her with a mock puzzled look. "And what kind is that?"

"The kind that feels like electric all over my body," she replied, running her hands over Dreya's bare skin.

"Correction: The kind that feels like electric all over *both* our bodies!" insisted Dreya kissing her, full and long, allowing their two magics to mingle along with their bodies.

"That's it, just like that!" Dreya gasped as Cat began gently caressing the tiny, delicate winglets that grew out of Dreya's shoulder blades. How could anyone think such beautiful things should be the object of scorn? Come to that, why should Dreya the Dark, who was scared of literally no-one, still feel like she had to hide them away? It wasn't right, but she didn't want to spoil the moment by voicing such feelings.

As if responding to some sense of Catriona's thoughts, Dreya whispered, "The way you touch me...you're the only person who's ever made me feel good about my body, that it's OK to be the way I am."

Cat looked deep into Dreya's eyes so she could see her reply held nothing but purest truth. "Dreya, you are beautiful and perfect the way you are. Don't ever doubt that."

"That's what I mean," insisted the sorceress. "When I'm with you, I never do."

Catriona gave herself to Dreya then, melting at her touch, wondering how anyone could ever think her cold and unfeeling.

"Hey, I've just had a thought," Dreya spoke up, pausing for a moment. "With our new Guardianship connection, you don't suppose it means Mandalee can feel everything we feel, do you?"

"Do you want me to go and ask?" Cat asked, mischievously.

"Don't you dare!"

"Then I suggest we give her a night to remember."

Dreya grinned. "Now that is a much better idea."

*****

Later that night, when Catriona had fallen asleep in her arms, Dreya gently extricated herself, pulled the covers back over her girlfriend and threw on her robes. Stepping out into the cold night air, she opened a Prismatic Sphere portal directly to Daelen's base on Phitonia. There she met up with Sara and Jessica who greeted her, warmly.

"Thanks so much for this, Dreya," Sara smiled.

"What for? I didn't do anything," the sorceress objected.

"Yeah, you did, love," Jessica insisted. "It never would have occurred to us that it was safe to come here, if not for you."

What Dreya had realised, from her time in three of Daelen's facilities on different worlds, was that the shadow warrior had changed the perception filter that surrounded them. Rather than simply hide what was within, each one was now a barrier, cutting them off from the rest of that world. That's what made it safe for the Chetsuan girls to be there. Sara described it as a 'containment field'. A phrase new to Dreya but it fitted perfectly. This was why Daelen planned to make his last stand against Kullos on his base on StormClaw Island on Tempestria – to help contain the power of Heaven's Surrender. Effectively, a second line of defence after his Wish barrier. If it could contain all that, then surely, as long as Sara and Jessica remained within its boundaries, there was no way they could infect any other Chetsuans. It wasn't much – a few acres of land, compared to a whole world – and they still couldn't interact with any of their people, but surely, Dreya suggested, it was better than nothing.

At first, both girls were thrilled with the idea, but as time had passed, it had become somewhat more bittersweet. There was a whole world out there – their world. A home that could never again be theirs. A world they could only glimpse, never touch. Sara likened it to being stuck in a goldfish bowl. Even so, they still agreed it was definitely better than nothing.

"Well, I'm sorry," Dreya broached, "but I'm afraid your visit here is at an end."

132

"It's time, then?" Sara inquired, wistfully.

The sorceress nodded. "Are you still OK with the plan, both of you?" she checked. "You don't have to do anything you don't want to."

"We know that, love, but we've made our choice, haven't we, sis?"

"Definitely," Sara affirmed. "I won't pretend I'm not nervous about it, but the idea of controlling a dragon, having power over the life of one of the creatures that's slaughtered our people, does have a certain appeal."

Chapter 18

Accepting their decision, Dreya left them for a moment, teleporting herself to the site of the former Citadel of Doom. She had told the dragons they were not allowed to rebuild the site. The ruins would serve as a reminder of what would happen if Mistress Dreya the Dark ever found out that a dragon had broken the truce and harmed any Chetsuans. There were always to be dragons stationed there, however, as she would appear without warning and expect an instant response to her commands. She didn't care who they were, just as she didn't care how they ran their affairs as long as they didn't harm Chetsuans. This time, she told them she wanted three fighter dragons to help her fight a war against an enemy who, if not stopped, would devastate their world, too.

"And believe me," she assured them, "he won't be anywhere near as reasonable as I am. One of you will have the honour of my presence on your back. The other two will be carrying a Chetsuan each." That caused a stir, so Dreya allowed a ball of crackling energy to glow and spark in her hand, growing in size and intensity. "I'm sorry," she growled, menacingly, "do any of you have a problem with that?" Her veiled threat had the desired response, quieting them down. "That's better." She allowed her magic to dissipate, harmlessly. "Be grateful that my girlfriend's got me in such a good mood right now. So, any volunteers?"

She picked three with varying abilities, mounted the fire-breather and opened a portal to Daelen's facility, instructing the other two dragons to follow hers in. They landed in Daelen's grounds, where Sara and Jessica mounted their dragons. Once in the air, it was time for another portal to Tempestria, specifically the Black Tower.

"Since you so kindly welcomed me into your home," she told her Chetsuan friends, "I think it's only fair that I show you mine for a few hours."

They set down in her grounds, where, as pre-arranged, Laethyn was waiting with his own dragon, Madroit. She didn't trust the dragons to behave if she left them alone with Sara and Jessica, and he was the only other person on Tempestria who knew anything about controlling dragons. His Black robes also helped – there was no way for the dragons to realise that his powers were no match for hers. Unfortunately, she didn't trust Laethyn, either, but her friends knew that, and they were well-armed and quite capable of handling him, if necessary. Plus, as a further precaution, she had reactivated some of Ulvarius' defences that had lain dormant for years. At the first sign of trouble, they were instructed to do whatever was necessary to protect Sara and Jessica. If they killed the dragons, well, there were plenty more where they came from, and for Laethyn, she cared nothing one way or the other.

*****

As Daelen surveyed the scene below him, he could see that the battle had turned decisively back in the allies' favour. Surrounded on all sides and assaulted by dragons from above, Kullos' forces were finally contained. It had taken a lot, but the allies were winning.

Dreya the Dark had proven to be an instrumental ally. Besides her innate power, her sharp mind was incredible. In a matter of weeks, she had united the Council, moulded them into a fighting force, opened the door to clerics and rallied together an army. In between all that, she had managed to conquer Phitonia just so that she could use dragons in this fight. It never would have occurred to Daelen. Her actions had clearly also won the hearts and minds of the two Chetsuan girls. They would follow her into the depths of hell to help fight the Keeper of the Underworld if she asked. In fact, she wouldn't even need to ask.

Teleporting down from her dragon, Dreya resumed her fight on the ground as a lethal shadow. She seemed invulnerable to conventional attacks. Warriors found their weapons useless; how does one fight a shadow, anyway? As he watched, he saw her step up to face a trio of renegade wizards. It was three against one, but they clearly didn't like those odds much because their eyes widened and, bowing once, they fled before her. They didn't get far; the three ghouls floated to intercept them and froze their souls. Running away was no longer an option, as far as Dreya was concerned. Had she been anyone else, they would have attacked, their intent had been clear. Intent was the same as deed. They only ran because they were scared of her. What was she supposed to do? Let them go so they could kill somebody else, instead? Daelen could well understand why she was the only mortal mage his dark clone had ever respected and feared.

Dreya's death knights seemed to be actually enjoying themselves, pitting their undead strength and skilful swordplay against Kullos' own champions. They were worthy opponents. The members of each side had even taken a moment to offer a knightly salute before engaging in their own private contest. Dreya's guards gradually gained the upper hand, however, and seemed to be playing with their opponents, content to fence them without going in for the kill. Suddenly, Daelen realised why: Dreya wanted to deal the death blows herself so she could absorb their power. In the future, he could easily believe that she would achieve her dark ambitions of power and become the Greatest Mage Who Ever Lived, in this world or any other, and the higher planes had better watch out, too.

Michael's forces, unlike Kullos', were handpicked for their skill and prowess, not just weight of numbers. They had trained for years, inspired by Ossian Miach Kaidool himself and the chance to fight beside him was a dream come true. They wanted to prove themselves worthy of the Champion of the Gods, and they were doing an admirable job.

Not to be outdone, Mandalee was like a living flame. She wasn't using her super-speed, because she couldn't afford to sacrifice stamina in such a long battle. Even without that power, though, Time seemed to slow down for her, and now that she was the White Guardian, she realised that the concept might be entirely literal. Perhaps by some new magical instinct, she really was slowing time. She made a mental note to ask Cat later, as she found a gap to throw her returning blade at a female warrior she had spotted trying to sneak up on Windell, who seemed to have become her shadow. She slit a throat with a dragonclaw dagger, before catching her returning blade on its way back with perfect timing.

Beside the assassin, Shyleen added tooth and claw to Mandalee's clerical magic and blades. It seemed to the ever-philosophical leopard that her bond with Mandalee had strengthened and grown since she became White Guardian. It was like they could see through each other's eyes, feel each other's heartbeat, anticipate each other's movement before it was committed to. They guarded and protected each other, deflecting blows that might have harmed the other. In short, more than ever, it felt like they were two parts of one whole being. The result to the enemy was devastating.

Ossian Miach Kaidool towered above all but a few demons, using his own brand of sword and sorcery. He was like a great rock on the shore: though the tide of the enemy washed over him and threatened to engulf him, still he could not be moved. Much of his magic was unconventional and all the more effective for it. Ravens of Death sent the enemy to their grave, while others were encased in petrified wood. Still more were bitten and stung by swarms of insects that had no interest whatsoever in his allies.

Finally, there was the beautiful Catriona Redfletching.

"Oh, how I will miss her," the shadow warrior muttered to himself with a wistful smile.

For her part, the druidess seemed to be thoroughly enjoying herself. For a while, she was a shapeshifting tour de force. Bear form to leopard, to wolf, to falcon, to owl. The enemy didn't know what they were fighting. She even made use of her mole form, burrowing under the sandy terrain, only to appear behind her attackers, shift to leopard form to spring at them, take them to ground and deliver the killing bite. He remembered her saying how her shapeshifting hurt her, but she would not allow that pain to stop her. Her inner strength was a marvel to behold, and he was grateful beyond words that he'd been granted the chance to know her, if only for a short time.

In her natural form, her magic and trickery confounded her enemies. Refusing to allow fear to touch her, she acted as though this whole battle were pure entertainment. It was a concert of magic put on entirely for her amusement, a show in which she was the star.

"All she lacks," he told himself, as Catriona taunted a renegade wizard, "is an audience to 'ooh' and 'ah' at the wonders she performs, to cheer and applaud her skill and presentation." Indeed, it was often not just what she did, but the flair with which she did it.

"You know how they say two heads are better than one?" Daelen heard her remark, conversationally, to a pair of enemy warriors. "Well, I think two heads just makes it all the more likely that you'll lose one of them." With a rainbow blade, she sliced cleanly through one of their necks, "or both," she added, continuing her stroke through the second one. They hadn't even tried to move – how were they to know a rainbow could be lethal?

A group of a dozen wizards tried to put a stop to her tricks with an anti-magic field. She rolled her eyes, adapted her magic and without even breaking it down, she scolded them, punctuating each word with a death.

"When. Will. You. Wizards. Learn. That. Anti. Magic. Fields. Are. Completely. Useless!"

She used her Faithless spell to place doubt in the minds of a pair of White clerics who were advancing on Mandalee. Justaria had mentioned there were a few of those – fanatics who believed that any magic that didn't come directly from their gods was blasphemy and saw Kullos as a means to destroy the heathens. Catriona cut them off from their gods and the magic they drew from them.

"That, on the other hand, works every time," she declared, as she cut them down,

An exasperated Catriona called over to Mandalee, "They just don't seem to be learning!"

"Cat, I don't think they're going to be learning anything anymore – they're dead," Mandalee pointed out.

Cat glanced over at her friend. "Oh yeah," she replied as if she'd just realised her friend was right. Turning back to the corpses, she shrugged. "Sorry."

Daelen allowed himself a smile, in spite of the situation. She was such a delight to watch…but he had a more pressing concern. Now that the battle was firmly under control and he could be sure they wouldn't need him; it was time to put an end to Kullos himself. As far as Daelen was concerned, this was his job and his alone.

Quietly, then, he slipped away, but he did not count on the sharp eyes and ears of a certain leopard.

Shyleen spotted him as he left and informed Mandalee, and thanks to their enhanced sympathic link, Cat and Dreya knew it, too. Thus, at some unspoken signal, the Three Guardians fought their way through the enemy ranks to meet together. Cat formed a Rainbow Road, arcing high above the battlefield, so they could confer without having to fight. A couple of particularly bold demons tried to follow, but Cat just nonchalantly pulled her bow and arrows out of her pocket dimension shooting both simultaneously and letting their bodies plunge back into the maelstrom of violence below.

"Sometimes you just have to do things the old-fashioned way," she sighed.

"Now, where do you suppose he's going just when things are getting interesting?" Mandalee wondered, watching Daelen disappear inside.

"To fight Kullos alone, I imagine," Dreya answered.

"While I still live and breathe? The hell he is!" Catriona insisted. Then she called out to Ossian Miach Kaidool, "Hey, Mickey!"

"Don't call me Mickey!" he shot back.

She ignored him. "We need to keep an eye on Daelen! We'll come back when we can. Do you think you lot can handle things here now?"

"Aye," he agreed. "I believe we can cope."

The words were no sooner out of his mouth than another blue portal opened.

Cat shot Dreya a worried glance, already knowing the answer even as she asked, "Is this another one of your schemes?"

The sorceress shook her head. "Nothing to do with me."

"Then I think we might be in trouble," Mandalee concluded.

Kullos' reinforcements, about five thousand of them, poured out of the portal and onto the battlefield.

"Then again," Michael reconsidered, "I may have spoken too soon."

Chapter 19

Justaria levitated up to the Guardians. Breathless, she advised Catriona, "You've still got a few hundred people trapped in the medical area. Release them. I'm convinced they're with us now. Kullos kept the more hardline elements inside his fortress."

"Are you sure?" Cat asked.

"Trust me. I've been in this camp for a long time. They realise you trapped them to save them, and Kullos just discarded them. That helped me convince them that Kullos has been lying to them. They want to fight on our side."

"The clerics should have mostly cured the sickness by now," Mandalee offered. "They might be tired and not at their best, but they're better than nothing."

"What if they betray us?" Cat questioned, suddenly very conscious that everyone – including one of the Triumvirate – was looking to her, a simple half-Faery druid girl to make these life and death decisions.

"A few hundred extra on their side won't make much difference," Dreya pointed out. "Our people are hopelessly outnumbered already. But that many on our side could buy enough time for us to get back."

"It's worth the risk, Cat," Mandalee counselled.

Even as they spoke, Cat saw that some of the reinforcements were trying to break through her glass barrier, and the way those on the inside were arming themselves, it did look like they were expecting execution more than rescue.

"Alright," she agreed and shattered the glass wall that had annexed that section, making sure the wind threw the shards of glass outwards so as not to injure their potential new allies. As the attacking forces shielded themselves, those new allies confirmed that potential, wasting no time in going on the offensive. Justaria levitated back down to lead them.

Then Mandalee turned to Dreya and asked, "Can you do something about the energy barrier? Our people need the freedom to move now." She didn't add, 'Or to retreat, if necessary' but it was heavily implied.

Dreya nodded and ordered her guards to stop playing with Kullos' knights and destroy them.

"It's a pity I won't get to absorb their power, but I'll just have to get enough from Kullos himself to compensate."

Catriona knew what that command had cost her girlfriend – she didn't like turning down power – so she rewarded her with a kiss.

"I love you, Dreya. You do the most wonderful things, sometimes."

Mandalee hid a smile as Dreya's marble skin flushed around her cheeks.

Kullos' death knights were soon no more, and Dreya's guards moved to the barrier. It was designed to kill any living thing that tried to leave, but her guards were not alive. Together, they reflected the power of the barrier back at itself, disrupting and finally collapsing it.

"I'll leave them and my ghouls here to help," Dreya offered.

"What about your pets?" Mandalee asked, referring to the dragons.

"I'll have to return them, I'm afraid," Dreya answered. "I can't guarantee to keep them under control if I'm not here. They're just as likely to kill our allies as anything else."

Calling the dragons over, she told Jessica and Sara to join them on Catriona's Rainbow Road.

"Trust me," Cat urged them, seeing Sara hesitate. "It's perfectly solid underfoot. I won't let you fall."

"Oh, don't be such a scaredy-cat, Sara!" her more adventurous sister complained as Sara began to tentatively dismount. "Get your arse off that dragon!" Backing up her words with actions, Jessica vaulted down off hers, adding, "There's a phrase I never thought I'd say!"

Not to be outdone, Sara took her own leap of faith and landed catlike on her feet.

"What about you?" Dreya asked Laethyn. "Are you keeping your dragon?"

"No," he replied, dismounting, casually. "Send him back with the others. He was useful for a while, but have you any idea how much dragons eat? This is one pet I just can't afford."

Jessica began wagging her finger at the wizard, scolding him. "Oi, Mister! A dragon is for life not just for Christmas!"

All the Tempestrians looked blank.

"Seriously?" Jessica complained, throwing her hands up in the air in exasperation. To Sara, she grumbled, "I think we've made a huge mistake coming to live here, sis – no-one's going to get my jokes!"

"Ignore my sister," Sara advised the others. "She thinks she's funny."

Dreya opened a portal back to Phitonia and ordered the dragons through it.

"Well, I suppose I'd better get back to the war," Laethyn decided, firing off his magic as he levitated down.

With him gone, Cat felt more at ease discussing what she now thought of as Guardian Business.

"Listen," she began, "we have to leave the battlefield. I don't like it, but this isn't our place. You feel it, don't you? Both of you?" she asked, looking pointedly at Mandalee and Dreya.

They both nodded.

"There's something else we have to do," Dreya replied, "otherwise none of this will matter."

"More like, somewhere we need to be," Mandalee suggested. "It's like there are co-ordinates in my head, except they don't make sense."

"You're right," Cat agreed, "and I think you've been right all along about Daelen destroying the world. He doesn't mean to, but as you always said, that makes no difference. I don't know the details, but I'm getting impressions bleeding through Time, that this has happened before, more than once. And it didn't end well. I also have the strangest feeling that this is the last chance. This time, White, Black and Red must work together with Daelen, or everything ends forever."

*****

The previous night, Catriona had woken up to find she was alone in her tent. That was no problem. She knew her girlfriend had things to do and quite frankly, so did she. Pulling the *Chronicles* out of her pocket dimension, she began to study it in more depth.

Reading between the lines of the note she had apparently left for herself under Calin's Tower, it was telling her that the Guardianship must be formed before Daelen's final battle with Kullos. Having done that, they surely needed to do something with their new powers, and that had to begin with understanding what those powers actually were.

But the battle was just hours away. How were they supposed to learn what to do and how to do it in so short a time? Cat was a quick study, but no-one was that quick.

*****

"I've got one of my ridiculous radical plans," she told her friends. "There isn't time to explain it, so you're just going to have to trust me, OK?"

"Of course," Dreya stated simply.

"Always," Mandalee affirmed.

"What about us?" Sara asked. "We want to help, too, don't we, Jess?"

"Totally," her sister agreed. "What can we do?"

"You can either go and help with the fight below or come with us. It's your choice," Cat told them.

"Oh, we're sticking with you," Sara insisted.

"Too right!" her sister nodded.

The companions heard a growl from below, which Mandalee translated as, "Shyleen volunteers to stay." The leopard knew she couldn't help with what they needed to do – she was better suited to fighting out in the open.

"It seems she's not the only animal volunteer," the sorceress spoke up. "Look, Cat!"

The druidess didn't need Dreya to point; she just followed the scream of agony and saw a small green snake removing her fangs from the leg of a renegade wizard.

"Pyrah!" Cat called out, delighted.

Her Ysirian friend had disappeared from the hold of the *Dolphin*, but that wasn't unusual. Pyrah came and went as she pleased. She often vanished for long periods, only to reappear just as suddenly.

The snake spoke in Catriona's mind, '*This seems like a good place for a nest, and this lot are in my way. Besides, my fangs need sharpening, and there's nothing like bone to do that.*'

That was by far the most detailed communication Catriona had ever heard from Pyrah. Another side-effect of the enhanced sympatic link that seemed to have formed since becoming a Guardian, she supposed. She hadn't heard the words, not like when she spoke to Shyleen in her language, but the concept images were so much sharper. She didn't have time to think any more about it, but it did prove useful, as she found she was able to connect with Michael's mind. It felt as if, by linking with her telepathically when they first met, he had formed a pathway that she could now sense.

Whatever the details, Cat was able to use it to reach out and ask, '*Well, Mickey, is that enough help? Can you handle this battle alone now, without getting yourselves killed?*'

She was reluctant to leave the battlefield when it could so readily shift the balance back to the enemy, but she knew the Guardians were needed elsewhere.

If Michael was surprised to hear her in his mind, it didn't come through in his 'voice' as he replied, '*To be honest, I think not, but I suppose we'll just have to take as many with us as possible.*'

"Keep holding them off!" Cat called down. "We'll come back and help you as soon as we can!" she promised. She lowered her voice, so only her friends could hear. "Somehow."

Just as they were about to leave, someone called out, "Mandalee! Wait!"

They turned to see Mandalee's friend, Windell, charging up Catriona's Rainbow Road, knocking aside any enemies that tried to grab him.

When he reached her side, he held out her Pureblade. "You should take it back. I've got a feeling you're going to need every weapon you can get where you're going."

"I can't leave you weaponless out here!" the assassin objected.

"Well, actually, I was hoping you might trade it in for a simpler sword that you *can* spare."

She took the Pureblade and handed him the best regular sword she had with her. It still wasn't a fair trade, though, and she told him so.

"Well, if it will make you happy, you could always give me something else, too," he suggested with a twinkle in his eye.

"Like what?" Mandalee wondered.

In fact, his body language, the way he stepped forward with an unspoken question in his eyes, she thought she knew what he was suggesting. But he couldn't mean that! Sure, they'd been getting along, and he'd seemed utterly unfazed by her gender identity.

When she'd brought it up, his only comment had been, "Of course, you're a woman. Obviously, you're a woman. Anybody who doubts that is an idiot. Why would you listen to idiots?"

But that surely didn't mean Windell was *interested* in her! Still, after swallowing, nervously, she gave him a tentative smile and a nod, saying, "OK, if you really want to."

He really did, so he moved closer, put his arm around her and kissed her full on the lips. She hesitated for a second or two as if she still couldn't quite believe what was happening, but then she decided to do what she did best: stop thinking about it, trust her instincts and just go for it. Pulling him even closer, she kissed him back, kissing as she had never kissed anyone before.

It wasn't love at first sight or any such ridiculous romantic notion. It was just two people who were attracted to each other seizing the moment, because they both knew how fragile life was, especially now. They were both fighters. They both danced with death every day of their lives, and if they waited until tomorrow, tomorrow might never come. And so, they kissed. The battle could wait, Kullos could wait, Time could wait. They were claiming this moment, this moment was theirs and nothing, no-one could take it from them.

At last, they broke the kiss, stepped apart and with a grin, Windell ran back down from the sky, calling back, "Seeya later!"

"Wow, girl!" Sara declared. "You have so pulled!"

"I'll say!" her sister agreed. "I haven't seen that much snogging since you and that elf boy!"

Cat lightly touched her friend's arm, bringing her back to the present. "Sorry," she whispered, "but we really need to go."

Mandalee smiled and nodded resolutely. She was ready.

Acting on a final impulse, just to add to Michael's irritation, as the five young women turned to leave, they waved at him and called out, "Bye, Mickey!"

145

He just growled in response and sheathed his sword in favour of bashing heads with his staff – it made a more satisfying sound.

Chapter 20

Catriona used her stoneshaper spell to seal up the fortress so no-one could follow them, although she couldn't rule out the possibility of there being other ways to enter. Sara and Jessica had their laser guns charged and ready, appointing themselves as those who would guard the Guardians. Then began the hunt for Daelen, Cat taking the lead in leopard form to silently sniff out the shadow warrior's scent trail. The fortress was dark, lit only by a few flaming wall-mounted torches and candles in chandeliers, creating a very gothic feel to the place.

Mandalee decided to use her Cat's Eyes spell. "It's all very well for you to see in the dark," she told her friend, "but it would help if the rest of us could, too."

The fortress was vast. Without Catriona's shapeshifting abilities, the girls could have searched the stronghold for hours without finding the right trail. Stone statues of various hellish creatures stood beneath tapestries and works of art from their world and others, from ages past and present.

As the companions followed the leopard, the only sounds were the soft jingle of the assassin's weapons and the whisper of Dreya's robes. Both she and Mandalee had instinctively withdrawn inside their hoods – a habit they both shared when preparing to face an unknown situation. Mandalee wondered what else they had in common, besides the obvious. The catlike Chetsuans were as silent as ghosts.

Catriona hadn't spent much time in leopard form and was still getting used to processing her feline senses. The scent wasn't as sharp as she would have expected, leading her to suspect they might not be matching Daelen's route perfectly. She was sure they were going in the right general direction, though, which was all that mattered.

Dreya was surprised to find that there were no guards in the area, apart from a dozen that Daelen had killed with his sword, near the entrance. Perhaps Kullos could not trust anyone to be close to him, and in his arrogance, he probably thought it unnecessary. His own powers were all he needed. There being nothing to do, the sorceress began to think about what she would have done in his place.

None of them noticed a handful of obsidian hellhound statues slowly and silently get down from their platforms, eyes glowing red.

*****

After a while, Dreya felt compelled to share her thoughts, commenting to her friends, "Y'know, I've been thinking, this is really sloppy. If I were Kullos, I would've at least left a few guard dogs around the place. Something with teeth and claws that could cut through armour, and hides that could deflect dragon claws. I'd probably make them magic resistant, too," the sorceress continued.

That's when the hellhounds attacked.

Dreya always travelled with magical defences, but the lead hound broke through them like they weren't there, biting into her left leg with vicious teeth. Her scream alerted the others, but it was too late for Mandalee. She was knocked to the ground, teeth flashing dangerously close to her throat; she thrust her right arm in the way and cried out as the hound's teeth rendered her flesh, even through the combat suit. Only Catriona and the Chetsuans with their catlike reflexes were quick enough to spring out of the way, so the hellhounds only nipped the furry tip of a leopard's tail. Sara and Jessica fired their weapons, but the beams just bounced off their hides. They hastily holstered them, lest they kill their friends by mistake. Dreya's prophecy about magic-resistance firmly in her mind, the druidess elected to remain in leopard form to fight. She was better armed this way – after all, the cat was nature's ultimate killing machine.

Mandalee didn't have the option of teeth, but she did have some serious claws. Her dragonclaw blade flashed into her left hand in an instant, which she raked across the hellhound's flank. The damage to the creature was minimal, but it did cause enough pain for it to whirl its head to try and bite at its source. That gave the assassin enough leverage to shift her weight and kick the mutt across the room. It hit the wall with a thud and a yelp. It recovered quickly, but the assassin was faster, standing and levelling her single-handed crossbow. She knew she would only get one shot – with her damaged right hand there was no way she could put a second bolt in place. If

148

she got it right, one shot was all she would need, and if she didn't…well, all her troubles would be over very quickly after that. She forced herself to hold back and wait.

At last, the hellhound sprang, and the bolt fired. The creature never even cried out, dying instantly. Unfortunately, Mandalee didn't realise it was a stone creature in its dormant state. It petrified in mid-air and momentum carried it on to knock Mandalee to the ground once more. Landing on top of her, the air rushed from her lungs, and she passed out. The statue teleported back to its rightful place, but after a few seconds, the magic respawned it. Once again, it advanced on the party.

Jessica and Sara had abandoned guns for swords, ferociously attacking the creatures. They were holding them at bay and had so far escaped serious injury, but they couldn't do this forever. One serious bite and it could all be over.

"Whose bright idea was it to come to this world, anyway?" Sara panted, delivering a killing blow.

"Sorry, love," Jessica replied, continuing her frenzied attack, exploiting an opening and scoring a kill of her own. It did nothing more than give them a moment to breathe, however, as the statues reanimated once more. "Fighting to save our new home sounded so good when we said it. Now we're here getting our arses kicked, I've got to say, I'm not as keen as I was."

Meanwhile, Catriona was on the offensive, claws flashing in the torchlight. The hellhound was no match for a leopard's agility. Time and again, its teeth found only fur and no flesh. Unfortunately, she knew the hellhound wouldn't tire; it could fight all day and all night – she couldn't. Besides, they needed to get to Daelen and Kullos before it was too late.

Dreya the Dark was not faring so well. Her best magic seemed to do nothing more than make it pause for a moment. Blood magic was of no help. Even her power words – DIE, FREEZE, BURN – had proven ineffective. She summoned a trio of skeletal warriors, but the hellhound had them in pieces in no time. She was about to do the unthinkable and call her dagger to hand, thereby admitting her magic had been defeated, when she saw what had happened to the ones the others had killed. Realising where the hounds had come from, she unfolded her power word, "STONE." The hound turned back to a statue before her eyes. Then, just to make sure, she added,

"SHATTER," and the statue exploded, spraying stone fragments in all directions.

She was just turning to see if her girlfriend needed any help when the impossible happened: the stone fragments rushed back together to form a whole creature again, only this time bits of it were stuck in the wrong places, making it all the more horrifying, but no less deadly as it came at her again. Dreya flexed her muscle to bring her dagger to hand from where it was hidden up her sleeve. It seemed there was no way magic could stop these creatures, but just then, an alarm went off in her head.

"Hold on," the sorceress muttered to herself, eyes narrowing, "something's not right here." A theory formed in her mind, but did she have the courage to put it to the test? She quickly decided her dagger wasn't going to be much help anyway, so her best chance lay in trusting her magical instincts. If she died, at least she would die in the embrace of magic. There was honour in that, she decided.

Mandalee came around just in time to see Dreya the Dark throw her dagger away and calmly kneel before the hellhound, exposing her throat to the predator.

"Do what you will," whispered the sorceress. "You can't hurt me." The hellhound rushed at her...and straight through her like a ghost. The insubstantial hellhound turned to stone once more and teleported back to its pedestal, showing no signs of returning to life.

"I knew it!" Dreya cried out triumphantly, getting to her feet. "Everyone stop fighting; they're not real!"

Trusting her lover implicitly, despite having not seen what had just happened, Catriona returned to her natural form and ceased all attempts to defend herself. The hellhound sprang and vanished. The others did likewise.

Mandalee patched herself up with a quick dose of magic and painkilling herbs, and Catriona used the last of the party's drinking water to heal Dreya's leg enough to stem the blood loss and allow her to walk.

"I refuse to ask how you did that," Mandalee huffed, stubbornly. Then, after a moment, her resolve broke. "How did you do that?"

"It suddenly hit me," Dreya explained, "how peculiar it was that Kullos should have left the exact same guards that I was thinking of. When the hellhound shattered and put itself back together all wrong, I realised there was no way physical magic would have got it wrong. It had to be illusion. We've got to keep a tight hold of our imaginations. Whatever we think up will probably appear and attack us. Keep telling yourselves: there's nothing here. Nothing at all. And if something does appear, remember it can only hurt us if we believe it's real."

"Why do you suppose Kullos' magic went wrong?" Sara wondered.

"The trouble with interactive illusion magic," Dreya explained, "is that it's tough to maintain if your mind is distracted. My guess is Daelen is causing him a few problems.

"Then it's begun," Mandalee said ominously.

"Come on, quick!" Cat insisted. "We haven't much time!"

She shifted back to leopard form, and they set off again.

*****

They reached the uppermost floor of a large inner antechamber with a high ceiling that clearly served as Kullos' throne room. Below them, a narrow corridor led away from the chamber, in the direction they had come, which made sense of the slightly muffled scent trail Cat had been following. Daelen must have taken the lower route.

There was a portal shimmering in the centre of the room, right on top of Kullos' throne, and it was closing. Even as the companions ran down the spiral stairs, Cat knew they'd never make it. She shifted to her falcon form and flew down, desperately, but even she couldn't make it in time and was forced to execute a muscle-wrenching stall in midair, lest she got stuck partway through the portal when it closed – a most unpleasant death. In the middle of her turn and twist, she felt something pop. The pain almost made her black out, but she fought to stay conscious. She could feel her grip on her bird form slipping away and she changed back a good twenty feet from the floor. She crash-landed with a violent impact that knocked the air from her lungs and broke several of her spell component pouches, spilling out their contents. She assessed the damage before attempting to get up. Coming on top of the injuries she had sustained in the battle, it was serious. Her left arm was

151

useless, and she didn't even want to think about the reason for the twinge in her back that jolted her with every step.

When her friends reached her, Dreya, scared out of her wits by what she had just seen, was livid.

"Of all the stupid, idiotic and downright dangerous stunts I've seen, that really was beyond belief! What in the name of all the levels of hell did you think you were going to achieve?"

"I had to reach the portal," Cat replied, weakly. "I knew you couldn't make it, so I had to try. Don't you realise? Daelen is on the other side of that thing, fighting Kullos alone. He's got to be stopped! Whatever happens to me is worth the risk. I haven't had time to fully figure out why, but I trust my instincts."

Dreya was unsympathetic. "If you'd stopped for a second, I could have told you that I can trace the destination of a portal even after it shuts. Through my extensive studies, I found there was a residual trace of magical disturbance, unique to the destination, that takes a few minutes to fade."

"Alright then, get to it!" Cat ordered. The druidess regretted speaking to her girlfriend that way, but time was short. She couldn't shake the feeling that they were just moments from disaster and only they could prevent it. And she hurt like hell. "Just make a micro-portal – big enough to analyse what's on the other side but too small to be seen."

"But surely we know where he's gone anyway," Jessica pointed out.

"Yeah," Mandalee agreed. "His base on StormClaw."

"I have a feeling it might not be as simple as that," Cat disputed, ruefully. "I've been trying to train Daelen to think strategically and judging by the way he killed those guards with his sword rather than waste his powers, I'm afraid he's started to listen."

Turning to Mandalee, the druidess asked, "Can you do anything? I've got nothing left to work with to heal myself, and I don't think I could manipulate my spell components with one hand, anyway."

"I won't lie to you," the cleric replied, fuming at her reckless actions, "you've really hurt yourself this time."

Come to that, she didn't exactly feel marvellous herself. She'd taken a few knocks, scrapes and lacerations in the heat of the battle, and despite her healing, the damage to her right arm wasn't as superficial as it looked. She didn't dare remove her body armour to find out – she was worried it might be the only thing holding her together. Dreya had fared better until the hellhounds attacked, but her leg was terribly mangled. The dark sorceress concealed things very well, but Mandalee was pretty sure her expert eye could detect injuries that the sorceress would never admit to having sustained.

"I can't heal you completely at this point," Mandalee continued. "Healing these kinds of injuries too fast does more harm than good. I can't even get your arm working properly."

"Mandalee," Cat growled, "stop telling me what you can't do and tell me what you can do!"

Mandalee was equally blunt. "I can get your arm working well enough for you to use your magic and maybe dull the pain a bit, but that's all. First, I need to put your shoulder back in place – it's dislocated."

"Do it."

"It's going to hurt," she warned.

Catriona glared at her best friend, and gritted her teeth. "It already hurts, just do it!"

Mandalee set about her limited ministrations, warning her friend, "Don't even think about any shapeshifting until you're properly healed. Some damage can never be fixed."

Cat promised to obey.

By the time Mandalee had finished, Dreya had already opened her micro-portal. They couldn't see it, but the Three Guardians could sense it. Acting on a sudden idea, Dreya asked Jessica if she had her phone with her.

Puzzled by the unexpected question, Jessica pulled it out of her pocket and looked at it. "Battery's a bit low, but it should be OK for a few hours, why?"

"I just thought, when we stop Kullos, it might be useful if we could prove it to that lot out there when we return. Capturing it all on video seems like a good way of doing that. May I?"

Jessica handed it over with a shrug. "Sure, why not? It's not like I can check my Twitter feed here anyway, is it, love?"

Before they could do any more, a pair of musclebound human warriors rounded a corner on their patrol. When they spotted the intruders, they each drew a formidable-looking sword and advanced.

"They're not illusions, are they?" Jessica checked.

"Not unless you've been daydreaming about fit guys with huge weapons, Jess," Sara quipped.

The others stared at her.

"That sounded better in my head," she conceded with a golden blush.

"Leave the jokes to me, eh, Sara dear?" her sister advised. Turning to the Guardians, she urged them not to waste their powers. "Leave them to us."

Sara agreed, "You just do your thing, and we'll guard your backs." The warriors were trying to intimidate them with fancy swordplay, flicking their blades from one hand, spinning wildly in the air, only to catch them deftly in the other. Locking eyes with her sister, Sara suggested, "Raiders?"

Jessica nodded. "You read my mind."

Nonchalantly, the pair drew their guns and shot them down.

"Nice shooting," Mandalee commended them, "but those guns make a lot of noise, and these walls echo a lot, so if there are any more around here…"

She didn't need to finish her sentence, as a dozen more guards came running.

"Oops!" the Chetsuans cried together.

"Want to borrow my dragonclaw blades?" the assassin asked.

"No need," Sara shook her head, as she and her sister holstered their guns once more.

"We've got our own," Jessica added.

With that, they both flicked their hidden knives into their hands and charged.

With full confidence in their bodyguards, the others got back down to Guardian business.

"There's something strange about the portal," Dreya reported, "or rather its destination. It's definitely StormClaw, but…" she trailed off, not knowing how to finish the sentence. "Mandalee," she prompted, "what do you sense from nature on the other side?" The sorceress knew her girlfriend was in too much pain to sense much of anything right now.

"Time," Mandalee replied. "Time is out of sync. Not as much as Earth, not a different speed, but…slightly in the past. Just about an hour."

Dreya swore. "He knew the place would be empty at that time because I mentioned how long I've had our Chetsuan friends in our world."

"You couldn't have known, Dreya," Cat reassured her. "Even you can't anticipate everything."

Mandalee realised Daelen's plan. "I forgot he had crude time travel. I would have just blundered through a portal to StormClaw as it is now, by which time the battle would be over. Too late for us to interfere. But does that mean everything's OK? I mean, the world obviously hasn't been destroyed."

Cat shook her head. "Doesn't work like that. Maybe the world wasn't destroyed because we did something, and if we don't figure out what that is and do it…"

"…then goodbye to everything," Mandalee finished.

"This is where your ridiculous radical plan comes in, isn't it?" Dreya realised.

Cat nodded. "He's changed the rules. This isn't a current crisis anymore, it's an Illegal Time Intervention. An hour in the past or a thousand years makes no difference. As Guardians, we can't allow that kind of interference."

Dreya remembered reading about this kind of scenario in the *Chronicles*. If the world on which they stood were destroyed in the past, then this would be an aberrant Timeline. With the walls of reality so weakened, the cosmos would be wide open to an incursion by the chaotic power of *IT*.

"What can we do?" Mandalee asked. This kind of thing wasn't her forte. She needed something she could stick her blades into.

Before she could reply, an alarm sounded, and more guards came running. The Chetsuans rushed forward to take them on, taking the battle into the narrow corridor where they could hold a line with just two of them.

Trusting in their ability to look after themselves, Catriona asserted, "Time is on our side now. We can make it work for us, but first, we need to create our new base of operations."

Chapter 21

Cat pointed out a section in the *Chronicles*:

To claim their Timeless state, the Guardians will create a place that can itself exist outside of Time, to which their powers shall be linked. If they are the right people, then one of them will have already created a place that can be adapted for this purpose:

A place that belongs to two worlds.
A place that belongs to none.
A place that is precious to all Three Guardians.
A place born of the greatest magic.
A place that does not exist.

*****

Of course, these Guardians were never going to operate from a dark underground base full of technology and flashing lights. They were a Faery sorceress, a half-Faery druid and a human Cleric of Nature. Together, they all had something in common: a love of nature.

"Dreya, close your micro-portal," she instructed. Dreya complied. "We need to travel to Daelen's Earth base, and we need to be there yesterday. Can you incorporate temporal co-ordinates into your magic?"

"Yesterday our time or Earth time?" Dreya checked.

"Earth time," Cat clarified. "About six hours our time. Safer that way."

"Why is that safer?" Mandalee asked.

"According to the *Chronicles*," Cat explained, "time travel to non-specific co-ordinates is dangerous."

Dreya nodded her agreement. "And it becomes exponentially more dangerous, the further you try to travel."

"Should be only minimal risk for six hours," Cat assured her friend.

Given that the risk of *not* doing it was the destruction of everything, Mandalee decided risk was relative.

Dreya concentrated and opened a Prismatic Sphere large enough to step through.

"What about those two?" Mandalee indicated Sara and Jessica. "We can't just leave them."

"We have to," Cat countered, regretfully. "They can't become Timeless, only we can. The temporal forces we're going to unleash would kill them. Once we're done, it might be OK, but not yet. Besides, we're going to be Time travellers; if all goes well, we can be back in five minutes from their perspectives."

"And if things don't go well?" the assassin asked, fearing she already knew the answer.

It was Dreya who replied, "Then it really won't matter where they are when the world ends."

Trying to hide the fear that she might be lying, Mandalee called out to the Chetsuans, "Keep holding them off. We'll be back in five minutes!"

The pair acknowledged that, and the Guardians stepped through the portal.

*****

Once on Earth, they closed the portal and headed for the only place that fitted what the *Chronicles* called for: Catriona's Meadow.

It was on Earth, but it was also a recreation of Catriona's Quarthonian childhood home on Tempestria. Two worlds. But since it was inside Daelen's containment field, his entire base was cut off from the rest of Earth, so in a way, the meadow belonged to no world at all. It was precious to all Three Guardians because of their love of nature and because Catriona created it. Creating it had been a labour of love for Cat, and as best friend and girlfriend, the other two Guardians shared that connection of love. The greatest magic. But it was a recreation of Catriona's childhood home that had itself been recreated by her Angel. A recreation, of a recreation, of a place that was long since gone. A place that did not exist.

Together, with the guidance of the *Chronicles*, the Three Guardians used the magic of all three flavours: wizard, druid and cleric, combined with higher planar energy from the Crystal Mage Staff. Cat believed the end of the world probably qualified as a 'dire emergency of worldwide cataclysmic proportions.' Working in harmony, they wove it all together and moved Catriona's Meadow away from Earth, away from all worlds, into the void between the mortal plane and that of the gods. Their own private realm where only the Guardians could exist, at least until they learned how to invite others to visit.

For the first time, the Guardians were as they were always meant to be: Timeless. Here, they could plan their next move without the constraints of reality, of space, of time.

"Now that we're here," Cat began, "there's something we need to learn to do because we need a consult."

"We need a what?" Dreya wondered.

"Well, as I said, I think this is our one last chance to get it right, so it would help if we knew what went wrong before. Besides, we don't have time to learn everything we need to know about being Guardians on our first day in the job."

"But we're Timeless now," Mandalee objected. "Doesn't that mean we have as much time as we like?" She paused. "Or am I making no sense, as usual?"

Cat gave her a wearied look. "I do wish you'd stop doubting yourself like that."

"It was a perfectly reasonable question," Dreya agreed, "and I think technically you're right, but there's a catch, isn't there, Cat?"

"More than one, actually," she confirmed. "For a start, Mandalee, we can't heal while we're Timeless because healing requires time. We'll just stay in our injured state forever. I don't know about you, but that doesn't appeal to me. Besides, if we stay here, we'll never know what happened to our world. Does it survive, or was it destroyed? Are our friends OK? What about Shyleen? You will never see her again if we don't leave here."

Mandalee was convinced. "So, what about this consult?" she wondered. "What's that all about?"

"Another good question," Dreya stated, encouragingly, "and this time I admit I don't get it, either. Who can we consult? We're the first Guardians on Tempestria."

Cat smiled the way she always did when she got to the heart of one of her plans. "That's where you're wrong, Dreya. We're not. We're just the first Guardians on *this* Tempestria. I've told you; this has all happened before. Those Guardians formed too late to save their world, but they're trying to help us save ours."

"That's what your letter said," Mandalee remembered. "The one from under Calin's Tower."

"Exactly. That's why I brought us here, so we can learn to open a Cosmic Rift to another reality, to where those other Guardians are. They've been Timeless for a long time, so they've had time to learn how to manipulate Time properly."

"Never thought I'd hear someone use the word time four times in one sentence," Dreya remarked with a wry smile. "Not one that made as much sense as that one, anyway."

"Oh, I can do way better than four, but—"

"—But we don't have time," Mandalee finished. Catriona nodded. "Right, how do we do this?"

They sat down together under the oak tree, Catriona in the middle, with the *Chronicles* open in her lap.

As they studied what was written, they discussed it freely. While the Guardians knew they couldn't stay in that Timeless place forever, it did feel good to be relieved of the constraints of Time…at least for a time.

At last, though, the Guardians were all clear on what to do. It was not so different from opening a Prismatic Sphere portal, except the destination co-ordinates were the ones in their heads – the ones that didn't make sense. The true difficulty lay in other aspects of the magic.

Opening a portal to another reality required more magic than Three Guardians had access to. It needed six. The co-ordinates made no sense because they were partway between the two realities. They had to take the Cosmic Rift that far, to that exact no-place, trusting that the Three on the other side would do the same and there hadn't been some miscommunication or mistranslation. The other catch was that they couldn't do it while Timeless because the magic required a Temporal element. In theory, they could choose any time and place as a starting point – it could make no difference to the other Guardians. In practice, though, there was only one possible choice: If they were going to stop Daelen, then they needed to be where the action was, on StormClaw. The Cosmic Rift would be stable for no more than an hour. That was the only hour in history when six Guardians could possibly work together to save the world. Therefore, it was decided that they needed to be on StormClaw just about thirty minutes before Daelen arrived, while their past selves

159

were in the thick of the fighting. The idea of being in two places at once was mind-blowing for the three companions, but they knew they had to get over it quickly. They were the Guardians; this was what they did, and they had a job to do.

*****

A portal took them to their destination on time, give or take a few minutes. Once there, they each took a few deep breaths to calm their nerves and began to work as one to open the first and only Cosmic Rift there could ever be.

It flickered a few times, as they fought the rules of their reality that decreed this was impossible, but gradually, reality gave way to their need, and the fabric tore open. The Guardians just prayed they could stitch it up again afterwards. The portal grew into a tunnel beyond time and space as they knew it, stretching in a direction for which they had no name until it encountered a force pushing back at its extreme end. Another identical tunnel was close by, and unknowable laws of physics decreed that some kind of repulsion force came into play, trying to prevent two separate realities from touching when they were never meant to. The three young women strained with the effort, imagining their counterparts doing the same. This had to work. It was the only chance for Tempestria. For the sake of everyone and everything that they cared about, this had to work, and no stupid cosmic forces were going to stop them.

Just when they were on the verge of exhaustion, the forces were finally overcome, and the two tunnels merged into one: the Cosmic Rift was complete.

Through the tunnel came a voice that sounded a lot like Catriona. "Hello? Are you the Guardians of Tempestria?"

"Er, yes, we are," Cat replied, a little uncertainly. "And I'm guessing, so are you."

"Cat! Perfect! Hello, me!" the voice called out greeting. "The Mandalee and Dreya on my side say 'hi' too, but they can't spare the magic needed to send their voices through the Rift. They're busy stopping this bubble of reality from collapsing. Look, I need to ask you something, and I know it's a hell of a way to start a conversation, but there's no polite way to say this: your world hasn't blown up yet, has it?"

"No," Cat assured her counterpart. "The fireworks don't start for another half hour or so. I'm calling because—"

"—because you need information, to gain knowledge," her counterpart finished, a touch of humour in her voice. "That's how this all started for us, isn't it? We just had to know. Quite right, of course."

"Can you tell us everything we need to know?" Cat asked. "Tell us how this all went wrong before, so we can avoid making the same mistakes."

"We can do better than tell you," came the voice. A beam of light seemed to travel through the Cosmic Rift, resolving into images in the air. It was like one of the movies their Chetsuan friends had taken them to on Earth, Cat realised, except it didn't require a screen. "Now, I suggest you all sit comfortably while I show you how Tempestria – my Tempestria – came to an end."

*****

Time for another interruption from yours truly, gentle reader. Arshes Megane – remember me? Your humble narrator? Well, in the interests of expediency, I'm not going to share the entire 'movie', along with the many asides, jokes, and misunderstandings it contained. Instead, if you'll forgive me, I will simply summarise myself.

In truth, the 'movie' was more of a series of clips and scenes – edited highlights, if you will – focussing on crucial moments on their Tempestria.

The first such scene began with the caption: *The Last Days of Tempestria.*

Catriona had spent two days running around Compton as a Trickster and fell into a demon trap set by Mandalee. However, on their world, she was trapped only once. From Mandalee's perspective, she'd wound up some girl, in revenge for wasting her time, but that's all. Nothing particularly memorable. She wasn't the first person to fall into one of her demon traps, nor would she be the last. It would be several years before they met again.

In time, Mandalee came to the attention of Justaria, Triumvirate Representative for the Balance. As a firm believer in promoting both diversity and promising young talent, she hired the young demon hunter's services a few times. Mandalee was grateful for the opportunity and developed a deep respect for the woman's fair-minded leadership.

Meanwhile, young Catriona had her first encounter with Dreya the Dark, seeking access to her library. Dreya was intrigued with her druid magic and agreed. They developed a positive professional relationship and eventually even a friendship.

Then Justaria went missing and given their separate connections to her, Catriona and Mandalee both chose to investigate, and so they met not only each other but Daelen StormTiger, too. The shadow warrior had also been looking into these strange disappearances, ever since he learned that higher planar energy was involved.

The movie scenes continued to show events very similar to those the three companions experienced on their Tempestria, except some of the details were different. Mandalee and Cat travelled overseas together and got to know each other, but while they were friends, it was never particularly deep or meaningful to either. Cat never knew about Mandalee's gender identity issues – Mandalee could pass so well by now, and it never entered Catriona's mind that she was unhappy with who she was. At the same time, Mandalee grew to like having a friend who simply saw her as a woman and she didn't want to risk that, so she never told her. At least, not before the world ended.

At the climax of this first act, there was a final confrontation between Kullos and Daelen, just as in my world. The crucial difference being that the institution of the Guardians had not happened. The movie showed Catriona unlocking the security on her staff, much as I described earlier, but she didn't have the *Chronicles*. In effect, then, gentle reader, she held a key with no idea what lock it was supposed to fit into.

There was nothing more she could do, so she focussed on the battle ahead, believing there would be time to explore the purpose of her staff when it was all over. She had no way of knowing that later would be too late because when it was all over, it would be all over for her whole world.

The battle against Kullos' forces raged, and Daelen fought hard, sapping his energy in the process until finally, he slipped away to fight Kullos alone as he always intended. At first, they fought inside the fortress itself, but Daelen managed to open a portal to StormClaw.

Kullos was too powerful to fight alone, and he managed to take the battle beyond the containment field that surrounded his grounds. Daelen was weakening, but with a final valiant effort, he grabbed Kullos' dimensional control device and used Heaven's Surrender. The Wish barrier could only contain the blast temporarily, and there was nothing anyone could do as the power escaped, killing Kullos and Daelen alike, and devastating Tempestria.

At first, there were survivors, including Cat, Dreya and Mandalee. The Heaven's Surrender blast pretty much ended the fighting. Whose side they were on suddenly seemed a moot point, given the end of the world. The peace didn't last long, however. Soon, people began to turn on each other, but it wasn't just former enemies. Friends and family were killing, maiming, torturing each other without thought or reason or remorse. Others were losing memories, entirely at random. It made no sense.

Cat managed to find her staff in the wreckage of Kullos' former base, and as a bonus, she also found the *Nameless Book*. Laethyn, now dead, had brought it to the battle, hoping to use the brute force of Daelen's beam cannon blasts to open it. It wasn't enough power for that, but Heaven's Surrender was, so all of its defences were now down and the conditions of Guardianship void. Catriona gathered her two friends, and together they became Guardians.

The containment field of Daelen's StormClaw island had so far kept the destruction out. Therefore, the Earth base was also intact. The Guardians created their base of operations outside Time, from Catriona's Meadow. They learned about Time Intervention and analysed Daelen's battle against Kullos. Doing so, they discovered the terrible truth: Kullos had been infected by the essence of *IT* – that was why he changed from Heroic Champion to Paranoid Villain. Kullos had, in turn, invented Heaven's Surrender, a weapon of true destruction. *IT* was loose in the world, turning life against life, while *IT* unmade the world. Nothing could stop *IT*.

Even as they showed the movie to their counterparts, those other Guardians were actively maintaining the containment field around their StormClaw. Otherwise, all connected worlds would be unmade. *IT* could even reach through the Rift and undo everything the Guardians were trying to achieve: the Salvation of Tempestria.

Not their Tempestria, gentle reader, for that was already lost. A new one. This Tempestria. My Tempestria.

The Catriona from their universe ('Alt-Cat', if you will) had one of her ridiculous radical plans: suspend Tempestria in its pre-Heaven's Surrender state, create a copy and tinker with the Timeline to prevent *IT* being released. This would count as Creation magic and was therefore impossible, at least under normal circumstances. However, the presence of *IT* was part of the problem, which made *IT* part of the solution: In the end, all failed Timelines would be unmade, as if they had never existed, leaving only one as if it had always been so. It wasn't just cheating, it was throwing the rulebook on the fire, but the chaotic power of *IT* meant the standard rules of order had been suspended.

Creation magic required a lot of power. Fortunately, there had just been a massive explosion of higher planar energy: Heaven's Surrender. Even so, there was sufficient power for only nine major Timeline Interventions in the new world.

The Black and White Guardians each identified two crisis points where killing Daelen might change things. The Red Guardian didn't think that was the answer and wanted to work co-operatively. In the end, they agreed to a compromise: The power would be divided into nine equal portions, three each. Each Guardian could use two parts for individual attempted Interventions, keeping a total of three portions in reserve for a final co-operative effort if the other attempts failed. To maintain the connection between worlds, Alt-Cat linked her Crystal Mage Staff with that of her counterpart. This had the side-effect that Cat would be aware that something was going on with Time and would be informed of the Interventions as they happened around her. Alt-Cat hoped this would help her get slightly ahead of the game.

Chapter 22

As the three companions watched, the movie introduced the next scene with the caption: *White Intervention 1.*

The White Guardian used one portion of energy to partially manifest as a white glowing image in our Tempestria, appearing to Mandalee and hiring her to kill Daelen. The scene flashed forward to the moment Daelen was weakened and vulnerable, having touched Catriona's staff. The White Assassin burst into view, and Cat tried to block her with ice and restrain her with the plants. But Mandalee was a Cleric of Nature, so all she had to do was ask the plants to let her go, and they did. Then, using her super-speed, she ran around Catriona's ice wall and killed the shadow warrior where he lay. But shadow warriors take a long time to die. They are light in a box and even when the mortal shell is damaged beyond repair, their light essence can remain viable for some time. Aden felt the death of his clone and saw his chance. Rushing to the scene, he absorbed Daelen's essence into himself, recombining. The shadow warrior killed both Mandalee and Catriona, destroying any chance for Guardians in that world. In the final battle, Aden got his hands on Heaven's Surrender and tried to detonate it while using Kullos' control device to re-Ascend, but Kullos held him back, determined to take him with him as he died. That world was unmade.

The following caption read: *Black Intervention 1.*

Learning from the White Guardian's mistake, the Black Guardian used one portion of energy to partially manifest as an apparition to Dreya, as a young child. She told her that if she worked on her magic with all of her being, then one day, she would suffer the bullying and taunting no longer. She would grow to become the Greatest Mage Who Ever Lived, but to achieve her ultimate goal, she would have to kill Daelen StormTiger and take his power for herself. Then, even shadow warriors would be no threat. The scene flashed forward to the moment Daelen's dark clone came to her Tower, seeking to take her as his pet. Dreya felt compelled to kill Daelen and cared not at all which one. Aden, weakened from his latest battle against his other half, could not stand against her. Once he was dead, she made sure to drain every last drop of higher planar energy. That made her more powerful than ever. She planned to offer her 'assistance' to the other Daelen as equal partners against Kullos. When Kullos was no longer a threat, if Daelen was still alive, she would kill him herself, and drain him of all remaining power, ending the danger of the shadow warriors forever. But Daelen didn't trust her and expected betrayal, so when the moment came, Daelen was able to use his little-used temporal powers to keep her out of it. Kullos was far too powerful for just one side of Daelen to handle and simply used Heaven's Surrender himself, so the world was unmade.

The third caption read: *White Intervention 2.*

What the White Guardian took from this, was that Daelen's misguided heroic nature was the problem. He knew he didn't have the power to take on Kullos without recombining with his other half. Yet he did it anyway. What would his dark clone do in that position? Using her second portion of higher planar energy, then, the White Guardian appeared to Mandalee while she was sailing on the *Dolphin*. She told her that shortly she would have a second opportunity to stop Daelen destroying the world. Flash forward a few hours, and Mandalee received a sympathic cry for help from Catriona over on the *StormChaser*. Pyrah, her Ysirian snake, had bitten Daelen, and he was going to die. Catriona did everything she could to get the two ships together, but once there, Mandalee refused to help Cat heal him. She was almost persuaded by Catriona's appeal to her cleric side, but the assassin in her won out. For the sake of the world, they had to let him die.

Cat was devastated, knowing Daelen's death was her fault – Pyrah would never have been there if not for her – but she could do nothing alone. The White Guardian reasoned that Daelen's essence was no use to Aden this time because the venom would kill him, too, but just in case, Mandalee weighed down Daelen's body and threw it overboard. Aden was no hero, and he wasn't stupid enough to face Kullos' growing power, so he simply opened a portal and ran away to another world. The White Guardian had hoped that Kullos, upon hearing about this, would have no reason to use Heaven's Surrender. She assumed he would simply use his control device to re-Ascend, never to bother Tempestria again, but she underestimated the depth of his malice. He detonated Heaven's Surrender and quickly re-Ascended to avoid the blast. Once again, Tempestria was unmade.

Up came the fourth caption: *Black Intervention 2*.

The Black Guardian decided that the recombined version of Daelen needed to die and told her counterpart that there was a golden opportunity to do that if she did not kill Aden at her Black Tower. Not quite. She just absorbed enough of his power to make him run to his other half and recombine. Dreya met with the recombined Daelen on the eve of the final battle. He was wary, but he recognised her power and appreciated her restraint in not killing Aden when she had the chance, so he agreed to discuss terms with her. At the moment Kullos' death knights attacked, however, Dreya seized her opportunity. With the element of surprise on her side, Dreya drew power from her own undead guards, and their combined power was enough to kill him. Absorbing his power, she took his place in the final battle and went after Kullos herself. However, lacking Daelen's experience, she didn't recognise the Heaven's Surrender device until it was too late. Kullos detonated it, and although Dreya stopped him from getting away, the world was unmade yet again.

Next caption: *Red Interventions 1&2*.

The Red Guardian didn't believe killing Daelen was the answer. She had allowed the other two Guardians to go first because her plans needed more preparation. By incorporating a kind of memory of their failures into her staff and linking it with its counterpart in her new world, echoes of these critical moments would resonate and help this world's Catriona to understand what was going on. The Red Guardian believed it was imperative that the Guardians be formed *before* the final battle against Kullos, so that they could intervene and save the world both *with* and *from* Daelen.

However, before that could happen, her plan lay much further back in history. Instead of two partial manifestations, she created a Mirror Image self-copy in the new world. After ageing up her appearance, the copy travelled back in time almost a thousand years, to when Daelen had first been split in two. The Red Guardian imbued this magical construct with the knowledge of the importance of her mission but also gave her free will to act independently. This was for practical reasons as much as moral ones – she couldn't maintain a connection across both universes and back in time.

Calling herself Rose, the sentient copy's primary objective was to leave clues that would help Catriona in the future. Secondary to that, she sought to gain knowledge and hopefully sow seeds that would help Catriona to gently influence him more when they eventually met.

She didn't expect to fall in love.

The very first time he told her he felt the same way, she had to share everything, at least about herself. He didn't care that she was really made of magic – he was light in a box. The Red Guardian believed the magic would sustain Rose for no more than five years, but when Rose told the shadow warrior, he took her to live with him on Earth. That would give them two decades together. During her time on Earth, she achieved one of her assigned Time Interventions – leaving the note for Catriona underneath Daelen's training centre and leaving clues to point towards it in her fiction writing.

At last, her time was up, and she had to say goodbye to Daelen. He understood something of the perils of Time travel, and before she left, he gave her a device that would wipe part of his memories. He would remember Rose, and he would recognise her style of magic in Catriona, but he wouldn't remember precisely who Rose was or have any foreknowledge of the future. This affected Daelen's reaction to Cat in the future because she subconsciously reminded him of Rose.

Returning to Tempestria, Rose placed another note under what would become Calin's Tower. This used up the Red Guardian's second Intervention, but Rose wasn't done. Not quite.

In addition to those two main Interventions, she still had just enough life left to make one further tiny tweak to the Timeline. Something so small that required almost no effort: she moved a tiny little spider slightly to one side, so it brushed past Catriona's ear at a crucial moment in Compton. Since Cat didn't like spiders, it made her jump, just as she was using what at the time was still new magic. Thanks to that distraction, she ended up stuck in a demon trap for a second time, this time naked and looking like Jacob. This precipitated Cat's second meeting with Mandalee, which was sure to be a memorable encounter.

None of this affected their free will. All she did was move a spider slightly, but it had a profound effect. Mandalee and Cat became close friends much earlier. This small action changed so much, yet still it was not enough.

The Cosmic Rift represented the Final Intervention for all Three Guardians, requiring every last drop of higher planar energy just to sustain it for one hour, half of which was already spent.

At the end of the movie, a final caption read: *All of the Guardians' actions have helped guide events to create the current version of Tempestria, but without further Intervention, nothing will change. Tempestria will still be unmade.*

*****

"What do we need to do?" Cat asked.

Her counterpart explained, "You, the Guardians, need to help Daelen and also stop him. Fight alongside him against Kullos, so Kullos cannot take the battle away from StormClaw. It must happen there."

Dreya broke into the conversation at that point.

"I have a question," she ventured. "Obviously, I'm new to how Time Interventions work, but logically, assuming our world's still here tomorrow, since your world will never have existed, all three of us here will have to nip back in Time and do what you did, to maintain current events, yes?"

"You're right, of course," Alt-Cat agreed. "Obviously, for you and Mandalee, things are simple enough. For Cat, it's somewhat more involved, but if she's anything like me, loving Daelen will be no hardship."

"Wow, this is awkward!" Mandalee remarked.

"Why?" queried Alt-Cat's voice through the rift. "What's the problem?"

"Well, I don't wish to sound possessive," Dreya replied acidly, "but I don't think it's unreasonable for me to be unhappy at the prospect of my girlfriend having a relationship with someone else!"

"Girlfriend?" Alt-Cat sounded puzzled. "Wait – you're together in your world?"

"Of course we are!" Catriona insisted. "How can you not know that?"

"We can't see the whole of Time, as you'll soon discover, only certain key points in history, and love is unpredictable by its very nature. Look, I can't tell you how to live your lives. I even gave my copy free will, so I'm not about to take yours away. You're all resourceful people, I'm sure you can work together to find another way to achieve the same results. That's the key to Time Intervention: the story may change, but the ending stays the same, yet sometimes moving a tiny spider an inch to the left is enough to change the world. You can worry about tomorrow's problems later. Right now, we need to focus on preserving your Tempestria, so that you have the luxury of a later. It's too late for our world, but if yours survives and you remember what we did to save it, then even if we are unmade, we still mattered. We made a difference. We existed. Even *IT* can't take that away from us."

"Can you teach us the magic we need?" Cat asked.

That was why she had wanted this consult in the first place. She believed they could spend an eternity in Catriona's Meadow and still have no idea what they were supposed to do. Far better to spend a few minutes talking to an expert who could help direct their focus.

"No need," her counterpart insisted. "This isn't about learning some specific secret spell. Just trust yourselves. All that matters is that Kullos dies today, there on your StormClaw. No escape, no portal, no Ascending, and no Heaven's Surrender. Only then can your world be safe."

"I don't suppose you can come over to help us a bit more hands-on?" Mandalee wondered, without hope.

"Can't risk it. We have no way of knowing the effect of having more than one version of anyone, let alone a Guardian, in the same place at the same time. Doing that with Time magic is strain enough on the cosmos but trying it with a Cosmic Rift is just asking for everything to collapse. I can send an object, though. That's safe enough. Here, catch!"

Tumbling through the Rift, came another Crystal Mage Staff.

"Thanks! Got it!" Cat declared, speaking a little too soon as, despite her best efforts to catch the staff, it promptly clattered to the ground. "More or less," she finished, sheepishly.

"You dropped it, didn't you?" Alt-Cat deadpanned. If they could have seen her, the Guardians were sure she would have been rolling her eyes.

"Yes, I did," Cat admitted. "This is why we never got picked for sports teams at school."

Her counterpart laughed, "That's true!"

"To be fair, you've only got one arm working right at the moment," Mandalee pointed out.

"Battle injuries?" Alt-Cat asked.

"Something like that, but you know I won't let it stop me. Anyway, you're sure it's safe for me to have two of these?" she asked her counterpart.

"Positive. Just throw it back through before the Rift closes, and it'll be fine. I have no use for its power, but you might need it and there's no time to wait for yours to recharge."

It was reassuring for Cat to learn that the power would return over time. She hadn't realised that before.

"Now you have everything you need to fight your battle."

"Maybe," Cat allowed, "but before the shadow warriors turn up, how about you quickly coach us in some of the basics of Guardian Temporal magic? Just in case we need to buy Time later."

Her counterpart readily agreed.

Chapter 23

As Daelen had approached Kullos' inner sanctum, preparing to face his gravest challenge, the only thought on his mind had been that he must not fail, to save all those that he cared about. He had made virtually no sound and lowered his power signature to make a stealthy approach. Kullos would expect him to attack the way he always did. He couldn't know that he'd been trained by an amazing mortal girl to think more clearly. Catriona had had quite the effect on him.

Further to that, he had a plan to keep her and the others out of this. When Daelen struck Kullos, he planned to do so swiftly, suddenly unleashing his power to stun him while he opened a Prismatic Sphere portal, not to StormClaw in this time frame, but the StormClaw of about an hour ago. He hadn't used his time travel powers for years, but as Jessica would probably say, it was like riding a bike. Besides, it didn't need to be perfect. Dreya had let it slip that the Chetsuans had been safely on Tempestria since last night, so there was a nice wide margin for error. One hour or two would make no difference. Either way, when Cat and the others tried to travel to StormClaw in the here and now, they would find the containment field had been changed to block them out. Then they would be safe.

Keeping to the shadows, creeping along the narrow corridor, Daelen had seen Kullos sitting on his throne, deep in concentration, putting together the pieces of what Daelen assumed must be his dimensional control device. It was fashioned into the shape of a sword, and it was becoming more and more complete in front of his eyes. He had no idea how he was doing it, and that wasn't just his lack of technical knowledge talking. He had never even heard of such a thing being done before, but he had told the truth about Kullos being a brilliant engineer before he became their Greatest Shadow Champion…before he 'gave in to chaos,' as Dreya liked to say.

Still thinking tactically, Daelen had decided to wait a few moments. He knew Cat and the others wouldn't leave the battlefield without first doing all they could to maximise their allies' chances. That would take time, so once again pulling on Catriona's training, he knew he could afford to be patient. The more complete the control device, the more stable would be the access to Heaven's Surrender, and by inference, the more stable the weapon itself would be. He used Kullos' own distracted state to creep carefully closer and closer.

Five more minutes, and the control device was as complete as it was ever going to be: Kullos held in his hand a fully forged sword, missing just one small detail. Like many swords of that quality, there was a socket built into the hilt, about an inch in diameter, where a jewel should fit, but it seemed Kullos didn't have that jewel. Still, the device was complete enough that it should work just fine for his purposes.

The time to strike was now.

Daelen burst out of hiding, powered up and slammed a cannon blast into his nemesis. He managed to grab the sword by the blade and wrest it from Kullos' grasp. It hurt like hell, even with the protection of the gloves of his combat suit, but he wasn't going to let pain stop him. Before Kullos could recover, Daelen opened his Time portal and knocked him through it. He didn't waste energy on closing the portal – it would close by itself in a minute. He shifted the sword to his other hand, this time holding it properly by the hilt. Through the portal, he thought he saw a familiar-looking bird diving towards the opening, but it closed too soon, and the bird was left stranded on the other side. That was it. No more interference…or so he thought.

*****

As he forced the battle closer to the centre of his facility, Kullos pulled more of his essence from where he'd left it in his pocket dimension so long ago. He didn't need to be touching his control device to do that. Proximity was enough. He grew to five times his normal size, ripping Daelen's base apart as he did so. In this case, size really didn't matter, except to make him harder to miss. The real problem was that a shadow warrior's natural state extended into extra dimensions which, in the mortal plane, were simply too small to contain their essence. That's why they had to shed those parts in the first place. The control device was supposed to help a shadow warrior reclaim his higher dimensions up there, not bring them down here. He could rip reality apart just by being here in his true form. Until that moment, Daelen had allowed himself the faintest hope that if he could keep hold of Kullos' control device, he wouldn't need Heaven's Surrender. Using that weapon required direct, physical contact, so if Kullos couldn't use it, Daelen had hoped that his recombined self would have the power to destroy his enemy without recourse to that weapon. That hope was now dashed. There was no other way.

Before he could do it, however, now that his base was in ruins, Daelen could see a blueish glow coming from outside, shimmering like some kind of portal. Even as he fought Kullos, trading beam cannon blasts, he flew high to investigate. To his astonishment, it was indeed a portal, but far larger than any he had seen before. It looked like it could consume his entire base and its grounds, it was so big. Standing in front of this portal, apparently unawed by the power arrayed around them, were three very pissed-off-looking young women, dressed in white, black and red.

"How are you here?" he demanded. "How is this even possible?"

"We are the Guardians of Time and Magic," they announced in unison. "You helped make this possible."

If Jessica were there, he was sure she'd be saying, 'Well, that's not creepy at all!'

He supposed he should have expected those three to find a way around his powers, but the shadow warrior had others that he was sure they couldn't counter. All he needed was an energy barrier and sources of power other than himself.

Feigning a retreat from Kullos' continued onslaught of power, as his enemy tried to regain the control device, Daelen moved the battle closer to the remains of his portal room. The room was ripped apart, but his portals were still there, shimmering away. They were dwarfed by the one the Guardians had opened, but he had six of them, each linking with another facility on another world. As he focused, he could connect his essence to the control systems that maintained all his permanent portals and pull that power into himself.

As the three young women watched, the portals flared open. They could see the power flowing from all those worlds as dark storm clouds seemed to cover the island. They prepared to join the fight, but Daelen began to glow with that same power. Daelen used

174

some of this energy to grow so he could match Kullos' new size, but he kept some back to use in the space between himself and the three mortals, who found that they were trapped behind some kind of magical seal.

"I'm sorry, Cat," he boomed, "but I must be sure that you and all those that I care for are safe! I must make sure that neither you nor anyone else will be hurt when he and I destroy one another. That means that I must do this alone!"

"No, you mustn't!" Cat snapped, viciously. "You are not going to fight alone. I won't allow it. Now let us in!"

Daelen ignored her, and continued, "I know you say power isn't everything, but I hope you can now see that sometimes power is precisely what you do need. In the end, it's the only way!

"After all this is over, any part of me that remains could be dangerous, so you'll have to put me in Michael's Tomb. He won't need it anymore – he'll be free at last!"

"But Daelen, you don't have to die!" Catriona implored him. "We can find another way if you just listen to me and let us in!"

"There is no other way, Cat," he insisted.

With that, the battle of the titans began anew.

"Kullos, you have taken so many lives. So many of the people of this world have died at your hands! No more. It ends here and now! I tried to stop you before, but I couldn't stop all of it. Now I can. The time has come to pay for all the lives you have taken!"

With an almost demonic scream, Daelen fired off his beam cannon pouring more of his power, more of his essence into it than ever before.

Kullos waved his hand, deflecting the deadly beam, so it hit only his side. Instead of taking a severe injury, Kullos received a deep gash, an open wound, but nothing more. This fight was not going to be short.

As Dreya and Mandalee watched the epic battle unfold, they could see that Daelen was clearly losing. Dreya and Mandalee combined magic and physical weapons to try to break through the barrier that Daelen had formed around them, but it was futile. Dreya was running out of spells and Mandalee was running out of weapons – something neither had believed could ever happen. Together with Catriona, they had one trick left up their collective sleeves, but even with the extra help and last-minute training from their otherworldly counterparts, they couldn't be sure of the results, so they were trying everything else first.

Cat tried to use the power of the barrier itself to feed her magic, but it wasn't an anti-magic field, it was magic mixed with technology, and she didn't know how to counter that by conventional magical means.

"No, Daelen!" she cried. "You've got to stop. Power is not the answer; you must find another way. Dear gods, it's going to happen all over again. Daelen, please! You're going to destroy everything! Listen to me!" she screamed, but the shadow warrior simply ignored her, assuming it to be nothing more than the distress of someone who loved him.

"Michael paid the price of death for me, so many times and for so long, but in the end, it was always going to come down to this: I always knew I'd die in my final battle."

"That's right, you will!" Kullos boomed, speaking for the first time. "Because I'm going to kill you and destroy this sickening world of matter, infested by these fleshy mortal creatures. This corporeal, mortal life is vile and disgusting. It's an infestation and must be exterminated. It was never meant to be!"

"Is that you talking, Kullos, or *IT*?" Cat challenged him.

"What!" both shadow warriors exclaimed at once.

"Yes, Daelen! *IT*!" Dreya shouted. "When I told you that he'd gone over to chaos rather than darkness, I didn't know how right I was!"

"That's why he went off the rails in the first place!" Mandalee told him.

"'Off the rails'?" Cat wondered, quietly, as an aside.

"Jessica expression," she whispered back.

Cat nodded.

"Is this true?" Daelen demanded of Kullos. "Did you surrender yourself to *IT*?"

"It was the only way to beat the Enemy!" Kullos insisted. "It still is! How else are we to defeat one of the Creator's elite warriors? You know I was an engineer. I tried everything, but there simply wasn't enough power in our entire realm to do anything more than beat her back. So, I had to think outside the box, outside the cosmos, beyond reality itself!"

*****

Kullos had thought that if the Enemy were unmade, there might even be a way to undo the terrible damage she had already inflicted on the shadow realm. In his lab, he had changed the focus of his research, working in secret, not to try and fight the Enemy, but to open up a small tear in the fabric of reality. Believe it or not, gentle reader, that was easier. Existence is more fragile than one might expect, considering it has the power to contain literally everything. He finally succeeded. It was a pinprick, no more, and Kullos had enough technical skill to block *IT* from actually entering except on his terms.

He made a deal – *IT* would give him the power to build a weapon capable of unmaking their Enemy, and in return, Kullos would do something for *IT*.

*****

"And what's that?" Daelen asked.

"Isn't it obvious?" Kullos replied. "Destroying this filthy, disgusting world and ending the stench of life that infests this whole mortal plane!"

"So, in answer to my question," Cat concluded, "it's *both* of you talking."

"You see, Daelen?" Mandalee called out. "Kullos and *IT* are of one mind – that can't be good!"

"Exactly!" Daelen agreed. "That's why I'm doing this – to destroy him and save your world! This is my Fate: to give my life for you!"

Cat rolled her eyes. "Oh, for pity's sake, Daelen, will you please give your ego a rest just for once?" she demanded, desperate to make him understand before it was too late. "You told me you're not a hero, so stop acting like one! This is not all about you, it's bigger than that! Let us in!" she screamed.

He continued to ignore her – she was just upset; she didn't know what she was saying.

"You need to listen to her, Daelen!" Dreya commanded, adding her voice to the chorus.

177

Mandalee tried to get through to the shadow warrior, saying, "She's already stopped both of us from making choices that would have ended the world. You have to let her stop you, too!"

Daelen did not respond. He'd said all he had to say. They didn't understand, but they would in time.

Turning to the other two Guardians, Cat threw her hands up in the air and growled. "Right, that's it. I've been ignored for the last time. There's no other choice. Agreed?"

"Agreed," they chorused.

"Stupid mortals!" Kullos roared. "He's not going to end the world! I am!"

Too late, they realised that while they'd been trying to get through to Daelen, Kullos had been building his power. By doing it slowly, carefully, he'd been able to power right up without anybody noticing. With a sudden burst of speed, he channelled that power at Daelen. It wasn't enough to kill him, but it stunned him enough to loosen his grip on the control device. In one move, Kullos had it in his possession.

"Thanks for the distraction, mortals – I couldn't have done it without you!"

*****

Catriona looked up from the *Chronicles* and raised her staff, ignoring the searing pain in her arm and called out, "Hear me! I am Catriona Redfletching: Red Guardian of Magic, Defender of Balance, Keeper of the Keys to Time, Bearer of the Chronicles of Magias. By the authority of the Great Ancient Archmage, I command you to stop!"

Her resounding voice seemed to fill the cosmos itself and made both Kullos and Daelen pause even before the Time magic began to take effect.

At her command, with the backing of her two companions, Time itself froze, not just around the battle scene, but everywhere within Daelen's containment field.

*****

This was how the Guardianship worked, gentle reader, how it still works: There are powers they can access individually, independently. Then there is a greater power that can be wielded through the co-operation of two. The only rule is that they must never be used against another Guardian, or the Guardianship shall be broken and can only be re-established under the terms that allowed their initial creation.

I am currently exploiting a loophole in that rule – Aunt Mandalee has not acted against the current Red and Black Guardians – I have. The White Guardian is just using her own independent powers, technically within the bounds of the *Chronicles*. I have Guardian-like abilities, but again, technically, I am not a Guardian, so I can act against those two, keep them locked in my bedroom, trapped in Time, and yet the Guardianship remains intact. Don't get me wrong, I'm breaking any number of laws, but I'm not breaking the letter of the law of the Guardianship.

Anyway, as I was saying, as you might have guessed, the ultimate power of the Guardians is something that can only be done with the agreement of all Three Guardians working together, which I continue to call the 'Power of Three' to wind them up. The Power of Three is exponentially greater than the Power of Two, but whether that could ever really stop me, I honestly don't know. In mock battles and simulations, they were powerful enough, but between you and me, gentle reader, I wasn't really trying. The whole idea is moot because I would never go against Aunt Mandalee. When I first told the Guardians my idea for an Illegal Time Intervention, if she had said 'no', that would have been an end to it. But in her view, it sounded too much like one of my mother's ridiculous radical plans for her to disagree. In my eyes – though not in the eyes of the law – the blessing of one of the Original Three counts more than the opposition of the other two.

Regardless, the Power of Three includes the power to Freeze Time and Manipulate Events within that Temporal Reference Field. (A technical term for move stuff about to their hearts' content.)

*****

"Was that speech strictly necessary?" Dreya asked.
"Well, maybe not necessary *as such*," Cat allowed.

"Flair for the dramatic, remember, Dreya?" Mandalee quipped.

"Of course."

"Listen, this isn't the time for jokes," Cat scolded them. "We have to join the battle whether Daelen likes it or not. We're the Guardians of Time and Magic; neither of them has the power to prevent us."

The barrier couldn't stop them either because it was not as constant as it appeared. It just flickered on and off so fast, you couldn't usually see it, but the Guardians could move Time along frame by frame until they found a nanosecond when there was a gap. Then they could cross the non-existent barrier.

"Quickly," Cat implored the others, "there isn't much time."

Mandalee spoke up to object to that. "Cat, if we've stopped time then surely there is no time, by which I mean time isn't an issue so we can take all the time we need…if you see what I mean." Damn, she wished she could explain these things better.

"Now you've both done four 'time's in one sentence," Dreya grumbled. "I'm having a go next!"

"It doesn't work like that, Mandalee." The druidess shook her head. "Look, I don't fully understand it yet myself; I'm acting mostly on instinct here, and I don't have time to explain. I just know we only get one shot at this and we have to act fast. And Dreya," she added, "I just told you this isn't the time for jokes."

Dreya, who seemed to have gone rather pale, shrugged. "It's the end of the world. This is the only time I've got."

"No," Cat disputed, frowning, "it's not the end of the world because we're going to stop it!"

"That's the thing," the sorceress replied. "I think it's a bit late for that: look."

Cat and Mandalee followed her pointed finger, and Mandalee gasped, "Dear gods! Is that what I think it is?"

"I believe so," Dreya replied.

What she had seen was that Kullos now had both hands full. One hand was holding his control device, while the other held something else, some other technology. None of them could positively identify the device, but within the Frozen Time field, it had flashed. Since it was pretty unlikely that Kullos had chosen this moment to take a selfie, they had to assume it was Heaven's

Surrender. Daelen, too, in the few seconds it had taken them to completely stop Time, had already begun to form a new energy barrier that must surely be the Wish. The fact that they were frozen in the moment after activation changed nothing: they had still been activated, and nothing could change that.

"Can't we go back a few seconds? Try again?" Mandalee asked.

Dreya went further, suggesting, "We should leave them like that for eternity. Just keep Time stopped in a bubble here. Think of it: two powerful renegades contained forever; threat ended. Why risk tampering with the situation?"

"I wish it were that simple, Dreya, I really do. But apart from anything else, I don't have the knowledge to achieve that. Time has stopped inside the bubble, but it hasn't for the rest of the universe, and the imbalance can't be maintained for long. Perhaps one day the magic you suggest may be possible, but here and now we have to act with what little we have and pray to any gods who will listen that it's enough. As for going back in Time and trying again, Mandalee, don't you think our counterparts would have done that if it were possible? I know I have ridiculous radical plans, but even I would try 'go back and change it' before 'let's make a whole new world'!"

"So, what can we do?" Mandalee pleaded.

"Don't worry," Cat grinned, "I have a ridiculous radical plan!"

"Oh, well that's alright, then," Dreya breathed, sounding much relieved.

"Absolutely!" Mandalee agreed, looking equally reassured. To Dreya, she remarked, "For a moment there, I was worried she might want to do something completely sensible."

Dreya's eyes widened in horror at the thought. "Then we'd really be in trouble!"

Chapter 24

Ignoring them, Cat briefly outlined her plan to her friends and to their counterparts on the other side of the Rift. This was going to rely on more co-operation. Cat hated to ask more of them, but Alt-Cat was dismissive.

"Our world is already lost. Trust me, you can't make things worse over here. Whatever we have left is yours."

The Guardians prepared to cast the magic and release the two combatants, but Mandalee wondered, "Can we really use this magic within the rules of the Council? Is it legal? Is it right…for any of us?"

"Frankly, Mandalee, I don't care," Cat insisted. "The rules were never designed with this in mind."

"Besides," Dreya put in, "there won't *be* a Council or anything else if we don't."

The Guardians stopped trying to apply their Time magic to the whole area, and just focussed in on the Heaven's Surrender and Wish barrier powers. They couldn't halt the detonation and still do what they needed to do, but it was slowed to an almost imperceptible crawl.

"You're too late!" Kullos laughed. "Slow it down all you want; it will just prolong your suffering! Your power won't be enough to stop my weapon, Daelen!"

As a trio, the Guardians chorused, "No, but ours will be!"

Dreya and Mandalee instantly went into battle, while Cat stepped up next to Daelen. "I told you I wouldn't let you do this alone."

"How did you break the power seals?" Daelen demanded.

"How many times, Daelen? Power isn't everything. There's always a way around it."

With the rush of exhilaration at what they were doing, she momentarily forgot her injuries, until a careless movement jarred her, painfully, making her wince.

"You're hurt," Daelen observed.

"Small accident, ruffled feathers, looks worse than it is," she lied.

Daelen, on the other hand, had almost drained himself fighting Kullos, yet he suddenly felt reinvigorated.

Catriona caught his gaze, and with a wink and a smirk, answered his unspoken question. "OK, maybe I sort of 'misplaced' a bit of Heaven's Surrender energy and used it, as you would say, to recharge your batteries."

"Is that in the rules?" the shadow warrior wondered.

Cat shrugged, innocently. "How should I know? I'm new at this Guardian thing, remember! Now, could you please help the others keep Kullos occupied? I'm busy saving the world."

Daelen moved away, launching wave after wave of attacks, visibly driving Kullos back. Even though his enemy was able to deflect many of his attacks, enough to avoid severe damage, the sheer ferocity and relentlessness began to wear Kullos down, especially with help from the other two. In many ways, it was just like the old days, except with two Guardians taking the place of Michael. Working together like this, Daelen realised something that had never occurred to him before: they were going to win this fight.

Dreya's magical flames seared into her enemy's side where he was already hurt and bleeding from Daelen's onslaught. She swiftly backed that up with multiple lightning bolts and poisoned darts coated with the best magical copy of Pyrah's venom that Catriona could create. Her magic didn't match Daelen's power, but she was highly skilled in anticipating and countering Kullos' deflections, even spinning her smart fireballs, so they hit in just the right spot. Her dark beam cannon really caught Kullos by surprise.

Mandalee caused a Flame Hammer to appear in her hand, still instinctively going for physical attacks, even when using magic. The opposing attacks from Dark wizard magic and the power of a cleric of Light seemed to cause a surprising amount of pain to Kullos, so she unsheathed her Pureblade with her left hand. It had been blessed and sanctified by clerics of Light and gifted to her more than two years ago when she saved some clerics from a powerful demon attack. It recognised her alignment to the Light and magically adjusted its weight and balance to suit the assassin. Kullos still continued to largely ignore her, though, considering her the lesser threat. Mandalee found that rather insulting.

"Time was when people took the threat of the White Assassin seriously!" she grumbled.

"I know how you feel," Dreya agreed. "He's pretty much ignoring me, too. It's highly offensive."

"Maybe we could make him change his mind," Mandalee suggested, then she used their sympathic link to convey her plan to the Dark sorceress, verbally adding, "Daelen told Cat that shadow warriors are like light in a box. Aren't you curious to see what that looks like?"

Dreya gave her a dark smile, and agreed, "Let's slice one open and find out."

The assassin dispelled her Flame Hammer, shifted her Pureblade to her right hand and flicked her dragonclaw dagger into her left. She stuck both weapons in Kullos' most serious wound and parted the flesh like she was carving a roasted duck. The oversize Kullos continued to ignore them. They were insects, parasites, nothing more. Dreya stepped up and focused a beam cannon blast deeper and deeper until it struck something akin to a nerve, sending Kullos into a kind of spasm. That proved highly dangerous as his power shot off in all directions at random. Mandalee ended up knocking Dreya bodily to the ground to get them both out of danger. She cursed at leaving one of her best weapons still embedded in his flesh, but she supposed she would just have to go and retrieve it later. Right at that moment, though, it was too dangerous to even attempt to get up. Still, they had done what they set out to do: Kullos had dropped his control device.

Daelen stepped up his power levels still further to cover them, drawing on reserves even he never knew he possessed.

Meanwhile, Cat was working new magic with the help of the *Chronicles* and her otherworld counterpart, acting with the full agreement of Mandalee and Dreya who loved her and trusted her enough to let her do whatever she thought was right. They didn't need to know all the details.

*****

It was all thanks to her Angel.

All those years ago, she had been given a clue that she only now understood. Her Angel had warned her not to tamper with that energy, 'Except in the event of some dire emergency of worldwide, cataclysmic proportions.'

184

Well, this undoubtedly qualified, but the problem was she'd had to draw power from the staff already. It had been necessary to create the Guardians' new base of operations from her Meadow, and there wasn't enough left to do what she needed to do now.

But what about the last part of her Angel's message: 'Even then, think twice'? After so many years, Cat finally realised she had been punctuating it wrong in her head.

What her Angel had really said was, "Even then, think: Twice."

Twice. Catriona could use the staff twice because there were two of them: hers and the one her counterpart had given her. Having the latter meant she had enough power on her side, but what about the other side? Cat could send her Crystal Mage Staff through the Rift in exchange, but where were they going to get power from to recharge it quickly? They were consuming the last of their Heaven's Surrender blast just to keep the Rift open, and their Tempestria was being unmade. But there was one other source of power.

When their counterparts became Guardians, they had created their own base of operations, their own Catriona's Meadow, using power from Alt-Cat's staff. Equally, then, they could do the reverse: if they collapsed part of it, that would recharge the staff enough for what they needed. Their Catriona's Meadow had been designed to be the Guardians' home. As such, it was a recreation of Daelen's entire grounds on StormClaw, about twenty-five square miles. Far larger than the one Cat had grown in Daelen's garden on Earth.

But this action meant that the last refuge of the people who were selflessly saving her world, would jettison all that extra space. According to Catriona's rough calculations, it would leave an area less than two hundred yards in any direction from the oak tree in the centre. That would be their whole world forever. Their prison.

They couldn't travel to another world because the world on which they were born would never have existed. Logically, if Tempestria never existed, the Guardians could not possibly exist, either. Only within their Timeless bubble of reality, their Catriona's Meadow, could that contradiction be nullified.

The worst thing was, Cat knew it was her fault. If only she'd been quicker, or if only she'd thought to take Time incrementally backwards instead of forwards to get through Daelen's power seals, then she could have stopped Kullos *before* he used Heaven's

Surrender. But even after all the clues, all the Time Interventions, everything her counterpart had done to help things along, Cat had still managed to be a fraction too late. She wouldn't have blamed the other world's Guardians for cutting their losses, but somehow, they were still determined to help.

"We're as one in this," Alt-Cat had assured her. "Don't blame yourself. You did everything you could, and really the cost isn't that high: a larger prison would still have been a prison. Tolerable for a while longer, perhaps, but not forever. We would always have chosen death after a while, and maybe you've brought that time closer than it would have been, but with our world unmade and gone forever, maybe that's a mercy. As one Faery to another, with the backing of my only two friends in existence, I give to you, freely, that which is precious. Execute the plan."

Cat wished her counterpart hadn't phrased it quite that way. She couldn't help thinking that was exactly what she was doing: executing them. Executing three innocent people. Heroes.

Still, there was nothing else for it. She had their consent and no other choice.

She threw her staff through the Rift so the other Guardians could charge it up. Everything had to be ready before they could finally act. After a few moments, it was done. She just needed Mandalee and Dreya to finish their job.

Using her super-speed, when Kullos was back under control of himself and still focussing on Daelen, the assassin quickly pulled her Pureblade from Kullos' side and returned to Dreya.

The sorceress called out to her girlfriend, "Can I borrow one of the flowers I gave you, please? I think this calls for fresh blood magic!"

The sorceress had left her dagger where she threw it in Kullos' fortress. There hadn't been time to waste trying to find it. Besides, the roses were infused with clerical and druid magic, too, which could make all the difference.

Cat reached into her pocket dimension and pulled a red rose out of the vase, tossing it to Dreya who caught it with a simple grace that Cat quietly envied.

Mandalee winced as Dreya embedded a thorn in her left index finger, although the sorceress herself gave no outward sign of discomfort.

Returning the rose, the Black Guardian channelled her magic through her blood and built up her power, adding as much higher planar energy into the mix as she could. Then she fired it at the control device, which Mandalee held firmly in her right hand. Dreya's control and precision, as well as Mandalee's weapon mastery and trust in her best friend's lover, were tested to the limit. Dreya had to take great care not to blow Mandalee's hand off, and Mandalee had to keep her right hand absolutely still even as she channelled all of her cleric powers from the Light end of the magical spectrum, from Shyleen, into her Pureblade in her left hand, swinging it around to strike the control device. Neither of them could afford to even flinch as both the control device and Pureblade shattered. Shards and fragments of metal flying in all directions.

Both women were left utterly exhausted.

"No!" Kullos roared.

Realising what they'd done, he tried to scramble for the fragments, but Cat smashed a bottle of water and grew an ice wall in his path. There was no escape for him now – without the control device, he couldn't Ascend, and if he opened a portal, he knew the Guardians would no longer hold back Time, and the Heaven's Surrender blast would catch up with him before he got anywhere. If he tried to kill the mortals, Time would definitely return to normal, and again the blast would consume him in an instant.

To Daelen, he ranted, "If I can't get away, then neither can you!"

Daelen never had any such intention, but he knew it was useless to tell Kullos that.

In an act of spite, Kullos used his powers to open half a dozen portals and move the fragments with his mind so they each flew through one of them before they closed.

Dreya immediately began analysing the residual magic, trying to determine where and when the fragments went. She could quickly tell some of the portals had temporal signatures and others went to worlds beyond Tempestria. It wasn't going to be easy to get accurate readings this close to the Rift, with so much Temporal magic flying around, but she would do her best. They would have to be found. The power in each fragment would be incredible and, worse, unstable, given the forces involved. There was no telling what might happen if people got their hands on even one.

"Cat! Notebook!" Dreya called over.

The sorceress had an excellent memory, but as always, she knew her limits. Cat threw it over to her, and Dreya began scribbling notes and rough calculations. She ended up with six sets of co-ordinates that should create sympathic impressions of the portals' destinations, but they would have to deal with that later. Right now, they were busy.

Now that Kullos was trapped, Cat and her counterpart could work together.

"Goodbye!" Cat called through the Rift.

There wasn't time for more – the energy was almost used up. The Rift could close any minute. Her counterpart had assured her that her two friends had a portal to their version of Catriona's Meadow – what was left of it – open and ready. The only place they could go where *IT* could not follow. As soon as Alt-Cat had played her part, she would have to use that portal to escape the blast that was coming her way.

On this side of the Rift, as the others watched the space around them, the ruins of Daelen's base within the containment field seemed to disappear and then reappear an instant later. It was as if they had all blinked at the same time. Everything was still as it was, except for two crucial details: the blast of Heaven's Surrender and Daelen's Wish barrier were gone.

Kullos noticed immediately. "That's impossible!"

"Not for us," Cat countered, breathing hard. "We've just done a little swap with some friends."

*****

Thanks to the containment field, they had been able to move the entire affected space through the Rift and swap it for the equivalent area on the other side, without touching anything beyond its boundaries. It was, in essence, the same magic they'd used to move Catriona's Meadow into its own private layer in the Cosmic Sandwich. It was just a question of scale. But if the Power of Three is exponentially more powerful than the Power of Two, gentle reader, you can imagine what the Power of Six was like.

On the original Tempestria, Heaven's Surrender had been detonated *outside* the containment field. Inside, thanks to the

Guardians' efforts, it was unaffected. On our Tempestria, it was the other way around. Since it was a simple like-for-like swap, there was no Creation magic involved, just as swapping staves was no problem. No rules were violated. At least, not cosmic ones.

*****

Catriona just hoped the other Guardians had made it to safety in time. She supposed she would never know.

"See, Daelen? I told you!" Cat remarked, cheekily, trying to distract herself from her own thoughts. "I said you didn't need to sacrifice yourself!" Sympathically, she sent, '*Kullos. Rift. Now.*' Hoping he would understand she meant him to knock Kullos into the Rift itself. It would send him to the other side, where the Guardians' Time magic was still keeping the new Heaven's Surrender power at bay. Once he was on the other side, she would cancel the Time magic entirely. The blast would destroy Kullos, and the Wish barrier would protect the Rift just in case it didn't quite close quickly enough.

"I guess you were right all along. Power really isn't everything." Daelen admitted as he grappled with his nemesis, pushing him ever closer to the Rift.

"You're finished, Kullos," he told him, "We've had our Final Battle, and you've lost! Give it up!"

But Kullos seemed to make up his mind about something and with a voice that was not his own, he replied, "Arrogant shadow warrior! This was never about you, or this world – those were only ever bonus prizes." Cat recognised the voice from when she unlocked the *Chronicles*, as the voice of *IT*. "The real target is defenceless before *IT*. Through her, *IT* might be banished forever, but now that will never happen. The Abomination shall never come to be, and *IT* will finally extinguish all of Creation!"

Pulling free from Daelen for an instant, Kullos used the last of his power to fire one final cannon blast at Catriona.

Time seemed to slow down for her, but it was only perception, not magic. She didn't have the necessary skill to weave Guardian magic in two worlds at once. Still, she had dealt with beam cannon blasts before. This was no different. After all, even before she became a Guardian, her magic already had a temporal element. All she needed was her sand.

With horror, though, just when she had committed herself, she realised she had none. The pouch in which she carried it must have ripped open when she crash-landed in Kullos' throne room. That meant no Nature's Mirror and no defence. If only she hadn't recklessly, futilely dived at Daelen's portal, perhaps she could have shapeshifted her way out of it, but her injuries made that impossible. There hadn't been time to heal, and due to the increased swelling and inflammation, she could barely move at all, now. Her friends couldn't help her, there was simply no time...no time to do anything...except die.

But Daelen had other ideas. Thinking nothing for himself, he opened himself up. This body wasn't really him. He wasn't human, not even remotely. He was light in a box and light could travel very fast. Ripping open his mortal body, he also had access to extra dimensions where Time moved differently. He gave every last bit of himself over to this one action – envelop and absorb the cannon blast, allowing it to do irreparable internal damage. Ignoring the searing agony, he took every last drop of power and used it to thrust himself forward, catapulting Kullos through the Rift. Cat cancelled all her Time magic and closed the Rift as fast as she could.

Before it closed completely, there seemed to be a further surge of energy that she couldn't identify. Cat worried it might be a small portion of the Heaven's Surrender blast, but a quick scan indicated no trace of *IT*. Their world was safe, even if Daelen was not. He somehow managed to pour his essence back into his mortal body, but the damage was done. Neither Cat nor Mandalee knew the first thing about healing a shadow warrior in that condition. There was nothing they could do.

Chapter 25

Catriona was in constant pain by now but put a mask on it for Daelen's benefit.

Mandalee had taken some pretty severe physical damage, including bruised ribs that hurt with every breath. She was still worried her right arm might just break off when she eventually removed her combat suit, but she dreaded to imagine how much worse things might have been without its protection.

Much of Dreya's battle damage was mental exhaustion and energy drain, but she also sported the beginnings of a black eye. When Mandalee had thrown them both to the ground as Kullos went wild, her face had had an unfortunate encounter with the hilt of one of her friend's many weapons. Still, better the hilt than the blade and certainly better than being blasted by Kullos' uncontrolled power. Also, a few flashes of magic had penetrated her shields, leading to burns on her body, and her leg was still terribly mangled from the hellhound. Of the four, only Mandalee was still on her feet.

"You guys look like hell," Daelen snarked from where he lay in a crumpled heap.

"Whereas you're in the peak of health, of course," Mandalee shot back, acidly.

His power and his life fading, he had reverted to his regular size. Despite his best efforts, blood and light were still leaking from his failing body. Still, he smiled as best he could.

"Seriously, you were amazing, all of you. I don't have the first clue what happened, but you were amazing."

Cat and Mandalee accepted his praise, graciously, but Dreya's response was to rub her injured leg unconsciously and reply with a rude noise.

"You do realise that I ended up losing the chance of absorbing power from Kullos' death knights through running after you," she complained. "And then you killed Kullos too fast for me to get any from him. People are going to start saying I did this out of the kindness of my own heart, from love or some such nonsense. I dread to think what that will do to my reputation."

"Drain mine," Daelen encouraged her. "Whatever power I have left, drain it from me – I don't need it anymore."

191

Dreya brightened at that, realising, "Then people will say 'Dreya the Dark descended on Daelen StormTiger like a vulture while he was dying and defenceless after he'd saved the world.' Yes, I like the sound of that."

She paused for a long moment as if considering, before giving her answer. "Very well, I accept."

She knelt beside him, placed her hand on his arm and began her power drain. By the time Dreya ceased, having absorbed her fill, his light had faded considerably.

"Now that you've done that, Dreya, are you up to opening another portal?" Cat asked her girlfriend.

It was going to be a tricky one – a portal to Kullos' fortress, in the exact same place as the one they used to get out, five minutes after they left. They had promised Sara and Jessica, after all, and it was only right that they should get to say their goodbyes to Daelen. Cat regretted there was no practical way to get to Michael. He'd known the shadow warrior longer than anyone.

Her plan wasn't entirely altruistic, of course – they needed help and medical attention. The logical place for that was Daelen's facility on Earth, assuming it was intact, and the only people who knew how to use that medical technology were the two Chetsuans.

"After we've healed up, we can go back to the battle a few minutes after we left and wrap things up there."

"Is all this Time manipulation in the rules?" the White Guardian wondered. "I've only just got my Council membership – I don't want it revoked."

Cat shrugged and instantly regretted it. "Why does everyone always expect me to know the rules? I've only been a Guardian as long as you have, I have no idea what the rules are, and frankly, I don't care. We have to help our friends and allies, you need to be reunited with Shyleen, and we're of no use to anyone in our current state. So, if we're breaking some rules, then the rules are wrong, not us."

Turning back to Dreya, she prompted, "So, can you do it?"

"You don't ask for much, do you?" Dreya grumbled. "Draining power doesn't mean I'm ready for mental gymnastics. Not only do I have to remember the exact spatial co-ordinates, but I also have to factor in our going back in Time and then add the time we've spent here, all without having an actual timepiece on me. Plus,

I have to do this after fighting the battle of my life, my mind in a million pieces and I have to make damn sure I don't make a mistake and arrive before we left, or I blow a hole in reality."

"You only tell us how complicated it is because you think we'll go 'wow' when you do it anyway."

"Besides," Mandalee put in, taking the opportunity to wind up the sorceress, "you're the Greatest Mage Who Ever Lived. You took the Black Tower in five minutes – this is peanuts to that."

Dreya sighed and shook her head. "You're going to be a thorn in my side the whole time we're Guardians, aren't you?"

Mandalee grinned. "Yep."

"So, how about it?" Cat asked her girlfriend, once more. "Will you do this for me?"

Six words.

Six words, spoken by the woman she loved. Six words that Dreya knew could only ever have one answer.

"Of course, I will, Cat," she replied. Then, turning to Mandalee, she added, "but the least you can do is help me."

"How? The most maths I do is deduction: If I start with fifty-seven enemies and I've killed thirty-two in five minutes, how long do I still need to keep fighting before I can go and have a drink? I certainly don't know anything about temporal-spatial co-ordinates."

"Maybe," Dreya allowed, "but you still have one advantage over Cat and me right now."

"And what's that?"

"You can stand up."

"Good point," she conceded, helping Dreya to her feet.

A moment later, a portal opened, and they could see the two Chetsuan girls fighting like a pair of wildcats, cutting down enemies as they came at them. They'd moved a bit from where the Guardians had left them, a few yards further down the narrow corridor before it opened up into Kullos' throne room. Using that chokepoint made enemy numbers irrelevant, and the sisters couldn't be outflanked. They'd tried using their telepathy, but there were too many. It would only take one to fake being under their control and they'd be dead.

Mandalee called to them through the open portal and with a final frenzied attack, forcing their enemies back a step, they ran like their tails were on fire to dive through to the other side.

A couple of enemy guards that were trying desperately to make it to the portal, each sprouted an arrow in their chests. As the portal closed, Mandalee looked for where the arrows had come from and saw Cat in tears. She had seen the danger, and with a supreme effort stood and fired her arrows with deadly accuracy, despite the cost to her body. Her bow clattered to the ground, swiftly followed by the girl herself. Her friends weren't sure if her tears were from agony or grief. The truth was both: standing and using her bow was more than her body could take. Her arm was now completely useless, the pain almost unbearable, and Daelen was fading fast.

"It's a shame you can't shapeshift at the moment," he croaked. "I would have quite liked to see that white rabbit one more time. It's OK, I don't expect miracles to happen just because I'm dying."

"You're right," she accepted, trying to smile. "I don't have that power right now, but you know what I always say about that?"

"Power isn't everything."

"Exactly. There's always a way around it, and miracles can happen if people make them happen." That's when she asked everyone to take their shoes off and give them to her. "And could somebody please help me with mine?"

Nobody questioned the random request. They just complied. Turning all the shoes upside down, sand fell out onto the ground – they had been fighting in a desert, after all. With her uninjured hand, Cat sprinkled the sand in the air and worked her magic, asking nature to please create a Mirror Image copy. One that was free from injuries.

When her duplicate appeared, she immediately changed into a white rabbit and hopped into comfortable stroking range for Daelen.

"Genius as ever, Cat," the shadow warrior declared, proudly. "Who else would have thought of that?"

Cat blushed but chose not to comment.

"But I was right all along, wasn't I? I had to sacrifice myself for you, after all."

"And in doing so, you made yourself what you always claimed you're not: a hero," Cat pointed out.

"If it helps," Mandalee volunteered, "I can tell everyone how insensitive, arrogant and egotistical you were when we first met."

"Yeah," Sara chimed in, "and we can say how you took a couple of alien girls away from their home and made them slave away for you, day after day."

"A proper Cinderella deal, it was," Jessica agreed. "Only without a ball or a prince."

"At least Sara got an elf boy to snog," Daelen pointed out.

"Yeah," Sara smiled through her tears, "but I still had to run away before midnight."

"Aww, rubbish!" her sister disputed. "We were at the afterparty for hours."

Sara rolled her eyes. "It was a figure of speech!"

The shadow warrior laughed, even though blood was now starting to fill his mouth.

"I'm glad you chose this world," he approved. "They'll look after you here."

"Of course we will," Dreya agreed. "There's space in my Tower until they get on their feet."

"An act of kindness from a Black robe?" Mandalee wondered, facetiously, knowing how her friend would react.

"Why do people always accuse me of that?" Dreya protested with an annoyed frown. "They're going to be looking after us for a while, first. I'm just paying my debts."

Daelen beckoned Catriona close, his voice fading, asking for one last thing.

Cat nodded and sang:[1]

Angels among us, stars in the night,
Watch o'er your sleep, shining so bright,
Safe in their light, as you close your eyes,
Love will surround you, 'til morning you rise.

Angels among us, shed you no tears,
Bright Angels guard you, quiet your fears,
Nature's embrace, is gentle and strong,
Love will surround you, all your life long.

---

[1] Fits to the tune of Rockabye Baby.

Her voice cracked on the last line. Daelen's life had indeed been long, but it was now over.

His final whispered words were, "I love you, my beautiful Cat."

"I love you, too," she whispered in return.

She knew Dreya would understand, under the circumstances.

*****

It took more than a week, Earth time, for the Three Guardians to feel well enough to prepare for their return. Dreya and Mandalee had been up and about first – the Cleric of Nature was happy to find her shopping bags full of Earth clothes where she'd left them. She managed to get through several new outfits in the last few days, and even Dreya felt comfortable enough around her friends to wear her little black velvet dress, making no attempt to cover her winglets.

Mandalee hadn't known about them until that moment, but she of all people wasn't going to judge someone else's body.

"That dress couldn't look more perfect on you," she told her.

She had bought it for Catriona, but now she couldn't imagine what she'd been thinking. It was in no way Cat's style, but she couldn't have found anything closer to Dreya's if she'd deliberately searched that entire shopping mall.

As if sensing something of her thoughts – which given their Guardian enhanced sympathic link was entirely possible – Dreya asked, "Did you know about us?"

She didn't think a magically backed promise would stop someone from guessing the truth if they'd already seen them together.

"Not consciously," Mandalee answered. "Maybe it flashed across my mind, but I just dismissed the possibility. To be honest, I don't think I would have understood if she had been able to tell me. I had too many preconceptions about you, Dreya, and I'm sorry about that. I really should know better."

Dreya dismissed that with a wave of her hand. "No apology necessary. I work hard to cultivate a certain reputation, so I can hardly blame you for believing it. You're a good friend to Cat, Mandalee, and…well…" she trailed off.

Mandalee understood it wasn't easy for Dreya to open up like this, so she let her have the time and space she needed, not pressing her to continue before she was ready.

At last, she did. "…I could do with a friend like that. I mean, I know we're going to be working together, and we're already sort of friends through Cat, but I'd like us to have something a little more…direct. Am I making any sense?"

Mandalee laughed, "I wonder about that all the time, so you're probably asking the wrong person. But seriously, Dreya, we're already something 'a little more direct'. You're my friend."

"Better than I could have hoped for," Dreya replied, embracing her. Breaking the hug, she held up a warning finger. "But if you dare tell anyone about this touching moment, I will have to kill you."

Mandalee knew the threat wasn't real, but she was nevertheless sincere, as she replied, "My lips are sealed."

*****

It was another couple of days before Catriona, with her more extensive injuries, was able to join them for long periods. To help pass the time, Jessica and Sara had introduced them to video games. They quickly agreed on a favourite, and in a reversal of their usual roles, Mandalee played a wizard while Dreya chose a demon hunter with a multitude of weapons.

It made them both laugh as Dreya kept saying, "Magic doesn't work like that!" and Mandalee came back with, "What about those ridiculous fighting moves? How are they even supposed to be possible?"

Solar panels and a generator had kept the lights on in the place, but with all the higher planar energy Daelen had taken, the portal room was now portal-less.

While Jessica had been in charge of medical care, Sara had put her tech skills to good use, editing the video Dreya had taken of Kullos' defeat, and putting it into a format that could be read by a device she'd picked up from Lavos, the world where people hunted dragons, rather than the other way around. It was a holographic projector, which could display the video in midair. Cat thought it was the technological equivalent of the magic the other Guardians had used. It should create quite a stir on the battlefield.

None of them was in top shape when they left, but any longer would have felt like an indulgence. They vowed to return, however. After all, even Guardians were surely entitled to holidays.

Cat opened the first portal to StormClaw on Tempestria, but she left the temporal portal to Dreya. She would learn that for herself later. Right now, Dreya had more experience, and they couldn't afford a mistake.

Despite the guards, they still agreed Kullos' fortress was the best place to start. There was no point in complicating things any further for the sorceress, and at least they knew what to expect. Even though it would only be ten to fifteen minutes, relatively speaking, since they left the battlefield, anything could have happened in that time.

The guards in the fortress were still there, but this time, they were faced with five intruders instead of two. With their varying strengths and powers, they quickly overwhelmed the guards and headed back the way they had come. Along the way, they passed by the remains of the now dormant hellhounds and Dreya retrieved her lost dagger. At last, they were outside, once more, where the battle raged on.

Running up high on one of Cat's Rainbow Roads, Sara activated the projector, so all could see how Kullos had not only failed but also completely lied about any promises he might have made to get people on his side. He'd just told them whatever they wanted to hear so that they would fight and die for him, while he got on with destroying the world.

For good measure, Dreya used her magic to project her voice. "Now, are you going to surrender or do I bring back the dragons?"

Within five minutes, almost all the mortal enemy forces had surrendered. The last few pockets of resistance were soon mopped up. Supernatural creatures were banished by the Council mages. Demons were encouraged to either Descend to the lower planes or face the army alone. All but a few chose the former.

The battle over, Catriona declared the Guardians were done, too. The clean-up, the aftermath, the pursuit of justice to separate those who were complicit from those who were forced – none of that had anything to do with them.

Dreya called the Triumvirate together – Justaria had been reinstated on the battlefield – and briefed them on the Guardianship. In time, the Guardians would have to be ratified by the Council, but that could wait.

Mandalee was reunited with Shyleen, who, Windell told her, had been looking after him.

Cat found Michael and broke the news of Daelen's death, apologising for being unable to let him be present at his side before he passed.

The demigod understood. He confided that he knew he had died because a particular block had removed itself from his mind, which could mean only one thing.

"Don't worry, I promise I will speak of it to no-one," he vowed. "I will take it to my grave – my permanent one, that is," he clarified. "It seems I have no further need of the one I've been using most of my life."

"Speaking of which," Cat put in, "we need to access your tomb, to keep Daelen's body secure, but first, we need to borrow you and your technology for another purpose."

"My technology and I are at your disposal. What are you planning?"

Before answering, she called her fellow Guardians over.

"Mandalee, I think it's time I came good on a very long-standing promise, don't you?"

Her friend smiled, excitedly. "I'm ready."

"Dreya, I'm relying on you, too."

"Always," she affirmed.

"Now, I know this is a deeply private thing for you, Mandalee, and you will have to be naked, so I'm keeping it to essential personnel only. Are you OK with that?"

Mandalee agreed. If it got her out of the body she hated, she could put up with just about anything for a short while.

Chapter 26

The four companions used a portal directly to Elvaria, rather than bother with another lengthy sea voyage. Justaria had agreed to return the chartered *Dolphin* ship back to Kingsville harbour and collect her horse from the stables there before going to do something about the damage to her home. Cat had promised to help with repairs when she was free.

As they entered the crypt, there on the northernmost tip of the Elvarian Peninsula, Dreya and Mandalee were suitably awed by the interior of Michael's Tomb, which would soon become Daelen's Tomb, instead. Catriona felt a little guilty about leaving her late friend's body more-or-less where he fell for so long. From a purely Tempestrian point of view, it had only been a couple of days, but with all the Time manipulation and the different time flow rate on Earth, it had been a lot longer for her. Still, from a practical point of view, she stood by her decision to focus on the living first.

As the druidess looked around at her surroundings, she was no less impressed than the others, just because it was her second visit.

Michael paused for a moment at the foot of the stairs.

"What's wrong?" Cat asked him.

"Oh, nothing, my dear, nothing," he assured her, patting her hand, affectionately. "It just occurred to me that I've never actually walked in the front door like this before. Every other time, I've been dead, carried in Daelen's arms. Next time, I will be carrying Daelen," he added, sadly. "You seem to have turned the world upside down, young lady, and I think that's a good thing, despite the cost."

Cat put a sympathetic arm around him – or at least as far as she could reach, given his generous frame – as they climbed the steps towards 'The Tower of Dreams'. She supposed the lower chamber, 'The Wishing Well', was now empty, but she had more restraint than to look, lest she trigger some additional security.

At last, they reached the top and entered through the door into the chamber that contained the Regeneration Casket and related technology.

Once inside, Michael did a 'thorough diagnostic on all systems' to make sure everything was working right. As soon as he confirmed all was well, Catriona once again gently reminded Mandalee that this did require her to be naked.

As she undressed, Michael turned his back to focus on the information on the screens, promising he would not look any more than was necessary. Mandalee would have been lying if she claimed she wasn't a bit nervous and uncomfortable, but if her friend told her this was essential to what they were trying to do for her, then she would swallow all that.

*****

At this point, gentle reader, I feel compelled to clarify something: I am not a voyeur.

As I gaze through Time, some things I can see clearly, while other things are hazy, depending on privacy settings as agreed under Council rules. Then there are moments like this, which are protected with 'Category 1 Content Filters'. That means time travellers can't see anything at all. In effect, it's like someone has turned off the screen, and all you're left with is the audio. Now, in this case, this is my Aunt Mandalee I'm talking about – we're family, and as such we've talked about her gender reassignment many times. Between her and Dreya, I understand the technicalities of how my mother achieved this for her friend, sealing forever what I've previously described as their 'friendship for the ages'.

That is how I can write this next scene – it's a reconstruction of events, rather than observation in the strictest sense.

*****

The first step was to create a Mirror Image copy of Mandalee's body. This was just a facsimile of her body, not her mind, and certainly not in any sense sapient.

Next, all three Guardians used their combined Temporal powers to gaze through Time, along Mandalee's own Timeline. Not specific events, but just a sympatic impression, the concept of her body's development, back through childhood, a baby, a foetus. Here, knowledge from Earth helped them enormously as, through their science and technology, they had a better understanding of that process than Tempestrians yet knew. Through that knowledge, they knew there was a moment when a kind of trigger signal was sent, which led to instructions for development along the biological male line. It was like a general giving an order to his second, to be passed all the way through the command chain. To stop it, all they needed to do was stop the original order, then the army would do nothing. Together, they could conceptualise that moment. Of course, this was all within nature's domain, so all Cat had to do with her druid magic was ask nature not to send that signal, don't give that order. Then development would continue according to the default female settings. It was a tiny change, far too small to be seen, but it could have a profound effect on Mandalee's Timeline. It could change practically every experience her friend had ever had.

Except, in this case, it could do no such thing, because they were only applying the changes to a Mirror Image copy.

The copy's body changed in front of their eyes until it was unquestionably biologically female. The changes to the face were subtle, so it was still recognisable as Mandalee.

It was as if the White Guardian were looking at the almost-identical twin sister she never really had. Or, to put it another way, it was the exact image of how she saw herself when mirrors weren't lying to her.

"I've done it this way partly for safety," Cat told her, "and partly so that you can see the end result before you commit to anything. This isn't about cosmetic changes, Mandalee, it's about bringing out the real you. I need to know you're going to be happy with this version of yourself. Nothing more will be done until you're sure this is what you want."

In truth, the moisture in her best friend's eyes spoke volumes, but she needed absolute verbal confirmation of consent before she would take one more step.

"This is what I've wanted my whole life. It's like I've always had this image of myself and now, for the first time, others can see it, too. What's next?"

The next step was the very first idea she'd ever had about this: shapeshifting. She'd never shapeshifted another real person before, but she knew she could do it. The only reason she hadn't done this for Mandalee previously was that she couldn't make it last for more than a few hours, and it had seemed cruel to give her what she wanted so badly, only to snatch it away again. This time, the temporary nature of this magic was the whole point: It would give Mandalee a chance to feel the changes as well as see them. The opportunity to get to know what it would be like to have that body as her own.

"I have to warn you," she cautioned, "this is going to hurt. A lot."

"I've been hurting all my life, Cat. Every time I see myself, I hurt. This will end that forever, so this pain is a price I'm happy to pay."

"Alright, just try to stay calm through this, breathe normally, and relax. Ready?"

Mandalee nodded, and Catriona began shaping her body to match that of the copy. The assassin felt like she was on fire. The only times the White Assassin had felt pain like this were when Shyleen was almost fatally wounded. Now, as then, she had to put that aside, focus on her training and not allow herself to panic. She shut her eyes against it, reassuring herself that everything was fine. The changes only took a moment, but it felt like hours before the pain faded. She'd known for years that her friend experienced pain when she shapeshifted, but she'd had no idea it was that bad. Yet she did it so freely. Her friend was truly indomitable.

Mandalee opened her eyes when Cat gently touched her arm.

"I'm done," she announced, unnecessarily, as the assassin could feel the changes.

"Anyone got a mirror?" Mandalee requested, realising that was the first time in her life she'd ever asked that.

"Allow me," Dreya volunteered. "Make me feel useful." Conjuring a full-length mirror so her friend could see everything, was child's play. It wouldn't be strong enough to deflect one of her beam cannons like one of Catriona's conjuring. It was just a simple mirror. "We can give you a moment to get used to your new body without us ogling you if you like," she suggested.

Mandalee shook her head. "On the contrary, I want you to look."

"Hey, are you making a pass at my girlfriend?" Cat demanded, indignantly, hands on hips.

Her friend laughed, "No, don't worry. I just want Dreya's eye for detail. I want to know if this body as perfect as I think it is."

"Looks great from this angle," Dreya assured her.

Michael remained fascinated by the technology directly in front of him.

Mandalee began to slowly turn around, to let the sorceress see all of her. "Feel free to keep saying things like that, Dreya."

Meanwhile, Cat continued to pretend to be annoyed.

"So, you want my girlfriend to stare at your naked body and compliment you as she does it? I'm beginning to think this was a bad idea. I'm creating my own competition."

"Tough!" Mandalee shot back. "I'm not backing out now. I want this to be me. Not just for an hour or two. Permanently. Please tell me you can do that."

"We wouldn't be here if I couldn't," Cat assured her. "At least, I can if Michael will actually turn around," she added, pointedly, "because this bit's down to him!"

Turning around, reluctantly, still trying desperately not to see what was now right in front of him, he guided Mandalee over to lay down in the Regeneration Casket, surrounded by its banks of flashing lights.

Clearing his throat, he explained, "This machine will do a deep scan of your body and store the pattern in its memory." Mandalee felt she understood at least some of those words. Enough to get the gist, anyway. "It can't scan Catriona's copy; it needs to be a real body to work. Don't be alarmed at the noises it makes, I assure you it's harmless. Please just stay completely still, or we'll have to do it all over again. One pass will take thirty minutes, which is a long time, I know, but unless you want to be here all day, I recommend you try and stay still. Dozing off is fine. Don't worry, I won't let you cook."

Mandalee smiled and assured him that while she wasn't the biggest fan of technology, she trusted him.

After pressing some buttons, he placed his hand on the palm sensor. In response, the machine sprang to life, buzzing with higher planar energy. Words and numbers scrolled down a screen like some kind of incantation. Cat and Dreya left the room so they wouldn't distract her and cause her to move.

About half an hour later, Mandalee woke up with a large, bony hand gently stroking her forehead. She opened her eyes to see Ossian Miach Kaidool standing over where she lay. She refused to let herself be startled. So what if he looked like a walking corpse with horns growing out of his skull-like head? He was kind and he was helping her, that was what mattered about him.

She smiled and quipped, "Am I cooked through already?"

Michael returned the smile. "Yes, my dear, you're all done."

Dreya, who had returned with Cat, remarked, "You certainly look pretty tasty from where I'm standing!"

Mandalee groaned at the terrible line.

"Will you stop flirting with my best friend, please?" Cat complained, cancelling Mandalee's copy, as it was no longer necessary.

Ignoring the banter, Michael told Mandalee what he'd done. "The scan was perfect, and I've stored it as the new default template."

Mandalee shook her head. "Yeah, all I'm hearing is blah, blah, blah. Just tell me what to do next."

Michael handed her a small box with two buttons – red and green.

"The red button completely and irrevocably erases all of your biological information from the memory banks." Seeing Mandalee's look of incomprehension, he rephrased that as, "It forgets everything we've just done."

"Why didn't you just say that in the first place?" Mandalee wondered. "What does the green button do?"

"The green one tells the system to analyse the stored changes and apply them to your body at a genetic level." Mandalee got that look again, so he clarified, "It will make this body permanent."

"See? Didn't hurt, did it?"

"Sorry, but it's important that you understand. Think carefully about your decision because this is a one-time-only deal. With Daelen gone, there's no way to recharge the system with higher planar energy with his signature. I had thought there might be enough for one more go after this, but I must have miscalculated because according to the readings, there's only enough for this one. Even purging the buffers will take energy, so you can't cancel now and then do it later. You can take all the time you need to make the decision, but—"

He never got any further before Mandalee hit green. The technology whirred and bleeped and flashed. Information on the display screens whizzed by so fast, she wondered how anyone was supposed to make sense of it.

At last, the hum dropped in both volume and pitch, as the Regeneration Casket powered down for the last time.

It wasn't easy to characterise the feeling. The closest thing she could think of was like a kind of tightening up. As if Catriona's shapeshifting magic had already begun to slightly wear off, and the technology of this Regeneration Casket had put everything back where it was supposed to be in her new body.

"—But you could also ignore everything I'm saying and do that," Michael finished.

"What?" Mandalee asked, incredulously. "Were you expecting some huge speech where I agonised over the decision? My old body sucked, this new one's awesome – what's to decide? Can I get up now?"

"If you like," he replied, "but you might want to take it slowly. Here, take my hand," he offered, but Mandalee was having none of it.

"I think you're forgetting who you're talking to," she insisted, jumping up and out of the machine, dancing around, feeling the exhilaration of finally being herself. "I'm the New Improved Mandalee: White Guardian, Cleric of Nature, assassin, demon hunter extraordinaire, fantastic dancer, phenomenal kisser, terrible cook, and I have the grace and agility of—" she was going to say, 'a cat', but she lost her balance and fell down. "—a drunk giraffe," she finished, having injured nothing more than her pride.

"As I was trying to tell you," Michael sighed, patiently, helping her gently to her feet. "Your body's different now. Your centre of gravity is different, your muscles are different. You can't just expect everything to work like it used to. Give yourself some time, and you will be all that you were and more. Just don't rush into it."

Mandalee blushed and forced herself to calm down. "OK, I promise I'll take it slow." She couldn't fight the smile of joy, though, as she declared, "Right, hugs all around!"

She started with Catriona.

"You finally did it," she whispered. "So many years ago, you promised you would, and you have. I can never, ever thank you enough for this."

Cat whispered back, "You're my friend. If turning the world upside down is what it takes to make you happy with who you are, then clearly the world is the wrong way up, and I need to fix it. Because that's what friends do."

Moving on to Dreya, she maintained, "I know you helped with this, probably more than you'll let on. Thank you."

"Just so you know, Dreya," Cat called out, "I'm watching where you're putting your hands."

"Best break the hug, Mandalee," the sorceress advised. "Girlfriend's getting jealous."

Moving on to Michael, she flung herself into his arms and thanked him over and over. He clearly had no idea what to do with a naked woman pressing against his body, but he took it in good part. "Yes, well," he flustered, clearing his throat. "Not that you don't look amazing, but perhaps you'd like to put some clothes on now?"

Nodding, she pulled her old familiar white leather out of her travel bag. As she unfolded it, something dropped out onto the floor: her mask. She hadn't worn it for so long, she'd almost forgotten about it. "Well, I don't need that anymore," she declared, emphatically.

Turning to Dreya, she asked, "Fancy giving one of your power words a workout?"

Dreya smiled. "I've got just the thing." Focussing her will on the mask, she unfolded her power word, "DISINTEGRATE," and it broke into a billion pieces that further broke into dust and vanished.

"Perfect," Mandalee approved with a sharp nod.

*****

With that, it was time to attend to the fallen shadow warrior.

Back outside, Dreya opened a portal and maintained it while Michael stepped through to have a few moments alone with his body before returning with him cradled in his arms. At last, Michael carried his old friend inside and up the steps as Daelen had carried him so many times. He finally lay Daelen down upon the bed at the heart of the machine that was now as lifeless as its occupant.

Dreya popped out for a moment to retrieve Sara and Jessica, and then they all spent a few moments paying their last respects, before returning back down the steps of what was now Daelen's Tomb and sealing the entrance. Then they walked through the grounds and went their separate ways, leaving the last shadow warrior to finally rest in peace.

Chapter 27

By now, gentle reader, you're probably wondering two things: How do I exist, given my father's death at the Fall of Kullos, and what all of this has to do with the danger that we currently face – the threat of the void-creature that has compelled me to take illegal action with my Time Intervention. Well, wonder no longer…

*****

It was about a week after the Fall of Kullos, and Dreya the Dark woke up in her Black Tower to discover she was in bed alone. That was unusual these days, but she supposed it was very like Cat to want to be up and about, now that all of her injuries had fully healed. The sorceress rose and opened a window, breathing deeply of the crisp, morning freshness. There was something in the air, something intangible that told her today was the day. As she dressed, she became more and more sure of it. All the interminable Council meetings that had plagued her existence the past few days were now done. The Guardians had been officially sanctioned in a typical bureaucratic waste of time, in Dreya's opinion.

How had Jessica put it?

"There's no putting the genie back into the bottle."

Sara had had to explain the allusion, but once she got it, the sorceress thought it rather apt. The Chetsuan twins were currently living in the Black Tower with Cat and herself until they had a chance to find their feet in this world and get a place of their own.

It would soon be time for the Three Guardians to start figuring out the extent of their new powers and what they were supposed to do with them, which meant this day might be the last that they had to themselves for a while. So yes, today was the day.

Dreya walked down the hallway and tapped lightly on a door. Sara opened it.

Speaking softly, Dreya offered, "Sorry to disturb you, but I just wanted to tell you – today's the day, so I'm going to need—"

"—Oh my gosh, you're actually doing it?" Jessica's voice interrupted, her voice bubbling with enthusiasm. "That's super exciting! Give us ten minutes, and we'll be right down, OK, love?"

Dreya thanked her and walked down the steps, following the sound of a spoon against a bowl, telling her Cat was having breakfast in the small sitting room.

She leaned against the door frame, lingering for a moment as she took in the picture before her: Catriona, her girlfriend. She thought back to the moment that upstart druid girl flew into her life, delivered flowers and proposed, sort of. Funny how things worked out, sometimes. Cat was brilliantly smart, wonderfully quirky and beautiful in body, in magic and most especially in spirit. In one way or another, she'd shared that spirit with a being from the higher planes who was like light in a box, an assassin and Cleric of Nature who shared her soul with a leopard god, and a Dark-aligned sorceress whom many considered a tyrant-in-waiting, with vestigial Piskey wings that most people ridiculed or reviled. Who else could have a spirit that big? She was amazing...

...She was also eating a large bowl of ice-cream, which was an odd choice for breakfast. Dreya frowned in puzzlement for a moment, but then dismissed it with a facial shrug. Cat was a big girl, and she could eat anything she liked.

Sensing Dreya's presence, Cat turned to her and smiled, which was like the sun bursting from behind the clouds.

"Good morning," Dreya greeted her, stepping over to where Catriona was sitting, and leaning close in invitation.

"Morning, Dreya," Cat returned, brightly, giving her the kiss that was sought.

"You were up early," Dreya observed.

"I was sick this morning," Cat stated, by way of reply.

"Aww," Dreya sympathised, preparing her own breakfast. "Do you think you're coming down with something?" she wondered. "You should call Mandalee, get her to check you over."

Catriona nodded. "I already called her, she'll be here any minute, but I'm pretty sure I know what she's going to say."

"Cat, are you self-diagnosing again?" Dreya admonished her. "You know that's never a good idea."

"In this case, I think I'm uniquely qualified to know what's going on."

The smile on her face was that of amusement. A look that told Dreya she was being obtuse, failing to see something that Catriona believed ought to be obvious.

"Dreya, listen to me," she insisted. "I was sick...*this morning!*" she emphasised.

Even then, it took a moment for Dreya's puzzled frown to shift to wide-eyed understanding.

"Oh!" she gasped. "Do you really think—?"

"—Well, we knew it was a possibility, and the timing fits."

Dreya nodded. "And it would explain the ice-cream breakfast," she quipped.

"Yeah," Cat laughed. Then she grew serious. "If I'm right, how do you feel about it?" Cat asked her.

Dreya immediately stopped what she was doing and moved over to sit beside her, letting her girlfriend see that what she was about to say was purest truth.

"I told you, you have my total support, whatever happens. You know that."

"Yes, I do," she assured her, smiling once more. "I just wanted to hear you say it. Last time, it was just sympathic."

*****

The 'last time', gentle reader, was a good six to eight weeks behind them, depending on how Catriona counted her time on Earth.

Catriona had just met Daelen StormTiger for the first time, outside Justaria's white cottage. Daelen's early-warning system that told him of any activity by Kullos or his own dark clone had been disabled due to some outside interference. That allowed his dark clone to catch him unprepared. Usually, he would have Ossian Miach Kaidool by his side, to tip the balance of power, but he was in stasis in his tomb, half a continent away.

Speaking to Catriona telepathically, fighting the pain of Pyrah's Ysirian sympathic barriers, Daelen fretted, '*If my clone and I fight all the way to Michael's tomb, we're going to leave a trail of devastation right across Elvaria.*'

'*Can't you teleport?*' Cat wondered.

'*Not with him here, we can block each other's powers,*' Daelen explained. '*That's why I need Michael in the first place.*'

'*So, you need me to get Michael for you? I have a friend who could teleport me there.*'

211

'*The defences won't let you pass without the right power signature,*' Daelen told her.

'*Actually, I have a sort of tool, a staff, that has higher planar energy inside it.*' she had told him and asked if that would work.

'*Maybe,*' Daelen allowed.

'*Maybe? We don't have time for maybe! There must be a way to make sure I get in!*'

'*There is one way, but there are risks to you. I can't allow it.*'

'*Not your call,*' she insisted. '*Be clear. Be concise. Get out of my head for thirty seconds. I decide.*'

While Cat kept his dark clone talking, Daelen did as she asked.

'*If I leave part of my essence inside your body, I will have no control over where it goes. It could enter your digestive system, causing stomach ache and nausea. It could enter your bones and cause painful inflammation, like arthritis that may not be reversible. It could enter your brain and link us telepathically, permanently hearing each other's every thought, both conscious and subconscious – and I'll admit I'm not always proud of some of the things my subconscious mind comes up with.*'

Catriona wasn't happy about some of her subconscious thoughts, either, so she would try not to hold his against him.

'*Trouble is, it might not be possible to tell those two kinds of thoughts apart,*' he warned her, before continuing his list of possible symptoms, '*which could affect your ability to concentrate, to think. It could cause dizziness, disrupt your sense of balance until you can't walk or even stand.*'

OK, this was starting to get scary, now.

'*And if I left my essence inside you for too long, you could start to grow into dimensions that your body isn't equipped to handle. I don't know what that would mean for you – it's never happened – you could even die. But I'll take it out of you long before there's a real risk of that.*'

'*Well, that's OK, then.*'

'*One more thing,*' he continued, hesitantly. '*I only mention this because you're young, female and, if you'll forgive me, presumably fertile…*'

When he was finished, Catriona swallowed, nervously, but quickly composed herself.

'*Thirty seconds.*' she insisted. '*Out of my head. You promised.*'

The instant he left her mind, she reached out to Dreya. Some of these complications could affect her, too.

In the end, though, Dreya simply projected, '*Support*', telling Cat it was her choice, and she would back her either way.

Catriona had chosen to do it, no matter the risk. She could not allow another child to lose their parents as she had. Not if she could prevent it. Besides, the chance to learn so much about Daelen's true nature was irresistible.

*****

The others all arrived at once. Sara and Jessica came down the stairs, just as Mandalee walked in the door, immediately asking, "OK, where's my patient?"

Mandalee was one of only a handful of people who had free access to the Black Tower. In fact, all of them were in that room.

"In here!" Cat called out to her best friend.

Mandalee walked in and greeted everyone with, "Morning, all!" Then, even as her friends returned the sentiment, she ushered Dreya away from Catriona's side so she could give her a private examination. Scrying for this particular condition was more intimate than her usual techniques. After a moment, she asked Cat, "Do I have the patient's permission to share?" Cat smiled and nodded. "In that case," Mandalee declared, "congratulations, Cat – you're pregnant!"

Cat jumped up and hugged her friend, tight. "Thank you!" she cried.

"I didn't do anything!" Mandalee objected. "I just delivered the news."

Next in line to hug the mother-to-be was Jessica, who quipped, "I reckon you'll be delivering something else before too long, love."

"How long is a Faery pregnancy, anyway?" Sara wondered, following her sister.

"Eight months for a full Faery," Cat answered, "add human blood, and it can be a week or two longer."

"But you're asking the wrong question," Mandalee told Sara. "What you should be asking is, 'How long is a pregnancy for a Timeless Guardian who is carrying a baby who is one-quarter human, one-quarter Faery and half higher planar being'?"

"The answer is, of course, nobody knows," Dreya concluded, embracing her girlfriend. "In fact, there's only one thing I know for sure about your pregnancy," she continued.

"And what's that?" Cat asked.

"Your baby is going to be amazing."

"Yes," Cat agreed, "she is."

"She?" Dreya wondered.

Cat shrugged. "Just a feeling."

"Well, whatever happens, you know you've got all the help you need in this room," Mandalee assured her.

Sara and Jessica murmured their agreement.

"There is just one thing I have to warn you about, though," the cleric stressed, in all seriousness. "For the sake of your baby's health, you're going to have to give up shapeshifting. I know you'll miss it, but there's no way to know what effect it might have as your baby develops inside you. Sorry. I hate to spoil the mood, but it's important."

Cat assured her she was right. "I will miss it," she agreed, "but I'll give it up for my child, no question. And it's not forever, right?"

Mandalee nodded. "Of course."

"Actually, now that I think about it," Dreya considered, as Cat gave in to her craving for more ice-cream, "I know another thing about your pregnancy – we're going to need a bigger icebox!"

The others laughed at that.

Dreya didn't think there was anybody outside this room, in front of whom she would feel comfortable opening up like this, but with these people, she could actually lower her otherwise constant guard.

"But I have something for you," she told Cat, "even better than ice-cream."

"The last time you said something like that," Cat recalled with her mouth full, "you came back with dragons." She swallowed, and concluded, "I have to say, Dreya, I'm not in the mood for dragons."

"It's not dragons," she assured her. "It's something I picked up on Earth when I went to that shopping mall with these two," she indicated the Chetsuans. "I've been planning to give it to you for a while, but I wanted the moment to be special. I woke up with the feeling that today was the day, and your news clinches it."

"Dreya, you're being enigmatic again," she objected, playfully. "We've talked about this." As an aside to the others, she explained, "She likes to be enigmatic, sometimes. She thinks it's one of her many attractive qualities."

"It is," Dreya maintained.

Cat gave her a mischievous smile. "I never said you were wrong."

"In that case, I shall continue."

With that, she invited everyone to follow her outside. As they did so, Jessica sneaked a small object into Dreya's pocket.

When they got outside, Cat saw that the three colour roses that had framed the Black Tower's doorway almost since the day they met, were now shaped into a heart. Mandalee, Sara and Jessica moved to stand at the base of the steps, but Dreya asked Cat to stay at the top with her so that they were standing within that heart frame.

"What's going on?" Cat asked with a blush.

"When you first came to me and challenged me to a contest of magic," Dreya began, "you put these red and white roses here. The next day, at my request, you moved the black ones here to join them. At the time, I called it a symbol of co-operation in magic. Looking back, I think, deep down, I just wanted my flowers to be close to yours because I wanted to be close to you. I also remember how you 'proposed' to me. Of course, I know it was just a slip of the tongue, but I like to think maybe it was a foreshadowing. From what we know of our counterparts on the old Tempestria, the Cat and Dreya there were never in love. Now, I can imagine all kinds of Timelines, but I can't understand how that one was ever possible."

Cat was listening to her girlfriend's speech, turning a deeper shade of red with every line. She had begun to guess where it was going but couldn't bring herself to pre-empt it. That would be highly presumptuous and potentially embarrassing if she were wrong. She was stunned by Dreya's open declaration of love. Yes, there were only three other people there, but even that would have been too much for the Dreya she'd first met to even contemplate.

"What I'm trying to say," Dreya continued, "is that while you proposed by accident, it was no mistake. From that first day, you've

215

been working your charm on me, so that – and I never thought I'd hear myself say this – you are the only thing that I care about more than my magic."

"Dreya!" Cat gasped, bringing her hand to her face.

She knew what Dreya's magic meant to her, and what that cost her to say.

Dreya dropped to one knee and opened a small box that she fished out of a pocket. The beautiful silver ring inside sported a blue gem that reminded Cat of the one atop her staff. Preparing to slip it onto the fourth finger of her girlfriend's left hand, she asked, "Catriona Redfletching, will you marry me?"

Tears in her eyes, Cat answered, "Yes! Yes, Dreya, I would love to marry you!"

Dreya slipped the ring onto her finger, and Cat pulled her to her feet so she could wrap her arms around her fiancée's neck and kiss her. Mandalee and Sara laughed, cheered and applauded, while Jessica was just overwhelmed with a flood of emotion.

"That was beautiful!" she sniffled. "I'm so happy for you two."

The two Chetsuans ran to embrace the happy couple, and Dreya explained how they had kept the ring for her, so Cat wouldn't accidentally find it before time.

Mandalee hung back for a moment until Cat beckoned her best friend over.

"You knew about this, didn't you? These flowers have your signature all over them."

Mandalee smiled. "It was all Dreya's idea. That's what counts. Her talents just don't extend to nature magic."

She had been working on it while her friends were away from the Tower, but Dreya had kept the changes hidden with illusion magic.

The sorceress came over to join them. "It was either Mandalee or my undead guards, and since Mandalee Blessed the red and white roses in the first place, it seemed appropriate."

"It's perfect," Cat told them. "It's absolutely perfect."

Epilogue

Moving away from that, gentle reader, I think it's time I brought you up to speed with what Aunt Mandalee is doing right now, from my perspective.

As you know, she's conducting an Illegal Time Intervention on my behalf, collecting my father from his walk just before his Ultimate Final Battle against Kullos. I thought she would bring him straight to me, which given my unique relationship with Time, will be a moment after I finish bringing my faithful readers fully up to date with everything that's happened since the Fall of Kullos. Instead, she's taken a bit of a detour.

*****

"Don't worry, nobody can see us," Mandalee assures Daelen.

Gazing on the scene below him, it's difficult for my father to take it all in, I can tell. He can see it's Elvaria, no question, specifically the area around Walminster where the old Council building is situated.

Gone are the standard medieval cottages and smoky chimneys. Gone are the days of horses for transport. Residential buildings can be whatever shape, colour and style the owners wish. A few change even as he watches. In the sky, transport pods race along Rainbow Roads that appear only when they need to, and transport pods provide instantaneous long-distance travel, including off-world, for those who can't transport themselves.

As they fly over the city, Aunt Mandalee shows my father what looks like a holographic concert in a nearby arena. These days, live events are routinely beamed to other stadiums around the world and beyond. Other citizens are seeking their own entertainment with smaller displays that appear above the palm of their hands. Still more people are pulling up tourist information, as well as interactive map images and directions out of thin air, as well as news and weather reports.

"Your Council building is about the only thing that hasn't changed since I last saw it," Daelen remarks as they circle back around again.

That, gentle reader, was about a thousand years ago...or, from Daelen's perspective, a few weeks.

The building's outward appearance hasn't changed because of its Protected status, but as Aunt Mandalee explains to my father, "It's not our Council building, anymore. It's the 'Commonwealth Regional Establishment for the Advancement of Magic.'"

"CREAM," Daelen says, realising the acronym.

You can blame me for that one, gentle reader. Long story short: there was a public consultation on the name. When it came down to a vote, my idea proved to be popular over the more sensible alternatives. Even so, certain officials continued to call it 'the Magic Research Building'. How boring is that?

Mandalee moves their time on a bit as mages leave CREAM, the workday completed. Some are wizards and sorceresses while others have clerical symbols embroidered on their robes. Still more carry pouches on belts, containing spell ingredients for druid magic. Security personnel are wearing combat suits like Mandalee's, while more workers wear a wide variety of other options.

Time moves on and rules change.

Mandalee returns the flow of time to normal. "Watch this."

A sorceress in a black dress is the last to step out of the building. She fishes a small item out of a pocket, which Daelen probably assumes is a key. I'm sure he's wondering quite what's going to be so exciting about someone locking up, but when she presses her thumb onto the device, the entire building disappears. In its place, stands a recreational park with a children's play area that kids quickly flock to.

"This is some amazing technology you have here," my father breathes in wonder.

Aunt Mandalee smiles, triumphantly, as if he's said exactly what she wanted him to.

"It's not technology, Daelen, it's magic," she tells him. "Don't worry, your mistake is understandable. After all, any sufficiently advanced form of magic would be indistinguishable from technology. All public and official buildings are open for business hours, plus extra for tourism, but outside of those hours, they're stored away in a pocket dimension. It helps us to maximise green space even in large cities like this. This kind of magic is used across the world, these days."

Mandalee moves the shadow warrior's attention to the children who are now playing happily, and the adults who are walking, chatting, and setting up picnics in the park that wasn't there a moment ago. Clearly, this is a typical, everyday experience for these people. Some of them appear human, some are Faery and others are a blend of the two – that's commonplace, now. There are aliens in the mix, too.

The White Guardian asks Daelen to focus on one particular teenage Faery girl, wearing a strappy top that shows off her tiny, delicate winglets. She's with a mixed group of six who are sitting and chatting together. Neither the girl nor anyone else is the slightest bit bothered by those wings. In fact, the boy sitting next to her, presumably her boyfriend, begins gently stroking them – an act the girl is clearly enjoying. They are too far away to hear their conversation, but from their body language, it seems as if there's some friendly teasing going on between her and a human girl sitting opposite her. As Daelen watches further, the kids casually shapeshift into leopard cubs. They start chasing and play fighting with each other. They shift back, laughing at the game before shifting into different animals and running around some more. Eventually, they decide to go somewhere else, so they all change into a variety of birds and begin to flock away.

"Your world is astonishing!" Daelen cries out. "I've never seen anything like it!"

Aunt Mandalee's smile is sad, and I know why. She's actually doing it, so I don't have to. She's going to show him everything. I can hardly bear to watch and relate this, but I know I must.

"This isn't our world, Daelen," says Mandalee. "Not anymore. Oh, I'm not saying it was paradise. We had our problems, same as always, but for the most part, life was good. Until today."

"Today?" Daelen wonders.

Aunt Mandalee hasn't chosen any old random day for her tour: This was the day everything changed.

At her request, my father follows Aunt Mandalee, flying through the sky, following the birds that meet up with another group along the way, doubling the flock size.

"More kids?" Daelen asks.

Mandalee confirms it. "This is just a couple of groups of teenagers meeting up for a harmless summer night of fun around the city: chatting, laughing, shapeshifting, playing with perfectly safe magic. Just enjoying being young and carefree, you know? Remember the Faery girl with the wings?" Daelen nods. "The girl who was teasing her was Erren, her best friend. I visited their class in school not long before this, to give a talk on demons. Erren came to talk to me afterwards. Walked up to me bold as brass and told me she wanted to be a demon hunter when she left school. She told me she had a free period next and asked if I had time to teach her some moves. Shyleen liked her, which was good enough for me, so I spent maybe twenty minutes with her. She was good, and I told her if she kept working and training hard, she'd have a bright future. I also told her to go out and enjoy herself because that balance is important."

"Good advice," Daelen agrees. He still doesn't understand why he's there. He will, all too soon. "And here she is doing exactly that."

Mandalee nods. "That was yesterday, relative to where we are now," she tells him. "I just met Erren yesterday. I'm not going to say she 'reminded me of me' or anything so cliché, but she made an impression. I want you to know that, Daelen." She's crying now. My father has no idea why. "She mattered. They all did, even the ones I didn't know. They all existed, and they all mattered."

"Of course they did, why—?"

He's fated never to get any further as the sky overhead grows black in an instant, not black as in night-time, but black as if the sky's been ripped apart to reveal nothingness beyond.

Out of that void, comes a Monster that Daelen has seen only twice before. It's one of very few things he's ever seen that genuinely terrifies him.

"Don't worry," Mandalee reassures him, "we have better techniques for hiding ourselves in Time, these days. There's no way he can see us or hurt us, but I can't say that about anyone else around here."

The void-creature pulls a great cannon out of a pocket dimension – it's enormous – and casually shoots the flock of birds below him. They blink out of existence in an instant, and the blast continues, uninterrupted.

"No!" Daelen cries out in horror. "What kind of monster would do this? They were kids! They were just kids!"

Mandalee puts her arm around him, offering what comfort she can, even in her own misery.

"I know. One of them was Erren. That bright future that I predicted she would have – gone in an instant, and I'm supposed to be a Guardian of Time!"

A long travel pod train gets caught in the blast as it continues its path to the ground, where it leaves a quarter-mile diameter crater.

His next target is the concert they saw earlier. Almost a thousand people dead or seriously injured. Emergency services respond – they, too, are caught in further cannon blasts. Wizards, sorceresses, clerics, druids, warriors, fighters of all descriptions try to stop the void-creature, but the cannon rips through shields and armour like they're not there.

Mandalee grabs Daelen's hand and pulls him through Time a bit more. Amid the carnage, most of the defenders have abandoned their futile battle in favour of trying to evacuate the area. Their place on the battlefield has been taken by three figures: one is Mandalee dressed, as now, in a white combat suit. The two alongside her are male – Daelen doesn't recognise them.

"The other Guardians," Mandalee explains.

"Following in Dreya and Cat's footsteps," Daelen remarks.

"Hardly!" Mandalee snorts, but cuts off any questions he might have about that, indicating that he should focus on the battle.

The three fight with Temporal magic, using every bit of skill and power they possess, and at last, something slows the creature down.

"We have to help!" Daelen cries, desperately, trying to spring forward, but Mandalee holds him back.

"We can't," she insists. "I'm already there, and you can't be here, yet."

"Can't you do something clever with Time magic?"

Mandalee shakes her head. "Even Time Intervention wouldn't bring back Erren or any of the others, because they never existed."

"Never existed?" Even as Daelen says the words, I can see he's realised what she means. "No!"

"Yes," Mandalee returns. "It's destruction magic. True destruction. He didn't just kill all those people, he unmade them."

Very few even remember them, gentle reader. Pretty much just the Guardians and me. Official records are Timelocked, these

221

days. They have to be to preserve them when the Guardians Intervene in Time. From those records, it is possible to prove the fact of Erren's sixteen years of life. But she never existed.

"I had to go to Erren's parents," Mandalee continues. She can't stop the tears and doesn't try to. "I had to give them Erren's records and break the news that not only had they lost a daughter, but they had also lost all memory of ever having a daughter. How in hell are they supposed to deal with that? How are any of them?"

Those records could tell them certain basic facts about Erren, but all the million family moments they shared are erased forever.

"I'm so sorry, Mandalee," Daelen offers. He knows it's inadequate, but what more has he to give? "I'm sorry this is happening to your world."

"So am I," Mandalee says, bitterly. "I'm sorry for everyone. I'm sorry for the victims, I'm sorry for their loved ones, I'm sorry for me, and I'm sorry for you."

"For me?" Daelen frowns. "Why are you sorry for me?"

Aunt Mandalee freezes the Timeframe and zooms in closer.

"Gaze into the void, Daelen." she tells him. "Think of it as a long, dark tunnel. There's something inside. It's difficult to see, but if you concentrate, really stare at it, let your eyes adjust, you will be able to make it out."

My father takes her advice, staring deep into the hole in the fabric of reality in which the void-creature stands.

At last, he sees it, and his world comes crashing down around him. "No!" he gasps, disbelieving. "It can't be!"

But it's undeniable: the figure standing deep within the void, intent on raining true destruction all around, the Monster that killed my mother's parents a thousand years ago, the so-called 'void-creature', he can see it clearly now.

"What kind of monster would do this?" Aunt Mandalee says, echoing his earlier remark. "You, Daelen. That's why I say I'm sorry for you: You are that monster."

*****

So now you understand, gentle reader, at least in part, the reason I embarked on this Illegal Time Intervention, asking Mandalee to take my father out of his Timestream and bring him here. The Monster that threatens us all, our world and all of Creation *is* my father. When the time is right, I will meet my father for the very first time in hopes that he can help me find a way to save the world...from him.

One thing I can't do, as I gaze through Time, is read my father's mind. I can tap into his telepathic communications and infer things from his words and actions, but his secrets remain his own, and I'm convinced he has many.

Above all, one thing about the story of the Fall of Kullos makes me suspicious. This is pure speculation, but I don't believe my father really knew as much about the Wish barrier as he claimed.

Neither do I think his choice of the Earth shopping mall as the venue for his revelation of this power and Heaven's Surrender was random. I can think of nowhere more distracting for a pair of Tempestrians of that age. Had it not been for those distractions, I am sure my mother would have picked up on a rather large inconsistency in his story.

He claimed, or at least implied, that he invented the Wish barrier as a defence against the great Enemy that had been trying to wipe out his people as she had so many others before.

But consider this, gentle reader: Does my father really seem like he had that level of technical expertise; he who went into every battle with all guns blazing?

Among the people he had hired to look after his facilities over the centuries, he had always had one with a good head for technology. Around the time of the Fall of Kullos, Sara had fulfilled that role. She had more technical expertise than he would ever have but she couldn't have invented the Wish power. Even in my time, such a thing would be beyond the resources of every world in the Commonwealth, worlds of high magic and high technology both.

Why would my father lie? I can't be sure. Maybe some secrets were too important to share with anyone, even my mother. The question is, if I'm right, who really created the power he called the Wish? Some other player that history has forgotten or omitted from its pages? I don't know, but I'm gambling that finding the answer to this question, among others, will bring us closer to ending the threat we now face.

But that's only part of the story. There's much more to come. Right now, I need a break to collect my thoughts and check on my captives, but when I return, I can tell you about the early exploits of the Original Three Guardians. Their victories, defeats, mistakes, and triumphs, and I will also begin to tell you about the most dangerous threat they ever faced: Purity of Angels.

A sneak preview of the sequel to
Shadows Fall

Fragmented Control

The Salvation of Tempestria
Book 4

Gary Stringer

Available Spring 2022

Chapter 1

The Guardians are getting creative. The two I've got locked in my bedroom, that is.

As you know, gentle reader, I've frozen my house in a bubble in Time, but it's challenging even for me to stop two Guardians from gaining a foothold and interfering with what I'm doing. I suppose I should have been suspicious, the way they suddenly went quiet, after working so hard to break through when I first put them in there. I naively thought they'd given up trying to beat me. Not so.

From my first instalment, gentle reader, you may recall that I wedged my bedroom door shut with my mother's old staff and cast an adaptive anti-magic field on my room. Now, you might wonder how I expected that to work, considering I later told you about my mother's discovery that anti-magic fields are useless. Well, the key lies in the word `adaptive`.

Back in the day, my mother's solution, later adopted by Aunt Dreya and eventually by pretty much everyone, was to determine the magical frequency. Then the mage could either adapt their own magic to use the anti-magic field itself and/or absorb its power into themselves. However, techniques evolve with time, and so did anti-magic fields. Now we use adaptive versions that change frequency at regular intervals to prevent tampering. But the two Guardians that I have imprisoned, the modern successors to Catriona and Dreya, were not picked by lottery. So, in the face of my `attack` (which I suppose it is, from their perspective), they got creative.

Their overriding opinion is that we should be out there actively working to stop the void-creature (a.k.a. Daelen StormTiger, my father). Dealing with current events. Aunt Mandalee and I believe that this is futile without help, hence our Illegal Time Intervention. Besides, since I've created my own Timeless zone here, there *are* no current events. That means there's no rush. I thought that would make them content to wait until I let them out, but I underestimated the power of ego.

Every True Guardian who has replaced one of the Original Three has suffered from inevitable comparisons, and, let's face it, my mother and Aunt Dreya were hard acts for anyone to follow. This means that the two in my bedroom have got something to prove. That's what drove them to try and break through my anti-magic field, running through the frequencies at random and punching through with a portal, of all things.

As Aunt Mandalee told Daelen, we don't use portals anymore – we have better techniques, now – but the brute force approach almost worked. The advantage of portals is that although the co-ordinates need to be precise, the frequency doesn't. The disadvantage is that they damage the fabric of reality, which is why they're banned except in an emergency. (Still, I can hardly blame them for doing something borderline illegal when they're convinced that they're trying to save the world.)

Unfortunately for them, they're forgetting who they're dealing with.

I'm not a Guardian; I'm unique. Although I appear to be a human woman (my Faery spots only emerge in hot sunshine), of about eighteen to twenty years, I'm nothing of the sort. From a Tempestrian point-of-view, my date of birth was almost a thousand years ago, but calculating my actual age is problematic, given Timelessness, Immortality and time spent on other worlds. Suffice to say I have far more life experience than my youthful exterior would suggest, and my true nature extends into places that humans can't perceive. That means I don't need to open the door to reach inside my bedroom. It's similar to what Kullos and Daelen were trying to do in their Final Battle, extending their higher planar nature, their essence, extending their 'light' outside their 'box'. Except I know how to do it gently, with care, control, and precision, so I don't risk tearing reality apart.

Let me put it to you this way, gentle reader: A two-dimensional royal family keep their two-dimensional crown jewels in a two-dimensional vault with a single two-dimensional door and protected by two-dimensional guards. One day, the guards capture a three-dimensional human trying to steal those crown jewels. They lock him up, but he escapes with those crown jewels. He didn't come through the door and he didn't breach the walls, so, question: How did the three-dimensional human escape his two-dimensional prison?

Answer: That three-dimensional human can reach into that two-dimensional vault without damaging anything, steal those crown jewels from above and escape the same way, because it's wide open in that dimension. It's wide open because those two-dimensional people can't perceive 'above' the way humans can.

Now, if they're *really clever* two-dimensional people, they might be able to intellectually grasp the *concept* of 'above'. They might even have magic or technology that operates in that dimension, but they can't perceive it.

In the same way, back in our plane of the cosmos, the Guardians' portals operate within the parts of reality that humans and other 'mortals' (for lack of a better term) can't perceive. But I can. I can exist there and effectively stand in their way so they can't access their portals. That's how I put a stop to their escape attempt. They'll probably try something else in a while, but for now, they are contained, and I can get back to telling my story.

To begin this instalment, gentle reader, I need to go back to the beginning. Yes, I know I've said that before, but I mean it literally this time. All the way back to the Cataclysm that began the cosmos.

*****

In the beginning, according to myth, the Creator Entity somehow annexed part of the void and created an ordered cosmos. As a balance to this Act of Creation, the *IT* Entity came into being in the void beyond the boundaries of everything. As the cosmos developed, it separated into the layers of what I continue to call the Great Cosmic Sandwich, and life came into being at all levels. At first, life forms were confined to their own native layers of the sandwich. Indeed, at first, lifeforms were blissfully unaware of the existence of other layers, but over time, sapient creatures evolved, some of which began to speculate that there might be more to Creation outside their experience. Among these, some particularly intelligent individuals started to devise ways to detect the undetectable. Much like my mother, they viewed 'you can't do that' as a challenge to do it anyway.

Eventually, it became possible to contact neighbouring planes. This was not always a good thing. Even with the best of intentions, there were misunderstandings. Those from the higher planes often considered themselves superior to those below, while the lower planes would often be jealous of the abundant energy resources of the higher levels.

The people of my age (that is, the age in which I live) are very much aware that Tempestria is one world among many in this middle layer of the sandwich. Many of these have joined together in a co-operative way, to form the Commonwealth. Moreover, we know that this plane is one of many more, each of which contains countless worlds, peoples and civilisations.

There is a tendency to view the lower planes as the primary source of trouble. The creatures we call demons continue to invade, as they pull energy from inter-planar forces – magic – and Ascend. Once here, they have an abundance of energy, which they mostly use to wreak havoc, maim, kill and even drag innocent mortals back down to their plane. The deeper their native plane, the more energy they need to come here. That's where summoning magic comes in, using the magic that's available here, wizards pull Greater Demons from the deeper levels of our sandwich. Once they are here, they can be very challenging to control because the energy demons require just to live, is very small compared to what they can now access.

Thankfully, gentle reader, there isn't enough energy in the whole mortal plane to summon the Keeper of the Underworld.

Before the war with the void-creature began, the people of my age generally didn't see the higher planes as a big problem. The Fall of Kullos was a thousand years behind us, and for a thousand years before that, the sum total of higher planar beings in our world mostly amounted to two shadow warriors (one of which was split into two clones), one Ysirian (Pyrah), one leopard god (Shyleen) and one demigod (Ossian Miach Kaidool, a.k.a. Michael). You can count them on the fingers of one hand, depending on how you count the shadow warriors and how many fingers your species has on one hand. Of these, history viewed only Kullos and Aden as a threat, whereas there had been uncountable demon attacks in history and pre-history, and (except perhaps for Tricksters) all have intended harm.

That has helped to create the misconception that, for the most part, the lower planes are `evil` and the higher planes are `good`.

But that wasn't always the case.

If you go back beyond two thousand Tempestrian years, though we know nothing of our world at that time, there is considerable evidence that higher planar beings came and went, freely. They interfered with countless other mortal worlds as they pleased, so it's reasonable to assume that our world was no exception. Often, these beings had the best of intentions, but to quote from the edicts of Balance, '*Power wielded in ignorance is dangerous, regardless of intent.*'

As you know from my previous instalments, gentle reader, a single shadow warrior was more dangerous than an army of demons. People could deal with demons – Aunt Mandalee is one of a long line of demon hunters – but until the time of the Fall of Kullos, no mortal had been able to stop a shadow warrior. The only reason that danger passed, was because Blessed Alycia threw up her barrier that kept higher planar beings from manifesting here. Of course, Shyleen found a loophole, thanks to her unique relationship with Mandalee, who willingly shared her soul. However, as I say, ours was not the only plane to suffer from attacks from higher levels.

According to legend, such trouble began with the Creator contacting the spread of Angels in the plane immediately below. The Creator actively encouraged those Angels, in the spirit of showing off, to explore the whole of Creation, see the beauty that had been Created, and extend the Creator's Blessing to all the peoples of the cosmos.

Angel sightings are abundant in stories throughout the whole of Creation. Every world we've encountered, both in and out of the Commonwealth, has such stories, and interactions with beings from higher planes suggest they may be truly universal. Of all these stories, though, only one is known to be literally true: the story of the Angel who called herself Purity.

Printed in Great Britain
by Amazon